The Sword of Zagan and Other Writings

The Sword of Zagan
and Other Writings

Clark Ashton Smith

Edited by Dr. W. C. Farmer

Introduction by S. T. Joshi

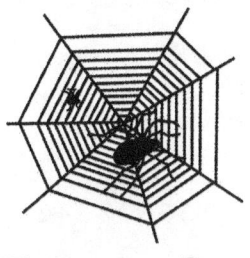

Hippocampus Press
New York

Published by Hippocampus Press
P.O. Box 641, New York, NY 10156.
http://www.hippocampuspress.com

Permission to publish this text has been granted by
CASiana, the Estate of Clark Ashton Smith.

Cover art and interior illustrations by Jason C. Eckhardt.
Cover design by Barbara Briggs Silbert.
Hippocampus Press logo designed by Anastasia Damianakos.

First Edition
1 3 5 7 9 8 6 4 2

ISBN 0-9721644-5-6

Contents

Introduction

When, in 1981, I came upon Clark Ashton Smith's juvenile novel *The Black Diamonds* among his private papers, recently deposited at the John Hay Library of Brown University, I could hardly have imagined that this work, substantial though it was, represented only the tip of the iceberg of Smith's bountiful early prose and poetic work. To be sure, the Clark Ashton Smith Papers contains a number of other, much shorter tales (some of them fragments) featuring the same general *Arabian Nights* atmosphere; but it would have taken a shrewd prognosticator to suspect that yet another novel, shorter than *The Black Diamonds* but nonetheless rich in style and incident, lurked unpublished, along with a sheaf of tales, poems, and fragments probably dating well prior to Smith's twentieth birthday.

The Sword of Zagan, at slightly over 39,000 words, is considerably shorter than the nearly 100,000-word length of *The Black Diamonds,* although it appears (from the greater maturity of its prose) to have been written sometime after the latter. And, it must be admitted, it is in many ways inferior to *The Black Diamonds,* a novel of extraordinarily convoluted plot, lively characters, and a delectable hint of the supernatural. By contrast, *The Sword of Zagan* is plainly an adventure story, resembling not so much the *Arabian Nights* as, perhaps, some of Kipling's tales set in India or the Middle East. An unusual amount of bloodletting occurs in the novel: the body-count is as high as in any of today's action films, and characters major and minor seem to die—or appear to die—with startling rapidity. And yet, one can sense a far greater technical assurance in the managing of prose, a paring down of incidents to those that have a direct bearing on the climax (aside from the awkwardly inserted "tales" in Chapter XVI), and a love-element that was apparently foreign to Smith's temperament while he was writing *The Black Diamonds.*

Several of the shorter tales also reveal noteworthy features—features that we can recognise from Smith's later prose work. "The Emir's Captive" is distinctive in that it manifestly takes the side of the Saracens in their battles against the British during the Crusades: let us recall that Smith could trace his ancestry directly back to English forbears through his British father. "The Haunted Gong," set in San Francisco's Chinatown, foreshadows many of Smith's later stories. As in such works as "The City of the Singing Flame" and "The Treader of the Dust," this real-world setting serves only as the springboard for imaginative voyages into far more exotic realms. "The Bronze Image" and "The Fulfilled Prophecy," set in India, again evoke Kipling—not merely the Kipling who wrote poignantly of both the British and the Indians in such works as *Kim,* but who probed the hidden realms of wonder and mystery lurking in the immense subcontinent in such tales as "At the End of the Passage" or "The Mark of the Beast." "The Haunted Chamber," though set in England, features an Indian character as a servant. It is also notable for being one of Smith's few tales utilizing what might be called the *pseudo-supernatural*, in which the supernatural (in this case, a ghost) is suggested, only to have the phenomenon explained away naturalistically at the end.

The numerous fragments in this collection give a hint of the prodigious fertility of a young imagination so bursting with ideas that they could not all be captured in finished prose. It is particularly regrettable that Smith did not—or perhaps could not—finish such substantial fragments as "The Opal of Delhi" (first version) and "The Guardian of the Temple," for they would certainly have taken their place among the more meritorious of Smith's early tales. And yet, it is very likely that these unfinished efforts were of significant formative value in teaching Smith the craft of fiction writing. As H. P. Lovecraft once said, the only practice for writing is writing; and it is only by trial and error that one can gain a concrete idea of what conceptions can be captured in prose or verse and what conceptions must, for lack of coherence or proper denouement, forever remain elusive.

Smith early on learned that some of his *Arabian Nights* conceptions could indeed best be encapsulated in verse. Kipling's verse may again have been a partial influence, but Edward FitzGerald's translation of the *Rubaiyat* is perhaps considerably more significant—and not only in regard to the a-a-b-a rhyme-scheme Smith adopted in some of his early poems. Interestingly, a fair proportion of this work—both the items gathered here and those that still remain unpublished in the Clark Ashton Smith Papers—are in a rather naively moralistic vein. Smith would quickly learn that the elementary morality found in "The River of Life" and "The Departed City" would not do in mature work: it is not that morality has no place in verse (or prose), but that it must be expressed with subtlety and indirection, and by means of image, metaphor, and symbol rather than by plain statement. Especially under the guidance of his mentor, George Sterling, Smith evolved the notion of "pure poetry" and exemplified it from his very first volume, *The Star-Treader and Other Poems* (1912), to his last.

The works in this volume were given by Smith, late in life, to his young friend W. C. Farmer (who also owns two of the four missing pages of *The Black Diamonds*, printed as an appendix). Miscellaneous as they are, the mere fact that Smith chose to bestow them upon a friend rather than merely destroy them suggests that he saw some value in them, even if that value was largely formative. As a means of providing a window into the early mind, heart, and imagination of Clark Ashton Smith, these works are of inestimable value; and not a few of them can claim an intrinsic value as well. How Smith's fantastic imagination metamorphosed from the exoticism of the East to the even more remote exoticism of interstellar space is something that scholars of his work must vchart; for us it is sufficient to read and appreciate these delectable works in the spirit in which they were intended—as the initial offerings of a creative mind that would soon take the entire cosmos as its haven.

—S. T. JOSHI

A Note on the Text

The Sword of Zagan was probably written when Smith was around fifteen of sixteen years of age. Other than the second page of the prologue, the manuscript is complete, and has been in a trunk in my possession since Clark gave it to me in the early summer of 1961.

Archaic and other unusual spellings have been largely retained, as have such spellings as "tho" and "thru" (indicative of Smith's brief utilization of "simple spelling") and such misspellings as "priviledge." "Janissaries" is the spelling early in the text, switched later to "janizaries." One may argue that the latter spelling is more "oriental." I have opted, however, for the more usual spelling of this term. His footnoting, using an asterisk, occurs on the page where the notation occurs in the manuscript.

The other works in this book are also presented with a minimum of editorial tampering. In some cases, editor's notes have been supplied to elucidate the origin or purpose of a given work. Some of the works exist in either published or unpublished form, most of the latter in the Clark Ashton Smith Papers in the John Hay Library, Brown University.

—W. C. FARMER

Acknowledgments

No undertaking of this size could have been accomplished without the assistance and encouragement of others.

First, my brother Noel, who notified me of the existence of the Web site, www.eldritchdark.com and that he had made fresh contact with an old friend and Smith devotee, Donald Sydney-Fryer.

Foremost among my assistants, my deepest appreciation goes to Ron Hilger and Scott Connors for actually flying from California to assist in transcribing many of the documents and for their infectious enthusiasm for the project.

Additionally, these two fellows put me in touch with Derrick Hussey, publisher, for whose many kindnesses I am deeply grateful.

Beyond the above, I could not have finished this task in time without the assistance of my good young friends Jonathan Simmons, an extremely bright and promising college student; Chris de la Paz, whom I have known for several years now, and who, with his family, were so very supportive of me while waiting for a Heart Transplant; and last, Clayton Luce. These young folks gave up their time to read the manuscripts for me to type into the computer, so as not to be looking back and forth, thus saving hours of very tiring work.

Finally, thanks to Rosie Cardenas who showed me how to justify margins, amazing! I'm still essentially a 3 × 5 alphabetized card scholar.

Of course, most of all I thank my beloved wife for her endless patience through this entire process—after 37 years it just gets better and better!

—W. C. F.

The Sword of Zagan

Prologue

It was in Benares, in the year of 1897, that I met Rama Kalindra Das. I had been sent up from Calcutta on business, in which the aforesaid Rama was to take a part. It is of little moment what that business was, as it has nothing whatever to do with this story.

As the transaction was of a somewhat important nature, in which other persons were interested in preventing, it was arranged that we should meet in secret. The temple of the Tirthankers was named as the rendezvous.

Therefore, on the following day I found myself at the temple, disguised as a wealthy down-country Zimindar, and on the lookout for another Zimindar from up-country, presumably from Allahabad, who was reputed to be a wealthy uncle of mine. At least so my confidential servant Mahbul had informed the Jain priests at the temple and the populace in general.

And because of this a puffing Bengali baboo from Calcutta who was close on my track missed his quarry and returned to his hotel swearing in bad English and inquiring of all whom he met if they had seen anything of a Sahib who went by the name of Lansing. While the aforesaid baboo was thus returning in high dudgeon, I was closeted with Rama Kalindra Das. In about two hours the transaction was finished, and all that the baboo might in future do was rendered useless. A little later we issued from the temple and started for a stroll towards the river front.

I was tolerably well acquainted with the streets of Benares and so was my friend, the supposed up-country Zimindar. We walked out on one of the ghats and watched the people bathing. They were constantly passing up and down, chattering as they went. Several great Brahmin umbrellas upreared themselves near where we sat, and the priests proceeded to ply their trade. Each devotee as he came from the river paid money and received the dab of paint on his forehead. Nearby a white-robed pundit was expounding the sacred writings to a group of people, most of whom were women. A palanquin was carried down to the water's edge and a rajah flashing with jewels and rich raiment stepped out. Near him walked a Sadhee, blind and naked save for his loin-cloth.

Together they passed us side by side—the rich and the poor, the blind and the seeing.

Laughing girls came up the steps carrying lotas of sacred water. They were Nautch-girls, probably attached to one of the Hindu temples. One, more beautiful than the rest, caught Rama's eye.

[*The remainder of the prologue is missing. The following is supplied by the editor based on his understanding of the author's intention.*]

He directed my attention to this divine being, and we both watched her for a few moments. Rama wondered aloud whether any girl had ever been so beautiful, and asserted that it was a great shame that virtue was not always be found in one so exquisite.

I assured him that such beauty must necessarily imply virtue, and a pure heart. We then entered a heated discussion debating this issue. At last he was forced to reveal secret information that would win the debate for him.

He revealed to me the existence of a certain manuscript which had been given him by an English friend of mine and fellow comrade in arms named Manning. Rama led me to his quarters where we surprised Manning by our arrival. After explaining the reason for our visit, Manning went to a locked cabinet, and there, well secreted amongst his belongings, wrapped in a worn sheepskin case, a weathered manuscript lay. Manning unwrapped the ancient documents and gave them to me with a word of caution concerning their great historical value, and advised that I should take it to my quarters to read at my leisure.   This self-same manuscript now lies transcribed before you; as to the answer to our debate, you may decide for yourself.

Chapter 1

It was in the year 1636 that I, Ali Zagan, son of Alzim Zagan, pasha of the province of Room-Elee, took leave of my father and journeyed to Istanboul.

With me, in my pouch, I carried a letter of introduction to the Sultan, which my father had given me. This letter requested the Sultan to give me a position as captain of the janissaries, I having asked my father to allow me to join this famous and priviledged corps.

As my father was in high favor with Narad IV, I had no fear that he would refuse to grant this request. Would to Allah that such had not been so! Still, I have but little to complain of. All this has been of my own doing, and I have gotten my just deserts. But I am not the only one. Many men have met the same fate. All of us are to die soon, but death has lost its terrors for me after all that I have seen and done. In Paradise, Heaven or Al Araf I shall meet [. . .] I know. It is the will of Allah that I should die for him sooner, and who shall say Him nay? As I said before I set out for Istanboul with the aforementioned letter in my possession.

I was alone in my journey, for I would take no attendants. But the way was not long for I had but fifty miles to go. I was mounted on a swift Arab steed, and had no doubt but that I would reach my destination by nightfall. And now, perhaps I had best tell something of myself. I am 28 years of age now, but I was twenty-three at the time spoken of at the beginning of this narrative. I am five feet ten inches in height and somewhat slim. My hair and eyes are black as coal and my face unusually dark for a Turk. Many would take me for an Arab but surely I am not. My father and mother and their parents before them were of pure Turkish blood. One of my ancestors was that Zagan, famous in our history, who forced the Sultan Mohammed II to order an immediate attack upon Constantinople. The result is familiar to everyone.

Many people call me handsome, and tho I do not wish to cause the reader to think me vain, I must say that in my private opinion, I think they are right. I was well, but modestly dressed, and in my possession was the scimitar used by Zagan at the siege of Constantinople, or Istanboul, as we call it now.

This sword had been handed down in our family, from son to son until it came into the possession of my father. At parting he gave it to me telling me to use it well, and only in defense of my country or ruler. Would to Allah that I had obeyed him! True, I would not be alive now, but a death for king or country is a glorious one, and not to be compared to that of a traitor.

Perhaps it is well that my parents are dead, for they never could have borne the great disgrace that is come upon me. And whose fault is it that I am thus disgraced? Partly mine, I must say, but I have the sweet privilege of laying the rest on other people's shoulders. Whose shoulders you will soon know.

About one in the afternoon I came to the top of a high hill, and beheld to the north, the glittering roofs and mosques of Istanboul. Between me and them lay a wide plain, ten miles in width, and the Bosphorus, a sheet of molten silver. To the east of the city, across the Golden Horn was Para, smaller, it is true, but equally as beautiful.

The Seraglio and its surroundings could be plainly seen owing to the clearness of the air. I reflected that I would be there ere the setting of the sun.

I had stopped my horse for a few moments to behold the scene, and I was now once more on my journey. Suddenly the clattering of hoofs broke upon my ear, and turning, I beheld a horseman coming up the hill. A moment later he was at my side and we had exchanged greetings. He was about my age, but of a lighter complexion and somewhat shorter. His horse was a huge black Arab, while mine was small.

We rode in silence for a few moments and then he broke it by saying:

"I am from Damascus and am the nephew of the pasha. My name is Abdul Alcorez. I am going to Istanboul."

"So am I," I replied, "I am the son of the pasha of Room-Elee, and a nephew of the Sultan. My name is Ali Zagan!"

"Why are you going to Istanboul?" was his next question.

"To join the janissaries. I have a letter of introduction from my father to the Sultan, asking him to make me a captain. Why are you going, I must ask?"

"For the same purpose. I, too, have a letter of introduction. If the Sultan grants my uncle's request, I, also, will be a captain."

"I hope so," was my reply.

Neither of us spoke for a few moments. Abdul was the first.

"Have you ever been in Istanboul before?" he asked.

"Yes. I went with my father two years ago. And you?"

"I was never there before."

"Then you will enjoy yourself," I replied.

"Kindly explain that."

"That is easily done," said I. "Having never been to Istanboul before, the novelty of it will cause you to enjoy it."

"So I suppose. But we shall soon see. If the effect is not as you have said, I shall call you a liar."

"I promise you that you shall have no cause to do so."

"Perhaps not. We shall see. I must have proof ere I believe."

"If all people required proof before they believed, there should be but little to believe."

"You speak the truth. Hereafter I shall not doubt your word."

"It would be best, Abdul. I assure you that I have never told a lie in all my life. I am unmarried."

Abdul burst into a laugh.

"Neither am I," said he. "Therefore you can take it that I am no more of a liar that yourself. When a man is married and his wife catches him speaking to some unmarried woman over a garden wall, he must needs concoct a falsehood to allay her suspicions. One falsehood leads to another, and when a man tells many you can never divine whether he is lying or speaking the truth. Therefore, say I, it is best to speak the truth except when a lie is necessary for the preservation of life and injures nothing except the liar's reputation."

"I agree with you," said I; "but if you talk like this any more I shall believe you are a philosopher."

"I am. Show me the man that isn't, or never has been and I'll show you an idiot."

"And would the idiot be the same person?"

"Of course. I do not know of an exception to the rule. I'll wager you never did either."

"As a matter of fact, I never bothered my head about it. So you can neither say that I have lost or won the wager."

We were now at the bottom of the hill and in a low plain or valley. There were many farms along the road and many fat cattle in the green pastures.

Occasionally we passed a vineyard with gaily dressed men and women picking the rich clusters of grapes. These gazed at us as we passed, but quickly resumed their work again, travelers being no rarity in that well-populated region.

Abdul rode along in silence, neither seeming to hear nor see anything that was taking place around us. For a long time I did not venture to break down his suddenly assumed veil of taciturnity. Perhaps I was too astonished. At any rate I did not attempt to do so.

It was only after we had traveled many miles that he spoke. We had just passed thru a village and were only a few miles from the banks of the Bosphorus. He suddenly slowed his horse to a walk. I did the same. I felt rather than knew that he was about to say something; what it was, I did not know.

"You are doubtless wondering why I have not spoken," said he.

"Yes," I replied; "go on."

"I have been meditating on a problem that has troubled me much lately."

"And what is the problem that it should occupy your mind so much that you know not what is taking place about you. I'll wager that you don't know we've just passed thru a town."

"You win!" replied he. "And now for this problem of mine."

"What is it?" I asked impatiently.

"A most extraordinary one," he replied.

"But what is its name?"

"That I do not know. But I'll state the facts of the case. It is not a very long story, and is somewhat startling."

"What is the woman's name?" I asked suddenly.

He was obviously startled.

"How do you know there's a woman in it?" he asked.

"Oh there generally is. There's a woman at the bottom of everything, and if you search long enough you'll find her. That is one rule to which there can be no exception."

"So you're a philosopher too, are you?" said Abdul. "I might have known it, for I can plainly see that you're not an idiot."

"Thanks to Allah, that's one thing I'm not," said I.

"Now I'll tell you that problem of mine," said Abdul. "As you said, there's a woman at the bottom of it. That much I freely admit. But there is something else, tho what it is I have not the faintest idea. This is the story:

"Two years ago I went to Beirut as the bearer of a letter from my uncle to a wealthy merchant, Ilderim Khan by name.

"And now comes the woman. Ilderim invited me to stay at his house for a few days and I, of course, accepted.

"On the second day, as I was strolling in the garden, I caught sight of a girl, about eighteen years of age. She was closely veiled, but I paid no attention to this fact, as it was nothing unusual. But I was afterwards destined to attach to it a special significance.

"Wishing to get a closer view of the girl I passed by her throwing a careless glance in her direction. I noticed that she was richly-garbed and very beautiful.

"To my great surprise she walked fast as if to overtake me. As she passed by she thrust into my hand a piece of paper, and went on as if nothing had happened.

"When she was gone I opened the paper and glanced at it. But the opening words caused me to thrust it into my pocket and walk on with an assumed air of indifference that I did not feel.

"After I had strolled about the garden for awhile I returned to the house. I noticed a fact that I had not observed before; namely, that there were several servants about the garden.

"Not until I was safe in my room did I take the paper from my pocket. Then I did so and read it all. Here was a problem indeed! The letter, if it could so be called, was as follows:

" 'I am watched constantly. I know that I am running a great risk in trying to give you this missive. From your face I know that you can be trusted. I am a niece of the Sultan, who has confined me here because I refuse to marry Bikri Mustapha, his friend. Meet me tonight, if possible, under the great cypress of Lebanon near the gate. There are many details that I cannot at present explain.'

" 'Fatima, niece of Murad'

"That afternoon a messenger arrived at the merchants house with a message from my uncle the pasha, ordering me to return immediately to Damascus. It seemed that my uncle had fallen sick with the fever and, believing that he was about to die, had sent for me.

"Of course, I had to set out for Damascus that very moment. My uncle recovered from the fever, contrary to the predictions of several Arabian physicians whom it seemed, had told him that he would die.

"Since then," Abdul went on, "I have neither heard nor seen anything of the Sultan's niece, Fatima, tho I often wonder what became of her. It is probable that she was forced to marry Bikri Mustapha."

"Of course," I said, "you are in love with her, and the problem you spoke of is: what became of her? Your answer is the most probable, as you say, but from her attempt to get you to help her escape it is obvious that she is a girl of spirit. If, therefore, she showed so much repugnance to a marriage with Bikri Mustapha, she may have killed herself in order to avoid becoming his wife."

We had now come to the banks of the Bosphorus. It was covered from one side to the other with ships and boats, and was crossed by several bridges. As we rode across one of these the sun sank into the west, and disappeared from sight. For a little while the golden light glimmered on the mosques, and then, with the cry of the muezzin announcing the hour of evening prayer, went out, and a dim twilight took its place.

Abdul and I went on thru the throng, and as dark now fell, rode thru the Sublime Porte and to the gates of the Seraglio.

Lights had begun to appear and the Sultan's palace was glimmering from end to end.

An eunuch took our horses and inquired as to what was our business with the Sultan.

Abdul replied and we were permitted to enter the Seraglio. Another slave met us, and after learning what we wanted, left the room.

In a few moments he returned with the news that the padishah would grant us an audience.

We were conducted thru many suites of rooms furnished in a manner I had never seen before. Their glories, and glittering, priceless treasures bedazzled my eyes and I knew not where I went. In one of the rooms we passed I heard laughter and the sound of music and dancing, and saw thru the open door for one fleeting moment a vision of Paradise. A second later it was gone and we had entered another apartment. Then we stopped and I knew that I was in the presence of the Sultan.

Chapter II

For at least ten seconds my brain was in a whirl. The brilliancy of the room we had entered surpassed all the others. The throne of the Sultan, formed of solid gold and silver, and studded with thousands of priceless jewels, surpassed in magnificence all thrones that I had ever heard or read of.

It was placed on a raised dais, about a foot from the floor. This dais, and also the entire floor of the room, was carpeted with priceless rugs, worth far more than their weight in gold. All of them were embroidered with brilliant and exquisite designs, representing scenes in the lives of dead Sultans. One was a representation of the siege of Constantinople, and another of the defeat of Bajazet by Tamerlane.

At these I was horrified, for, as everyone knows, our religion forbids the representation of the human form. I at last set it down to some drunken freak of the Sultan's, or to the influence of Bikri Mustapha.

But to go on with the story.

On the Sultan's right side stood Bikri Mustapha, attired in all the glories that money could buy, and on his left, the Grand Vizier, who was a little more modestly clothed.

The room was lighted by countless lamps of gold and silver, suspended from the ceiling by long chains of the same metals.

An indescribably sweet and subtle perfume pervaded the room and exerted a strange effect upon my senses. At first the apartment and all its occupants seemed to sway to and fro as in an earthquake. Then came a sensation of lightness, of floating in air, then I seemed to recover my senses, and everything was as normal as ever.

Tapestries, embroidered with trees and flowers were hung on the walls, covering them with softness and beauty as if to conceal the base wood and stone. On each side the dais stood six guards, armed to the teeth, and gorgeously dressed. There were also two in front.

Murad bade us advance, and Abdul, being first, went to him, and kneeling, presented him with his letter. The padishah read it in silence and then beckoned to me to come forward. I did so and presented him with my letter. After reading it he said to us:

"A week ago there was a mutiny among the janissaries, which we had to put down by strong measures. Three captains are now in Hell as a result, and their places have not yet been filled. You may fill two of them. Take this ring to the agha, whom you will find at the barracks and tell him that it is our will that each of you be given a company to command."

Murad took from his finger a heavy signet ring and gave it to me. We immediately left the throne-room and made our way out of the palace, guided by a very polite eunuch.

My heart sang with joy as I rode thru the Sublime Porte, and I have no doubt but that Abdul's did likewise.

Here I was, a captain of janissaries, five minutes after I had presented my father's letter to the Sultan. It is but little wonder that my heart sang with joy.

And yet it would have been far better for me as I observed before, if that petition had not been so easily granted. Had I known what was in store for me in the near future, I should not have been so joyful. It is well that we poor mortals are unable to tell what will befall us on the morrow. If we did, we should be continually miserable.

It was now getting very dark and we had a hard time finding our way to the barracks. At last we reached them, and after showing the padishah's signet to a suspicious sentry, rode thru the gates into the grounds surrounding the barracks. The moon had risen and I saw my future home for the first time in the glimmer of moonlight. It made a most weird impression on me at the time.

Picture to yourself a number of high buildings rising out of the ground and making a half circle about a large, bare, deserted yard. Picture these buildings as ghostly quiet, and picture the whole in bright moonlight, with your own black shadow and that of your horse on the ground before you; and you will perhaps glean some vague impression of what I saw.

Abdul rode boldly up to the door of the building which the sentry had informed us was occupied by the agha and the captains.

Dismounting, he knocked loudly on the door, one, twice, thrice. After a few moments it was opened by a half-dressed captain, who demanded sharply what the devil we wanted.

Abdul informed him as politely as he could under the circumstances. The fellow called loudly, and a soldier appeared as if from nowhere and led away our horses.

The captain then bade us follow him and led us up a narrow and winding staircase to the second and highest floor of the house.

He knocked on a door and a voice replied, bidding who was without to enter. The captain quickly obeyed by opening the door and stepping in. We followed his example and found ourselves in a large, but plainly furnished room. It was lighted by two lamps of brass, suspended from the ceiling by chains of the same material.

A man of middle age, with gray hair and beard was seated at the table, engaged in writing a letter or something else of the same sort. He looked up sharply as we entered and then bent to his work again. But in that moment I had caught a good look at his face and had fixed it indelibly in my memory. It was a firm but kindly face, and yet had about it no signs of weakness. The nose was prominent and slightly aquiline, and the eyes were of a dark gray color. The chin was firm and strong, the mouth somewhat large, and the face in general, somewhat pale for a Turk. Such was Ismail Pasha, the agah of the Janissaries.

After he had finished writing he looked up and spoke. "What do you wish?" was his question. Abdul gave him the padishah's signet ring and told our story. Ismail listened in silence.

"Your names?" he asked at the finish.

"Abdul Alcorez," said that person.

"Ali Zagan," said I.

"Are you not a descendent of that Zagan, famous in our history for advising Mohammed II to attack Istanbul?" said the agha.

"I am," I replied.

"Abeuka," said Ismail, "take these men to their rooms. In the morning I shall give them particulars as regards their companies, who are at present commanded by men belonging to them. Ali and Abdul will learn the drill, and when that is done, take command. Begone!"

Chapter III

On the following morning I awoke, feeling greatly refreshed by my sleep. It had been deep and peaceful and utterly devoid of dreams of the future. At first this struck me as strange, but I concluded after a little reflection that it was due to the fact that I had ridden long and far on the day before.

It has afterwards seemed strange to me that my mind should have been occupied by such trivialities on the morn of a new era in my life, yet it was so. I cannot satisfactorily explain it, so I must set it down to some eccentricity of character or temperament.

But I shall not weary the reader by citing any more instances of this sort. I have said enough about it already. I shall go on with the story and leave its thread unbroken, if it can be said that I have not yet broken it. I am uncertain on that point myself, and shall leave the final decision to the judgment of the reader.

Scarcely had I risen and dressed myself when Abdul and Abeuka entered. For the first time I had a good look at the fellow. He was short, tho not fat and was a very pleasant looking fellow. I judged that he was about twenty-five years of age. He had short, black hair and his face was as dark as my own. He ears were large and somewhat prominent but were somewhat constrained by a huge red turban.

"Did you sleep well?" was Abdul's first question.

"Very soundly," I replied. "Where do we eat?"

"In the officers' dining room, of course, stupid," said Abeuka; "But I forget that you are new here," he went on, half-apologetically.

We left the room and went downstairs to the dining room, where the agha and the captains were already seated.

The meal was a somewhat pleasant one, and after it was over, some of the captains instructed Abdul and I in the drill. The exercises were very simple, and that afternoon we took command of our respective companies. They were formed of well-dressed, well-fed, and well-paid men, most of whom had joined the corps because of the priviledges it afforded. There were about five hundred to each company, the entire force at Constantinople being about fifteen thousand. The rest of the corps were scattered throughout the Turkish Empire. The entire force consisted of 100,000 janissaries and about 400,000 irregular troops called Jamaks who were attached to the corps and fought beside them in the line.

The barracks of the janissaries at Istanboul were separated from those of the other troops, consisting of the cavalry and infantry and the Bashi-Bazouks. There were only two companies, or regiments of Jamaks with us at the time, and these were under the control of the agha.

The exercises of the troops occupied about two hours, and when they were over, Abdul and I found that we were at liberty to do as we pleased for the rest of the day.

Therefore we left the barracks and in our gay uniforms as captains of janissaries we walked along the streets of Constantinople, discussing idly whatever subject caught our attention.

"Did you notice," I asked, when the conversation began to flag, "the discontented looks on the faces of the men?"

"Yes," replied Abdul. "It is rather strange. What do you make of it?"

"I think this is likely to be another mutiny," I remarked. "There was one not long ago."

"If there is I'll do all I can to stop it," was the reply.

"But this is likely to be very serious one. I noticed the discontent in every company, including the two regiments of Jamacks."

"But it can be easily put down."

"I hardly think so. Many of the captains, too, wear a surly expression. I also noted many winks and nudges that passed between them at breakfast this morning."

"This is serious," said Abdul. "Did you count how many of them looked dissatisfied?"

"There are forty-three officers including the agha and ourselves. Out of these forty-three I counted thirty-six who looked dissatisfied. Many of them, I think, took some part in the last insurrection, tho they were not so conspicuous as to attract the Sultan's notice. Only the ringleaders were punished."

"We had better speak to the agha of this to-night." said Abdul. "It is likely to be as serious as you at first said."

"We had better wait till we have something more substantial than our suspicions," I said. "There will be no mutiny immediately."

"Perhaps not. We can only watch and wait. We are sure to learn something more ere long."

A moment later our attention was attracted by something else and we forgot all about the prospective mutiny we had just been discussing.

As we passed before the stand of a sword-seller to look at the weapons he displayed, a man in the uniform of the Bostanji, or the Sultan's gardeners, walked rapidly up to Abdul, and whispered something in his ear. The man was tall and stalwart and was panting from running.

Abdul spoke to him a little while, and I could see by the glances cast in my direction that they were speaking of me. At last Abdul came to me. "This fellow has news of the princess Fatima," he said. "Come with us and he will tell all."

We walked off down the street utterly regardless of the antics of the sword-seller, who was shouting after us to ask if we wanted a weapon.

Scarcely had the Bostanji spoken a dozen words when we heard a hue and cry behind us, and looking back saw half-a-dozen men in the Bostanji uniform coming toward us, shouting, "Stop! Thief!"

"We are pursued," cried the messenger, as he started off at a run. Abdul and I followed at his heels. It was well that we did so, for had we stopped the Bostanjis would have had us in less time than it takes to tell this!

Street after street we transversed at a wild pace, in immanent danger of being stopped at any moment by those we passed.

The cry of "Stop Thief," grew fainter as we went on, and at last we heard it no more. We sank down, completely exhausted, on the steps of a large building.

When we had recovered our breath the messenger went on with his tale. The substance of it was somewhat as follows: The princess Fatima, whom the Sultan kept a close prisoner in the palace, had bribed him to convey a message to a young captain of janissaries, named Abdul Alcorez. He had left the palace, closely pursued, and had set out for the barracks. There he had learned that the captain was absent and had set out in search of him.

The message was as follows: "Enter the palace grounds tonight. You can surmount the wall in some way. Come to the east side of the Seraglio, and wait for me under the large cedars of Lebanon that you will find there. I shall come to meet you at the stroke of twelve, unless I am prevented by some unforeseen happening. Bring my cousin, Ali Zagan with you. My uncle, the Sultan grows more enraged at my refusal to wed Bikri Mustapha. He loves me too well to compel me to do so by force, so he seeks to tire me out by confinement. He will find the task harder than he thinks. You can freely trust the messenger."

"Well," said Abdul to me, "What think you of this, Ali! Shall we attempt it?"

"Of course," I replied. "I thought you were in love with the lady."

"I am," said Abdul, his face flushing.

"And I am her cousin," I said.

"Then we shall attempt it. A light ladder will do the work well, and we can carry it over the wall with us."

At that moment we heard the sound of many feet, and a moment afterwards our late pursuers came round the nearest corner. They caught sight of us, and spreading out in a thin line to prevent our escaping, came at us with drawn swords.

"There is no escape that way," said Abdul, running up to the top of the steps. Here our feet were on a level with the heads of the Bostanjis in the street. Several pistol shots rang out, and we saw that fighting would not help us. So we flung our united strength against the door of the house. It was strong and was evidently well bolted from within. At last it began to crack.

The Bostanjis, swords in their hands, were half-way up the steps. We pushed harder, and the door began to break. A moment later it broke in, with the three of us on top. One pursuer had now reached the top of the steps.

We were on our feet in a thrice, and facing them with cocked pistols. They fired first, but in their excitement, missed us.

Abdul and I fired simultaneously and two of the enemy fell.

The Bostanjis now fired and another man staggered back, carrying one of his comrades with him. The number of our opponents was now reduced to eight. We had been singularly lucky, and had remained unhurt ourselves.

We had now drawn our other pistols, and as the enemy came on, fired into their midst. Two of them went down, shot thru the head, and another staggered down the steps with a broken arm. We now had only five to contend with.

Wild with rage the remaining five flung themselves upon us. We met them with drawn scimitars and one went down under our strokes.

The tide of battle now began to ebb. The Bostanji who had brought us the message of the princess, fell with a blade in his heart. Before the striker could draw it out I had cut him down. He fell with a cloven shoulder.

The odds were now three to two. Both of us received slight wounds, but we managed to put another of our antagonists out of the combat.

The two who now remained to fight us began to lose heart, and we would undoubtedly have killed them had it not been for the arrival of reinforcements. I heard a wild shout from the street, and looking over my opponent's arm, saw twenty Bostanjis, coming towards us. The first of them had already reached the foot of the stairs.

"Resistance is useless," I yelled to Abdul. For answer he made a wild stroke at his opponent and cut off his sword arm half-way between the wrist and elbow. The fellow dropped as if he had been shot and the blood gushed in torrents from his wound.

A moment later the two us of made at the remaining one. He did not wait to receive our onslaught, but raced wildly down the stairs to his companions, leaving his sword behind him in his flight.

With a quick movement, Abdul picked it up, and stepping out in full sight of the Bostanjis, flung it point foremost, down amongst them. One fell with the blade half-way thru his right shoulder. A shout of rage rose from the whole twenty, and a dozen bullets flew past Abdul, one taking a little piece out of his ear. The others imbedded themselves in the wood-work over the door.

My friend lifted his fingers to his nose with a derisive gesture and then stepped calmly back to my side. "Come," said he, "we must get out of this."

We ran to the other end of the room. There we found an open door and going thru, found ourselves confronted by an astonished servant who had undoubtedly come to see what the noise was about. Abdul drew one of his empty pistols, and pointing it at the man's head, said:

"One word from you and I'll shoot you dead. Lead us out of this place and say nothing to those who pursue us. If you do, I'll come back some day and blow your brains out. I think you understand."

It was very evident that the servant understood, for he was trembling noticeably and beads of sweat were gathering on his forehead. He led the way out of the room, and we followed unquestioning, knowing nothing as to what would happen next.

Chapter IV

After traversing several richly furnished rooms we found ourselves con-fronted by a large, massive iron door. The trembling servant shot back the bolts and the three of us stepped out into an extensive garden, to find our-selves confronted by a dozen furious Bostanjis.

The astonishment was mutual. The soldiers fell back in amazement at our unexpected appearance. Before they could recover from their surprise, Abdul and I, and the slave sprang back into the house, and slammed and bolted the great door.

A moment later we heard them hurl their bodies upon it with wild cries. It was of no use. Batter it as they would the door did not budge an inch. After a few moments the rain of blows ceased and our enemies ap-parently drew back. Their exclamations of rage came to us and we knew that we were between two fires, the Bostanjis in the front of the house and those in the garden.

Already we could hear the yells of the former as they searched room af-ter room, and their shrieks of disappointment when it was found that their objects were not there. We heard the stamping of feet overhead and knew that if we did not do something ere long, all hope of escape would vanish.

"Hide us! Hide us!" whispered Abdul at the servant in an agonized tone. The man ran quickly from the room and we followed him with drawn swords. In the next apartment we came upon two of the enemy. I cut one of them down, and before the other could cry out we had him on the floor, and gagged and bound. We made him stand on his feet and walk in front of us with the servant.

Finally we entered a room like the others in every respect except that it contained several large pictures. These were of animals and flowers. The slave stepped up to one of these, and pushing it aside, disclosed a large cavity, or closet in the wall. We pushed our prisoner in and followed him. The cavity was large enough to stand up in and was about ten feet in length by six in width.

"If you tell them we're here we'll come out and shoot you," was Abdul's parting injunction to the slave. That person, who was still very badly frightened, let fall the picture, leaving us in total darkness.

We heard the pattering of his footsteps as he ran from the room. That he fully believed us capable of carrying out our threats was shown by the fright he was in. We had little fear that he would betray us unless on pain of death. So we sat down, one on each side our prisoner, resigned to a long period of anxious waiting. Abdul cut a slit in the picture, so as to admit light, and we noticed for the first time what sort of a man our captive was.

He was of medium height and very plain-looking. In every respect but one he was a most commonplace kind of person. That respect was his large black eyes. They gleamed at us with malice, rage and cunning displayed in their depths. We saw at once that he was a dangerous man.

"You shall die first if your comrades find us," said Abdul to him in a whisper. The fellow nodded and his face assumed an expression of contempt. The black eyes glared at us with redoubled hate. This intensity of expression frightened me. I saw at once that he possessed the power of mesmerism. This fact I communicated to Abdul in a low whisper. Abdul shrugged his shoulders in contempt, as if to say: "He can't make me go to sleep."

We quietly reloaded our pistols and then deprived our prisoner of all his weapons. They consisted of an exceptionally sharp scimitar, a long yataghan, or dagger, and a brace of large pistols. These we found to be loaded. Each of us took one and slipped it into his sash. We determined that at least six of the Bostanjis would die ere they killed us.

Five long minutes passed away, five long minutes full to the brim with agony and suspense. At last we heard the patter of feet and knew that several persons had entered the room.

We heard them as they searched it from end to end, and heard their exclamations of disappointment when they discovered that it was unoccupied.

"It's the last room in the house," said one of them. "Where on earth can those two devils have gone to?"

"They've probably vanished," said another. "One of them is the Devil and the other is one of his chief assistants. You've doubtless heard that the devil possesses the faculty of disappearing whenever he wishes to. It is not unlikely that his assistants have the same faculty, too."

"Then there is no use trying to kill or capture the devil," said a third. "I vote that we give it up."

"The Devil doubtless had some companions with him when he descended to Hell!" said the first, facetiously, referring no doubt to the dead Bostanjis.

"Come on," said the second, "We'd best get out of this before he returns for some more." They all laughed at this, but still they did not leave. They lingered for a few moments, exchanging remarks with each other, which were highly uncomplimentary to Abdul and myself.

It is very improbable that we should have been discovered had it not been that one of the three Bostanjis threw his dagger at the picture behind which we were concealed.

The weapon passed thru the cloth and grazed my cheek, leaving upon it a gash three inches long, the scar of which I bear to this day.

A cry of amazement rose from the Bostanjis, and two shots rang out. The bullets passed thru as the dagger had done. One passed thru the top of my turban and the other bored a neat hole exactly in the middle of our prisoner's forehead. He dropped without a sound.

Abdul and I drew our pistols and fired simultaneously. The two shots made a sound like the explosion of a musket.

One of our antagonists uttered a cry of rage, and we knew that our shots had taken effect. With a pistol in each hand we burst thru the painting and upon our enemies.

Both of us fired at once, the four pistols going off at the same time. A Bostanji fell to the floor with a groan. He was the one we had wounded just before. The other two fled but we did not seek to follow them. We reloaded our weapons and walked to the window at the end of the room. I stood guard with a weapon in each hand while Abdul hacked at the grating with his sword.

Just as it dropped out, half a dozen of our pursuers entered the room, having been attracted hither by the sound of pistol shots.

On finding themselves covered by a brace of pistols, they hesitated, and fell back. They did not dare attack me, for each one thought that he would get shot.

The delay gave us our opportunity to escape. Abdul sheathed his scimitar and vaulted thru the window. I fired my weapons into the midst of the Bostanjis, stuck them in my belt, and followed my friend. I saw that the shots had taken effect, but whether anyone was killed I am to this day unaware.

Sufficient to say that as I went thru the window, my antagonists fired at me. Their shots were not without effect. One of them grazed my neck, leaving a long furrow, another bored a hole thru my turban, touching the head and shaving off a tuft of hair, and a third splintered the window sill.

The delay gave us our opportunity to escape

Abdul and I alighted in the top of a cypress tree about ten feet below the window. There we stayed for a few moments while we disentangled ourselves from the boughs, making targets of ourselves for numerous bullets from the window above. None of these did any damage, however, unless it was to the tree. Several little twigs, dangerously near my head, were neatly lopped off. I shall always consider it a miracle that neither of us was hit.

We had in the meanwhile attracted the attention of several Bostanjis in the garden below. These began to shout for their comrades and shoot at us. After a little deliberation we determined that, as it was only about fifteen feet to the ground, we had best jump down amongst them.

The aforesaid action was duly put into practice and the two of us landed fairly on top of one of the enemy. That person promptly doubled up with a yell, and fell to the ground with the two of us on top and the breath knocked out of him.

He did not rise again, but we did, and very quickly, too, I must say.

We cut our way thru the midst of the Bostanjis, wounding several of them, and, as the target for a score of bullets, raced at top speed for the garden wall. This, fortunately for us, was only about seven feet high, and we succeeded in reaching the top of it before our pursuers got within striking range.

A moment later we were in the street, and running for our lives. Unfortunately we had no idea of direction, and as a matter of course, took the wrong one.

It landed us in front of the house and right in the midst of a score of the enemy. We turned and ran the other direction but were met by an equal number who blocked the street so that we could not possibly pass. Thus we were caught between two fires with nothing to do but fight to the death.

The whole forty closed in on us from opposite sides and we backed against a wall with loaded pistols in our hands. On they came with a wild yell, determined to end the fight then and there.

We fired amongst them as they came and several fell. The riot came on with redoubled fury. When they were within ten feet of us we fired our last shots and threw the weapons in their faces. The shots were not without effect, but no one dropped this time.

We drew our swords and a moment later they were upon us. For almost two minutes we managed to hold them off. I think that we killed several, but I know not how many. Abdul fell with a sword in his left shoulder, and a moment later I was struck down. I saw the flash of a sword-blade above me, felt a sharp pain as it descended, and then the whole world grew red. I thrust out wildly and heard a shriek. Then all was darkness and I reeled and fell. I heard dimly the sound of many voices and then all was still, and I knew nothing.

I came to with a terrible pain in my head. I opened my eyes and saw where I was. I was lying in a street, and Abdul was bending over me. The pale moonlight disclosed his features to me and I saw that he was very pale. His clothing was red with blood.

I sat up feeling very stiff. Abdul regarded me anxiously. "They left us here for dead," said he. "You've been unconscious about five hours, I should say. The Bostanjis may be back for our bodies at any moment. Can you walk?"

For answer I rose slowly to my feet. I was still very weak and faint. I could scarcely stand up.

"That was a terrible blow on your head that you received," said Abdul. "It is a wonder that you were not killed. You have lost a great amount of blood."

"How is your shoulder," I asked, in a very faint voice.

"Very sore, Ali. But it isn't the worst wound that I got. Those Bostanjis were not content with nearly cutting my arm off. Look at this."

He drew aside his cloak and unbuttoned his jacket, disclosing a horrible wound in the right side, just under the shoulder.

"There was no vital organ touched," he said. "But our late friends evidently thought that there was. Come on; we'd best be getting out of this, ere they return."

We walked slowly off down the street, gradually regaining our strength as we went. By the time we reached the shores of the Bosphorus I was feeling much better, and I have no doubt but that Abdul was, too. The cold night air was like a draught of wine to us, and its effects were certainly much better.

We now strolled off towards the Seraglio. Half an hour's walking brought us to the high wall enclosing it. This wall was about twenty feet in height.

Abdul and I having determined to keep the appointment with Fatima, if possible, tho we thought it extremely unlikely that she could get out of the Sultan's palace that night after all that had happened, began to devise some means of scaling the wall. If Fatima had heard that we had been killed it was not likely that she would be waiting for us under the three cypresses. But we determined to carry out our part and so did it forthwith.

We walked along the wall till we came to a tree growing close to it. Up this we climbed, tho it was a particularly thick tree and devoid of limbs for the first fifteen feet.

Breathless and faint from our exertions we at last reached the first limb. We rested a few moments and then went on. A few seconds later we were on a level with the tops of the wall, but the wall was about six feet away, and no limb extended towards it at that point. The first limb that did so was about ten feet above our heads, and that was certainly too far to drop.

The only thing to do was leap, and leap we did. We landed safely on top the wall, which was about five feet in thickness. Having rested a moment we leaped down and made a run towards the east side of the Seraglio.

Chapter V

The garden was very dark. The tall trees shut out the moonlight and it fell upon us only in streaks or spots. Here and there we came upon an open place, and in it we could see very well. Not a cloud obscured the sky and the moon was large and full.

We caught an occasional glimpse of the lights in the palace as we went along, but this was seldom. The trees were for the most part cypresses and oaks, but there were a few pines and mulberry trees.

Many of the cypresses were two hundred years old. The gnarled and twisted trunks gave their surroundings a weird, strange appearance, and when viewed for the first time in moonlight, would cause a person's hair to stand on end.

Indeed, and I am not ashamed to confess it, Abdul and I would not have been astonished if a ghost had suddenly appeared before us.

Two hundred yards of cypresses, oaks, pines, and other trees, with many thick bushes of various kinds, brought us to the east side of the Seraglio. There, close to its walls, and not ten feet away from them, rose the three cypresses which were the largest and oldest in that place. The tallest of them rose fifty feet from the ground and was at least eight feet in diameter. The trunk was undivided for fifteen feet and then it branched into five separate trunks, each of them as large as an ordinary tree.

Twenty feet above our heads was a barred window. That window, Abdul concluded, was the window of the princess' room. "Why else," he argued, "should it be barred? I don't think she's in the harem, with the Sultan's wives and daughters," he concluded.

"I'll soon find who's in that room," he went on in a whisper. "I can climb this tree, I think. If I stand on your shoulders I can reach that little limb. Once on that, I can climb into the crotch. The rest will be easy."

This plan we proceeded to carry out.

Abdul was soon in the crotch of the tree, and selecting the branch nearest the Seraglio, went up it. Five minutes later he stood by my side once more.

"Was the princess there?" I asked.

"Yes," he replied. "She did not see me, tho and I dared not call to her for fear there was someone else in the room."

"What are we to do?" I asked.

"Wait till midnight and then climb the tree. It isn't likely that there will be anyone else with her then."

"But how can we both climb the tree?"

"We'll have to find a rope. There must be one somewhere in this garden. The gardeners would need one in climbing trees."

We proceeded to search the grounds in a radius of a hundred yards. Not a rope was forthcoming. I was about to give up the hunt in vain, when a low cry from Abdul brought me running to where he was.

"This is luck," he said. "Here's a fifteen foot ladder. We won't need to climb that cypress now."

Five minutes later the ladder was leaning against the side of the Seraglio directly beneath Fatima's window, and we were congratulating each other upon not having made any noise in the operation of placing it there.

There was nothing to do now but wait for the stroke of twelve. It was about 8 o'clock.

"I'm going to sleep a couple of hours," whispered Abdul. "Wake me up at ten and then you can sleep till twelve." He dropped to the sward and a moment later was fast asleep. How the minutes dragged! Each seemed an age to me. I was desperately tired and still a little faint. It took all my will-power to prevent myself from falling asleep. At times I reeled and staggered, and seemed to be falling on the brink of the world. Everything would go dark all of a sudden, and I would find myself falling. The motion, coupled with the will-power would waken me again, only to repeat the same performance once more.

At last, when I seemed to have lived for a million of years, ten o'clock came. I hurriedly awoke Abdul and then fell into a deep, dreamless sleep. I seem to have slept but a few minutes when Abdul jerked me to my feet by the ear.

"What's the matter?" I said dully, not yet fully awakened. "It isn't twelve yet, is it?"

"Yes, it is," he replied, "and I've been trying to wake you up for the last five minutes."

He walked over to the ladder and went up it like a cat. I followed him, and before long we were under the princess' window. We stood side by side, the ladder being some three feet in width.

The moon had set and there was very little light. What light there was was completely shut off by the cypresses. Their branches were almost within reach. We both looked into the room, but could see nothing. We could, however, hear the gentle breathing of someone, presumably the princess Fatima herself.

Abdul whistled softly. There was no response. He took a small pebble from his pocket and flung it into the room. For answer there came an exclamation of surprise, in a feminine voice, followed by the sound of someone rising, as if from a couch.

We heard the patter of feet and a little scream as the princess espied us. Then she came to the window. She was fully dressed, but was unveiled. "Are you the ghost of Abdul Alcorez?" she asked, in a voice filled with melody.

"Princess," said Abdul, "I am that person in the flesh, not his ghost. This man with me is your cousin, Ali Zagan. He is no more of a ghost than I."

"I heard that you were both killed by the Bostanjis," said Fatima.

"The Bostanjis thought they had killed us," said Abdul. "But if they should meet us again they would learn something to the contrary. It seems to me that the killing was mostly on the other side."

"So I heard," said Fatima. "I think you did quite right in killing them. I heard also that they killed my messenger. But let us get down to business. I have summoned you here, as you have doubtless guessed ere this, to help me to escape if you will. I knew that I was exposing both of you to great danger, but I felt sure that you would run the risk."

"Of course we'll help you, if you'll show us how," said Abdul.

The princess disappeared and soon returned with a large, heavy file. "My messenger managed to smuggle this in to me," she said.

"I meant to file these bars in two myself, but I learnt that you were dead, and that broke up my plans completely. I also have a rope here with which I was to lower myself to the ground. Without your aid I did not think myself capable of escaping from the garden, and I could not bribe the Bostanjis to help me."

Abdul was busy filing the bars in two now.

"Be quiet," enjoined the princess. Two of the Bostanjis sleep just outside the door. You can hear them snoring."

The snoring in question was somewhat loud and I could hear it well, altho it was separated from us by a room and a heavy, thick door.

In half an hour three of the bars were on the ground below and Abdul and I were in Fatima's room, conversing with her in low tones. She lit a taper, and I saw her face well for the first time.

It was a very beautiful face, far more beautiful than Abdul had told me it was. The complexion was a light brown, and was certainly most lovely to behold. The eyes, large and black as the wings of the night (to use a poet's phrase) were deep and strong.

Anyone looking into them could see reflected, as in a mirror of the soul, the thoughts in the brain behind. Her chin, small and dimpled, gave, with the crimson, bow-shaped mouth, an expression of piquancy to the whole face. The ears were small, like sea shells, and lay close to the head.

The hair resembled the wing of the raven more than anything else and was confined in a net.

Fatima's form was to my eye, perfect. She was small, not much over five feet, and somewhat slim. The ideals of the Orient call for plumpness, but my ideals do not. In that respect, and in no other, am I different from the average Oriental.

We were about to leave. Suddenly a loud rap came upon the door and someone yelled in a harsh voice to be admitted. I recognized the voice as that of Bikri Mustapha, the princess' lover. What he wanted at that time of night I did not know, and I could only guess at it.

The three of us sprang for the window. But we could not all emerge at the same time.

Hearing sounds within and finding that the princess did not intend to admit him he kicked the door open and sword in hand, stalked into the room, followed by the two guards, who were but half awakened.

They halted at sight of us, evidently much astonished. As it was clearly impossible for us to escape, we stepped back into the room, prepared to meet our fate. Abdul and I drew our scimitars and advanced towards Bikri and his companions.

Bikri was evidently in a drunken rage and very angry. The two Bostanjis were more amazed than anything else. They hardly knew what to do.

Bikri Mustapha, the drunkard, the king's boon companion was a stout man, very fat, and red-faced, a typical inebriate. I knew him to be a dissolute man, whose every base passion was satisfied by the padishah. He had evidently been drinking very heavily, for he staggered as he walked and his voice was thick when he spoke. "What means this?" he roared, rushing at us. "Know you not that I am to marry the princess. What are you doing here anyway? I'll kill you!" He punctuated his last words with a clumsy rush at Abdul.

Emboldened by his example the two Bostanjis attacked me. But they were not yet fully awake, and their swordplay was clumsier even that that of Bikri Mustapha.

Still I found it hard to beat them off. I was desperately tired and faint and my arms longed for rest. But there was nothing for it but to fight.

As I fought, I became desperate and attacked one of my enemies with great ferocity. His foot slipped and he went down with a cloven skull. No sound escaped his lips.

I now turned my undivided attention to the remaining Bostanji. That person was a better swordsman than his comrade, and gave me more trouble than I had anticipated. But he, too, went down at last.

Leaning on my bloody sword I turned to see how Abdul was faring. He was having decidedly the best of the fight, for the drunken Bikri, altho he was a fine swordsman, could do little against the fiery janissary. But what he could do he did with a will.

The swords of the two clashed together again and again, and neither received a wound. Five minutes passed away and at the end the drunkard was almost spent. He panted with fatigue and rage, and made a wild rush at Abdul determined to end the combat then and there. He overreached himself and stumbled against the chair. His sword flew from his hand and clattered to the floor. He recovered himself and made a mad attempt to regain it.

Abdul flung aside his own weapon and rushed at Bikri with clenched fists. His right arm shot out and the drunkard sank to the floor with a groan and lay senseless.

My friend seized the fellow's turban, unrolled it, and bound his arms to his side. He then went over to the bodies of the dead Bostanjis and appropriated their headgear. They were wearing turbans at the time, instead of the bonnets which are their distinguishing feature. Abdul then gagged Bikri and bound his legs together. He then placed him in a sitting position and came over to where Fatima and I were waiting.

"He won't recover for several minutes," he said to us. "They won't find him till morning."

"What does your highness intend to do when you have escaped from here?" I asked of the princess.

"There is a certain tailor, who lives in Pera whom my father patronized," she said. "To him I shall go. I have no doubt but that he will hide me."

"Come then, we must be going," remarked Abdul, climbing out of the window. We followed him, the princess preceding me, and a few moments later we stood on the solid ground. Abdul and I took the ladder, and with the princess behind us, made our way to the garden wall. We placed the ladder against it and were soon atop the wall itself.

To haul up the ladder and let it down on the other side was not a hard task. We then climbed down and made off in the direction of the Golden Horn. A few minutes' walk brought us to the main bridge. It was not long before we had entered Pera and had, under the guidance of Fatima, made our way to the tailor's house.

Abdul knocked and we were admitted by the tailor. To him we related our tale, and asked him if he would hide the princess. After some deliberation he replied in the affirmative. Fatima was duly received into his family, and it was agreed that she should be passed off as the tailor's daughter.

"I must thank you very much for your help," said Fatima at parting. "Without you, I could never have escaped from the clutches of my uncle. You must come to see me whenever you can."

It was now about two o'clock. Abdul and I made the best of our way back to the barracks and were admitted by a very suspicious sentry. We instantly returned to our rooms and slept soundly the remainder of the night.

Chapter VI

I awoke on the following morning with a very tired feeling. It was about all I could do to rise from my bed and dress myself. I tottered down stairs to the dining room looking more like a vagabond that an officer of janissaries. My face was bound up with a handkerchief and the rest of my wounds were similarly bandaged. My uniform, or rather clothes, for it could scarcely be called a uniform, was stiff with blood in many places.

My neck, where I had received the bullet wound of the day before, was equally as stiff. It was an effort for me to turn my head from side to side. It was with a sinking heart that I met the curious glances of my brother officers and anticipated the running volley of questions that was to follow.

The agha said nothing. He merely looked at me a moment and then returned to his eating. I was not the first man that had come home in the same condition; if the barracks can properly be called "home."

The glances of the officers were at that moment directed towards Abdul who tottered into the room in a more dilapidated condition than myself, and dropped silently into a chair.

To him, also, the agha said nothing. He was not surprised. It was not the agha's character to be surprised at anything. One look at his stolid face would reveal that to the most profound ignoramus.

"What is the matter with you two, anyway?" asked Abeuka, taking a large mouthful of bread. "You look as if you'd been in a cat-fight. What's the trouble? Did you have a quarrel about a girl?"

Abdul scowled at him and winked at me across the table. To the questioner he said nothing.

"I must be right," said Abeuka. "Abdul and Ali have had a fight. What's her name, Ali?"

I glared at him and returned Abdul's wink.

"Haven't you a tongue in your head?" asked our tormentor.

"Yes," replied Abdul; "I have also a sword in my scabbard." He tapped the hilt significantly and Abeuka subsided for the time being.

For a few moments no one said anything. There was no sound in the room save that of eating. The officers still continued to subject us to their looks of curiosity, but beyond that nothing was said or done.

Abeuka spoke at last. "You are very hot-tempered, Abdul," he observed.

"A very unnecessary observation," sneered Abdul.

"Perhaps unnecessary, but not absolutely so."

"What mean you?—Oh, well, we must not bother ourselves about such trifles. They can take care of themselves."

"I must beg your pardon for my silly words."

"Such as it is, I cannot but grant it. It is, however, entirely superfluous."

Abdul and Abeuka clasped hands. "My apology is then accepted," he said. Turning to me, he said: "And your forgiveness, Ali?"

"Is freely given you," I said. "All three of us have been somewhat foolish."

"And now, I entreat of you, tell us the true source of these wounds!"

Abdul glanced over at me. He winked solemnly three times, very slowly and distinctly. To Abeuka he said not a word.

Abeuka repeated his question.

"Our prudence and good sense bids us keep that to ourselves," said Abdul at last, seeing that there was but one way out of it, that of point-blank refusal to tell. This refusal, however, he couched in terms that could not possibly be offensive.

"Then you refuse to gratify our curiosity," said Abeuka.

"Yes," replied Abdul, "that is the long and short of it. I entreat of you, if you have any sense of politeness, not to ask us again."

"I shall not," said Abeuka, relapsing into silence. To all intents and purposes he was thinking deeply.

Looking at his face, I saw that his suspicions had been aroused. From Abdul's refusal to acquaint him with the story of how we had gotten our wounds, he had concluded that we had something of importance, which if revealed would do great harm to somebody. What the secret was, was what puzzled him.

I looked attentively at Abdul to gain his attention. Having gotten it, I raised my middle and forefingers in the air, extended as far apart at I could get them, in the form of a fork.

After some meditation Abdul assured me, by a nod of his head that he understood what I meant. No one at the table had observed this little by-play, we having timed our actions the those moments when all eyes were turned away from us.

As my readers may not understand what was meant by the fork, I will tell them that I intimated to Abdul that he must tell Abeuka a lie to direct his suspicions from the true form of our secret. The sign of a forked tongue, indicated by two distended fingers has been used among savages from time immemorial. It is evident that pantomime must have been the first language of the human race.

And now to go on with this tale. After indicating to me that he understood what I meant, Abdul turned to Abeuka.

"I am somewhat reticent in telling you how we received these hurts," he said in an apologetic tone. "With Ali's consent I will now tell you the true story." At this announcement everyone at the table, the agha included, brightened up and stared in anticipation at the speaker.

I indicated my consent to Abdul, and he went on. For an example of lying, the following is, in my estimation, a masterpiece. Do not think for a moment, my dear reader, that I approve of falsehoods. But I think it best to tell one rather than hazard two lives, and the honor and freedom of a princess. Others may have different opinions, but I am convinced that mine is the only rational one. This falsehood will also prove that necessity is the mother of invention, and also prove it in a most literal way. (This is not intended for a pun.)

The story was as follows:

"Yesterday Ali and I met the daughter of an innkeeper. As she was very pretty, and wore no veil, we fell in love with her. Her father was a Greek Christian, named Alexis Constantius. The girl's name, we learned, was Olga.

"Now, my friends, as you all know, Ali and I are the best of friends so I said to him, 'Ali, we'll not get jealous of each other, but go to the girl's father and let him choose which he'll take for his girl's husband. And, perhaps, he won't have either of us. At any rate, the chances are the same.'

"Well, Ali agreed to this, and we followed the girl home. We soon found her father and laid the case before him in very eloquent terms. He was much impressed by the stories we told of our great wealth and riches, but, for the soul of him, couldn't tell which suited him best. So he took us to the girl and told her to choose.

" 'I don't want either of them,'" says she, with a contemptuous toss of her head.

" 'But, Olga, you *must* choose,' says old Alexis. 'They are both rich men and one is the Sultan's nephew.'

" 'I'll not marry a Mohammedan,' says Olga. 'And besides, how do you know they're telling the truth?'

" 'But look at their uniforms. That is sufficient proof that they are captains.'

" 'A person need not be a captain to possess a captain's uniform,' says the girl.

"That scared Alexis. He told us that we must produce proof of our statements.

"So we took out the Sultan's signet ring, which we still had, and showed it to him. That convinced him that we were telling no lies.

" 'Come again, to-morrow,' says he, and I'll tell you what I think of it. I know not yet which of you will make the best husband for my daughter.'

"We took this for a dismissal and went out, feeling pretty well satisfied. We had done better than we thought to do."

"Well done, Abdul," said Abeuka. "You convinced him al-right. Now what happened next?"

"Well," said Abdul, going on. "It was late at night when we started home, about nine I should say. Half-way to the barracks we were waylaid by one Alexandre Pouffski and a band of young Greeks. It seemed, as this fellow told us later that he was a rejected suitor for Olga's hand, and hearing of our success, had determined to put an end to us ere either got the girl.

"They attacked us and we backed up against a wall and drew our swords. We held them off awhile, but finally we had to give up. We fell to the ground breathing hard, while Alexandre told us what he thought of us. He cursed us very thoroughly, but I dare not repeat the blasphemies he used, for fear that God will strike me dead. He cursed the prophet, the Alkoran and all that has to do with the true religion. Yes, my brothers, this infidel dared to do it. Had he fallen dead on the spot I should not have been astonished. His words seemed to strike me dumb. And Ali has told me that it was the same with him.

"We did not hear him to the last, for we fell in a dead faint, partly caused by our loss of blood, and partly by the blasphemies of this infidel.

"Taking us for dead, the whole band left and when we recovered the street was deserted. We made the best of our way to the barracks and fell asleep instantly."

"Is that all?" asked Abeuka.

"Yes," said Abdul. "Do you want any more?"

At this point the agha interfered.

"Your tale would be very plausible if it were not for one little particular," he said. "The Sultan's signet ring was left in my possession by you on the night that you came here. I do not think that he gave you a duplicate!"

Chapter VII

A thunder-bolt entering the room could not have surprised us more. We sat back in our chairs, the very picture of discomfiture.

Everyone, with the exception of Abdul and I, laughed outrageously, the agha included. Before they had done we two rose from the table and walked out. Abdul's cheeks, I noticed were burning with shame, and he has since told me that mine were a perfect reflection.

Be it as it was, we were very angry, Abdul at himself for his clumsiness, and I at everything in general and nothing in particular except myself.

"All hope is gone," said Abdul, "Abeuka will be more suspicious than ever. Depend upon it, he'll never stop till he discovers our secret. I read it in his face. He will hear of the fight with the Bostanjis and the disappearance of the princess and will connect us with it all. And to make matters worse, they have a pretty good description of us. I don't think Bikri Mustapha would recognize us if he saw us, but the Bostanjis will. If we're not arrested to-day, I don't know what I'm talking about!"

"But what can we do?" said I.

"We can run away," returned Abdul.

"Never!" said I. "Remember, Abdul, that we are soldiers."

Abdul sighed. "That's the worst of it," he said. "We lose our honor if we desert. We are pledged to fight for his Majesty. Still if it were not for my uncle, I would not stay in Istanboul ten minutes. The thought of the dishonor it would bring upon him, deters me from such an act. Still, if we're not arrested by this afternoon, we had better go over to Pera and stay there for the night. But that is extremely unlikely. What's this?"

At that moment we discerned two horsemen enter the barrack grounds with several men walking behind. As they drew nearer, I saw the Bikri Mustapha was one of them and that the other was the Sultan himself. The men behind were Bostanjis, one of whom I recognized as one of my late opponents. There were five of them in all.

"As I thought," whispered Abdul, "they've come for us, bringing men who will identify us."

"Betray no uneasiness," I replied, "but look as unconcerned as possible. Feign surprise if they accost us. Perhaps, after all they'll not recognize us. There are other officers here who resemble us."

"Not much chance of a mistake," my companion replied bitterly, surveying his bandaged neck and blood-stained uniform. "No, but there's a chance. Come, let's walk slowly towards the barracks. We can enter and reach my room ere they catch us."

"What good will that do?"

"It would be a respite."

"I shall see the whole thing thru. Run if you want to. I'm going to put a bold face on the matter and deny every charge they can make."

"So shall I," I rejoined.

We strolled unconcernedly towards the riders and betrayed much surprise when they came up to us. It was well-done, well-acted, but to no use.

The Bostanjis rapidly surrounded us to prevent all attempts at escape. The Sultan, and Bikri Mustapha, after the latter had scowled savagely at Abdul, rode on to the barracks.

"What do you think you're doing?" said Abdul, staring one of the Bostanjis in the eye. "I'd like to know what right you have to treat us in this manner. By ———, if you don't let us go I'll cut your head off!"

"We have been ordered by our master, the padishah, to arrest you," said the man addressed. "As to why, you know that as well as I do."

"Indeed I don't," said Abdul, nonchalantly. "I wish you'd explain."

The Bostanji vouchsafed no reply and at a motion from him, his comrades seized us and bound us with ropes. Thru it all, we preserved an injured, surprised air, as of persons subjected to an outrage, of whose cause they are ignorant.

I was not frightened, only excited to an undue degree. I knew the fate that we would meet, and yet was singularly unafraid. I know not what to set it down to. My modesty forbids me to boast that it was my courage, so I must say that I think it due to—oh well, it matters nothing. Such things can take care of themselves.

As to Abdul's state of mind, I know nothing, so I must go on with the story.

A few moments after our arrest, the Sultan and Bikri Mustapha returned bringing the agha with them. They came up to where we were and the agha spoke.

"Young men," he said, "I am heartily sorry for what you have done. I had formed a very good opinion of you, and now I find that your actions have torn it into a thousand fragments. I think it just that you should meet any punishment that his Majesty may think it best to sentence you to."

The Sultan's speech was somewhat the same, tho briefer. Bikri Mustapha said nothing, but his expression was more eloquent than words.

"I must now request your swords," said the padishah.

We drew them and handed them to his Majesty. That person handed them to Bikri Mustapha. After bestowing a horrible grimace upon us, he took Abdul's weapon across his knees, spat upon it, snapped it in two and flung it away.

He then made ready to deal with mine in the same way. I stood looking on in speechless agony, while the rude Bostanjis and some of the janissaries, who had been attracted by unusual sounds, stood looking on, laughing at our disgrace. Prominent among them was Abeuka, and upon him I bestowed a glance that would have soured milk. He laughed again, and his companions joined in with him.

"Silence!" roared the agha, angrily. Abeuka and his facetious companions immediately subsided. I now turned to look at Bikri Mustapha, who was making an attempt to break my sword. The tough Damascus steel, tempered and hardened by a process unknown to mankind in these degenerate days, would not even bend. Bikri swore furiously. I laughed with joy and the padishah, the agha, and the Bostanjis, stood looking on in evident embarrassment.

It was very comical. Words fail to express Bikri's actions, or rather contortions. He twisted first this way and that, blaspheming all the while, cursing the sword, the steel it was made from, its maker and the day he was born on, and all his relations and ancestors back to Adam, and every one of his descendents. He also included me in the category, and all my relations and forefathers, the day I was born on, the day I was to die on, and every individual day of my life. He cursed me sleeping, waking, fighting, sitting still, frowning, smiling, and eating. In short, he cursed nearly everything.

He wound up by damning me, living and dead, and committed me to eternal perdition. With his last words, he flung the scimitar away, and coming up to me, still swearing, caught me by my mustache, and spat on it.

My arms being bound, I could only kick at him. This I did very effectively and he sat down on the ground, howling madly. The Bostanjis dragged me off and he got up, cursing more volubly than ever. He then went up to the padishah who had been much amused by what took place, and asked permission to kill me on the spot.

This request Murad refused, saying that he could do it later, when the trial was over, and that he could also have the pleasure of beheading Abdul.

Bikri eagerly accepted this permission, and kneeling before the Sultan, kissed his foot. Every eye was upon him and no one was watching me. I lifted my foot with a right good will, and kicked him as hard as I could. He fell prostrate, banging his pate with great force, against Murad's shins.

Both of them emitted yells that would have awakened the Seven Sleepers of the Christians, and immediately fixed upon me as the cause of their discomfiture.

They came at me furiously, but the Sultan recollected his dignity at the last moment, and stepped back with a frown upon his countenance. Not so with Bikri Mustapha. He came right on, bound upon ending me there and then. It was all very amusing. One of the captains of the janissaries who had been looking on, stepped up silently behind me, without being observed by the guards, and at the crucial moment, cut the bonds which bound my arms. He then stepped back amongst his comrades, who all fell a-laughing at his bold exploit, and prepared to watch what followed.

At the crucial moment, as I before remarked, the ropes fell from my body. I lifted my arm in time to parry Bikri's fist, and the next moment, knocked him down. He rose, bellowing with rage, and came at me again. He had lost all self-control, and struck wildly and fast. As a consequence he was again knocked down. The Sultan, in spite of himself, fell to laughing and had to be carried away by the agha and the Grand Vizier.

The Grand Vizier returned at the very moment that Bikri again rose to his feet, and ordered the Bostanjis to seize me. They, however, bore Bikri and the Grand Vizier a number of grudges, and simply declined to obey. The formed a ring around us, to prevent us escaping.

Abdul, who had been looking on all the time took no part in the contest except to mutter words of encouragement.

Bikri Mustapha got decidedly the worst of the fight. Six times I knocked him down and on the seventh he did not rise again. He lay quietly on his back, his face covered with bruises and breathing like a porpoise. He was half-unconscious.

At that moment Ismail Pasha, and the padishah returned. "Seize Zagan!" roared Murad. "Mutinous wretches, see you not that he is unbound?"

The Bostanjis came at me and again tied my arms, tho more securely this time. They took my pistols and yataghan, and gave them into the care of the agha.

Bikri had by this time risen to his feet, and after making an ineffectual attempt to burn me into cinders with his ferocious scowl, returned to the padishah. I noticed that he was tottering and that he was likely to fall at any time.

Supported by the Grand Vizier, he walked very well, and avowed his intention of returning to the Seraglio.

The procession immediately set forth from the barracks grounds and towards the palace. Abdul and I were closely guarded and made no attempt to escape.

Much attention was attracted by us, and a great crowd followed after. Amongst them were a number of janissaries. About half-way to the Seraglio, they set upon our guards and hacked several of them to pieces. The freed us immediately and one thrust a sword into my hand. Upon looking at it more closely I found that it was my own!

"Shall we escape?" Abdul whispered in my ear. The janissaries stood about us, imploring us to go while there was yet time. Already we heard the galloping of hoofs and knew that reinforcements, attracted by the unusual commotion, would soon arrive.

"Come," I replied, and escorted by half-a-dozen of our friends, we made our way quickly thru the crowd, which recognizing us, opened a way, and closed immediately behind to prevent the passage of any foes.

We at length emerged and after thanking our rescuers most hastily, set out we knew not where.

As we went our blood, excited by the riot, began to cool down. A sense of honor returned, and with it a knowledge of the disgrace that would fall upon us.

"I am going to the Seraglio," I said. "I do not wish to be a deserter, a fugitive from justice!"

"And I go with you," said Abdul, resolutely, with a set face. I'd rather face any death than have the stigma of 'deserter' attached to my name."

And forthwith we bent our steps towards the palace, well knowing that we were thrusting our heads into the jaws of death.

But we thought not of that, but of our honor, which was as yet comparatively unstained. An hours walking brought us to the gates. We were just in time to see the Sultan, the Grand Vizier, Bikri Mustapha, and what remained of our guards, enter.

The two of us walked resolutely up to the sentry and asked for admittance. The fellow knew us well, and readily let us in, on our statement that we had important business with the padishah.

We caught up with the Sultan and his escort, just as they reached the Seraglio. Bikri, hearing rapid footsteps, turned and saw us. His amazement is beyond the power of my pen to express.

We stepped past him, drew our swords, and kneeling before the Sultan, presented them to him, hilt foremost.

His face was a mixture of admiration and astonishment. "You are very brave men," he exclaimed fervently, evidently unable to think of anything else to say.

"Your majesty," I said, " we humbly beg your pardon for escaping. Our friends hurried us away under the excitement of the moment, and we scarcely knew what we did. When our senses returned, we came here with them."

"You have done well," said the Sultan. "Men like you are the kind that Turkey needs. If all my soldiers had your courage they would be invincible."

"Your Majesty," I replied, "we did only what we considered our duty."

"Your Majesty," said Bikri, stepping up to the Sultan, "these men have surrendered themselves, merely for the purpose of making a favorable impression on your mind, so as to prepare you for pardoning them."

"Silence!" roared Murad. "Wretch, go to your room! Appear not in my sight to-day, lest thy form offend me, and I be not responsible for my deeds!"

Bikri slunk away, casting a malignant glance in our direction as he went. I knew that he would not love us any better, after the manner in which we had brought him into the Sultan's disfavor.

"If you will tell me the whole truth about my niece's disappearance, and your own part in it, and her whereabouts, I will grant you a full pardon," said his Majesty, turning to us.

"If your majesty will promise that the princess be not compelled to marry Bikri Mustapha," said I.

"I swear it on the Koran!" said Murad, laying his hand on a copy of the book, which had been produced by the Grand Vizier.

Therefore, without hesitation, Abdul and I told the true story of all that had happened after the Bostanji had brought us Fatima's message, up to the time of our arrest.

"You did much wrong," said the Sultan, when we had finished, "but love," and he smiled, "is responsible for much."

Abdul and I blushed at this, and freely acknowledged that we loved the princess.

"You can come to see her at any time you wish, " he said. "I should be proud to have either of you as her husband. But the princess herself must choose as to that. I promise you once again that Bikri shall not wed her."

He then called for pen and ink and paper and wrote a note to the agha, briefly stating that we were forgiven.

This he entrusted to our care and bade us begone, after telling us that he would send a messenger to the princess, with her pardon and a request to return to court.

We expressed our most heartfelt thanks to the padishah and left the Seraglio, with joyful step.

We at length arrived at the barracks, and were met with shouts of joy by our comrades. Going immediately before the agha, we presented him with the Sultan's note.

"I am glad that it is so," he said cordially, as we left the room. "We cannot afford to lose men like you."

Outside the door we were met by the officers, who were very anxious to hear the true story of our adventures.

That night we told them, and were wildly applauded at every incident. There was so much carousing, that the common soldiers concluded their officers had gone mad, and some of them ran to see what was the matter.

No sooner had they looked in and seen Abdul and I sitting on empty wine casks, relating our tale to a wildly applauding audience, than they needs must enter.

Nor did the officers throw them out. They were received with shouts of joy and allowed to stay as long as they pleased.

About midnight most of us were so drunk that we fell asleep, and those who had sufficient strength left to drag themselves away to their rooms, did so. Abdul and I were among the latter.

Chapter VIII

It was three days ere Abdul and I availed ourselves of his Majesty's permission. On the afternoon of the third day, we set out for the Seraglio.

On our arrival, we were graciously received by the Sultan.

"It only remains for her to choose which of you she'll have for her husband," said he. "I don't know which of you is the favored one, but I know that she loves one of you. You'll have to ask her about it. As to myself, I'll have nothing to do with the affair. Keep an eye on Bikri. He'll do you an injury if he sees a chance."

Somewhat astonished by this speech, we were ushered into the presence of the princess.

She was seated on a divan, attended by several eunuchs, one of whom was fanning her with a long-handled fan, for the weather was excessively hot.

Fatima immediately spied us, and with a smile, bade us be seated. As the divan was the only visible seat in the apartment, Abdul and I made bold to place ourselves by her side, one on each side.

Fatima immediately spied us, and with a smile, bade us be seated.

As she seemed to be waiting for us to speak, I motioned Abdul to do so. For awhile, the conversation was somewhat strained, all three of us being extremely embarrassed.

"I suppose you are anxious to know what happened to me after you left the tailor's house," she said at last. Abdul and I intimated that we were. "Well, I suppose I must tell you the story. There is not much to it, but it may interest you."

"Of course, of course," we chorused.

"I slept very ill that night and awoke in the morning with a slight headache. The tailor's wife was very kind to me, and after a while I began to feel at ease.

"Judge of my surprise that afternoon when two of the Sultan's gardeners entered and demanded the princess. I was ready to die of fright, thinking that I would be sewn up in a sack, with cats to tear out my eyes, and thrown into the Bosphorus.

"Coming up to where I stood, trembling with fear, they salaamed profoundly, and informed me that his Majesty had granted me a free pardon, and that I was not to marry Bikri Mustapha. I was overjoyed at this, and after thanking the tailor and his wife for their kindness, I was conducted back to the Seraglio.

"The padishah greeted me kindly, and forgave me for my wild escapade. He also seconded the promise that I was not to marry Bikri Mustapha, and here, my dear friends, you find me."

The ice was broken. After that our conversation flowed smoothly and easily. There was no more embarrassment to contend with.

Abdul and I led gradually to the main point. That the reader can guess for himself. I shall only say that the two of us were violently in love with Fatima. Strange as it may seem to you, we were not jealous of each other. We knew, or thought we knew, that both of us had an equal chance to win the princess' favor.

For half and hour we conversed on various things, finally leading up to that of love. Here we had an animated discussion. The princess maintained that love had no place in marriage; that wealth and power were the main things. Abdul joined in with her and I was left to fight them both alone. The eunuchs had been dismissed, but I knew that they were lurking outside the door to hear everything that was said. Such it is in the palace of the Sultan, eternal suspicion and watching, and trust in nobody.

But now to return to our discussion.

"Most happy marriages," said the princess, "have been made, not for love, but for wealth. In such unions as these, there being no love, there can consequently be no jealousy. Suppose the wife takes a liking to another man; suppose they run away from the husband. Neither the wife nor the husband can have anything to complain of. She has the person she loves, and he has the wealth that he married her for, without the encumbrance of a wife. Tho such a happening is obviously immoral, it satisfies all parties concerned."

"Your argument is very cold-blooded," I said, "and besides it has many faults. The runaway wife might become dissatisfied with her seducer, or he with her. Unhappiness would be the only result. Besides, it is too immoral. You said that in a marriage for wealth, there being no love, there could be no jealousy. You are right about that, but there are other things besides jealousy which can interrupt the course of happiness. What happiness can result from the union of two such people! They become angry with one another over the smallest happening, they quarrel on any little provocation. Consequently they are always in a state of dissatisfaction with one another. If they loved each other, all these little things would be overlooked, and a reconciliation be made even after a big quarrel."

"You reason very well, Ali," said the princess, "and I must admit that you picked my poor argument into pieces in short order. What to say next I don't know. I can think of nothing to support my tottering standard."

"Why not admit defeat," I said. "Surely there is no disgrace in that. You only waste your strength in useless endeavour if you struggle more. Save it till a future time."

"It is good advice," she replied, smiling, "and I'm inclined to surrender. Abdul may carry on the fight if he so wishes."

"I have no wish to do so," said that person, winking at me. "If my leader submits, I too, must do so."

The subtle flattery of this was not lost upon Fatima. That I noticed by the reddening of her cheeks.

"Abdul must think me a very paragon in argument," was the sweet remark.

"I do," said Abdul, fervently.

At this point I could not restrain my sarcastic tongue. The words were out of my mouth ere I understood their meaning. "People who are in love always think that of the object of their affections," I said.

Abdul glared at me. The princess looked at the floor, her face scarlet with indignation. The cat was surely out of the bag now!

"Ali is right," said my friend, "I love you, Fatima!"

The princess said nothing. Finally she raised her eyes and directed them at me.

"I love you, too," I said in a low voice. "Forgive me for my rash words. They were spoken in an injudicious moment. Believe me, I said them ere I knew what I was about."

For answer Fatima rose from the divan and walked slowly towards the door. She looked at neither of us, but straight ahead. Finally she disappeared.

"Bungler!" said Abdul, furiously the moment she was gone. "What'll she think of us now?"

"If she thinks anything of us," I said, "her love will not by cooled by my remark. She may be offended for a time, but it can last no more than a few hours." Abdul said nothing, and we went out, feeling decidedly gloomy and ill-at-ease with the world in general.

His Majesty remarked our gloomy expressions. "Better luck next time, my friends," he said gaily. "There is more than one way to skin an animal."

The rest of that day no sun shone for us. If it did, we were utterly oblivious of it. Our comrades at the barracks soon discovered that something was amiss, and readily guessed the cause. Abeuka was inclined to twit us about it. That was what brought on the trouble. "Wouldn't the princess have either of you?" he asked.

"That's none of your business," said Abdul, hotly. "I'd thank you to leave me alone."

But the captain was not to be suppressed. "I'll wager you ten piastres that I'm right," he said.

"And I'll wager you my life that you're wrong," said Abdul, springing up, with his hand on his sword-hilt. I knew well that tone that he spoke in boded ill for the taunter. But I said nothing, feeling very angry at Abeuka.

Abeuka also had a quick temper. He liked neither of us over-well, tho he had been somewhat friendly, and wanted only and excuse to vent his feelings. He glared at Abdul. Abdul returned the glare. For a moment neither said anything.

Finally a quick movement from Abdul brought the matter to a head. He moved his arm suddenly and gave Abeuka a resounding slap on the left cheek. Abeuka's face turned white, not with fear, but with anger. "You are the challenger," he said, "but I allow you to choose the weapons, time and place."

"I have challenged you," said Abdul, "and you must make the choice."

"I choose pistols, this room and the present moment," said Abeuka.

He took his station at one end of the room, and Abdul at the other. They gave me the pistols to load. I acted as my friend's second, and another officer as Abeuka's.

There was deathly silence for a moment. The captains were ranged on either side the combatants, all alert and interested. It was seldom that a duel was fought among the janissaries.

All eyes were riveted on me as I loaded the pistols. I then handed one to each of the antagonists. But instead of balls, I had loaded each with a lead-colored pellet of paper! I did not choose that either of the two captains should be hurt, especially Abdul.

I then held up my turban. "One—two—three!" The turban dropped. Both fired at once. Abdul's bullet struck his enemy in the face and fell harmlessly to the floor. Abeuka's shot took Abdul in the center of his chest. Both were greatly astonished.

The bullets were picked up and inspected more closely. It was then found that they were of paper. Every one laughed with the exception of Abdul and his opponent. "This is one of your tricks, Ali," said the former, angrily.

This time each of them loaded his own pistol, determined not to trust me again.

I now raised the turban once more. "One—two—three!" Down went the turban. Abdul raised his pistol like a flash and fired. Abeuka's weapon, shivered into pieces, fell to the floor. His hand was not touched!

There was a chorus of applause. "You are a good shot, Abdul," said many. Abeuka's face was white with fear. He saw there was no chance in fighting this man. He stepped forward to where Abdul stood. "I apologize," he cried.

"And I accept your apology," replied Abdul, gravely. The two shook hands and were friends once more. After that, Abeuka did not venture to tease Abdul. He knew only too well what the result would be. But the fight was not without its aftermath.

The agha entered, attracted hither by the sound of firing. He looked at us and immediately detected the duelists; Abdul with the smoking pistol in his hand, and Abeuka's pale face with a red mark upon it where the paper bullet had struck. The shattered pistol on the floor did not escape his eyes.

"What means this?" he asked sternly. The two duelists told him the story. "It must not happen again," he said, as he went out. "His Majesty has forbidden all dueling amongst soldiers."

And now, ere I go on to a more important portion of the story, let me give a little incident which occurred at the barracks that evening. It may serve to illustrate the kind of humor current among the soldiers.

A certain captain named Ahab was one of the main factors. He was a medium-sized man, neither short nor tall, and had come from Scutari. He was a practical joker among the officers, and was perhaps the only one.

The agha had risen from the table somewhat earlier than usual and the officers were left to themselves. Ahab, thinking that no one was looking, took a small snake from his bosom. It was of a harmless sort, about half an inch in thickness, and over two feet long. The name of it I have forgotten, but it does not matter.

Holding the snake in his hands he leaned towards Abdul, who sat beside him, and was at that moment looking the other direction, he slipped the reptile down his back, and within his shirt. I alone saw him, but I said nothing at the time.

Abdul leapt to his feet with a cry of amazement, and clutched wildly at his back. All of us laughed loudly at his predicament, the joker included. Indeed, he excelled us all in that particular.

At last Abdul got a hold on the snake's tail. The snake wiggled himself loose and leisurely crawled down Abdul's body, emerging at last from the bottom of his pantaloons. Abdul grabbed it by the neck as it came out and at last secured it safely. He then turned about and demanded furiously who the joker was. I pointed at Ahab.

My friend seized the unluckly humorist by the collar, and administered to him a sound thrashing, using the snake as a whip.

Ahab yelled and squirmed to escape, but in vain. Abdul did not release him till he was thoroughly bastinadoed. He got up, much crestfallen and regained his seat, amidst roars of laughter. No more practical jokes were played on Abdul after that.

Chapter IX

A week had passed by. It had been a very quiet week devoid of any important events in our lives. We had been to see Fatima twice, but she was very cold and distant. My rash words seemed to have offended her.

We saw Bikri Mustapha several times. He was as malignant towards us as possible and neglected no opportunity of displaying his hate for us. I shall not weary the reader by a recital of this man's little acts of meanness. They are utterly unnecessary, for the reader has already been given several pieces of his conduct.

And now to get down to business. On Monday afternoon of the second week, Abdul and I found ourselves starting for the palace. It was exactly three o'clock when we set out.

I shall never forget that memorable journey. I have in my mind's eye the scene that confronted us as we went along. A dull blue, half-purple sky overhead, narrow streets, monotonous houses, much alike as to appearance, and seemingly deserted. Here and there a market-place and a row of gay bazaars, with great crowds of gaily-clothed people of every class and nationality, from the veiled Turkish woman of high rank, to the Armenian beggar at the street corner.

At last we came to a long, dark alley. A person with outstretched arms could easily have touched both sides of it at once. Above our heads some fifteen feet or so, the roofs of the houses almost met, but left a streak of sky, a foot in width. Here all was silence save for the barking of an occasional mangy cur. Below our feet was refuse and filth and at one side a gutter of dirty water. The alley was shrouded in semi-darkness, and was some seventy feet in length. The odors were almost unendurable.

About the center of this place we met our fate. I have a dim recollection of several figures with bludgeons in their hands, springing out from a corner, and of a stinging blow on the head. After that, all was oblivion and silence.

When I came to I found myself lying on a couch. I recovered slowly, scarcely knowing what had happened. My first feeling was a pain in the head. After that I quickly awakened and finally sat up with a full knowledge of what had happened to me.

Upon looking around, I saw that I was in a medium-sized, well-furnished room. A richly covered couch served as my bed. On the other side of the room I saw a similar one with the body of a man lying upon it. Upon closer inspection I discovered that it was my friend Abdul. There was a lump on his head the size of a goose-egg, and he was perfectly senseless. His heart beat slowly and his face was very pale.

There were two windows in the room, both being in the side. They were heavily barred, and the bars were six inches apart. The furniture of the room, besides the two couches, consisted of a couple of tables, a number of rugs, and three or four chairs of European fashion. The walls were tapestried with rich tapestries, embroidered with flowers, and other objects of nature. There was only one door, and that was in the side opposite to the windows. There were several large pictures of landscapes, one of them of Japanese workmanship, and a small statue.

The door was of thick cedar, and very heavily barred and bolted. All my efforts to open it were in vain. I then went to the window and looked out. At least twenty-five feet below me was a garden planted with all variety of trees and flowers and surrounded by a high wall. I soon perceived that I was in the top floor of some house. I then walked over to the tables and inspected them. They were of oak and carved with all manner of designs. On one of these I found half-a-dozen books and as many more manuscripts, and on the other a platter of meat and bread and a large jug of water.

By this time I saw that Abdul was manifesting signs of recovery. He rolled over several times, and finally off the couch. The fall, tho it was only a couple of feet, thoroughly awakened him. He struggled slowly to his feet and finally perceived me. "Where are we, Ali?" said he, "and what has happened?"

"As to where we are, I know no more than you," I replied. "But I may to able to give some answer to the other question. I think we have been knocked on the head."

For the first time, Abdul perceived his wound. "I've been hit with a bludgeon," said he. "I wonder if your good friend, Bikri Mustapha, is concerned in this."

As if in answer to the question, the door opened and Bikri Mustapha stepped in. He was richly attired and seemed well-pleased with himself and the world in general, or at least anyone would take it that way. He bowed profoundly upon entering and then seemed to wait for us to speak.

"How came my friend and I in this place?" Abdul asked.

"By my orders," said Bikri, smiling till he almost grinned.

"And why?"

"Because I wished it to be so."

"And why did you wish it to be so?"

"Because I don't want either of you to marry the princess," replied Bikri with a shameless grin.

"What do you intend to do with us?"

"Kill you, of course."

"And when, may I ask?"

"Immediately," said Bikri. A second later he whistled shrilly and we heard the sound of running feet. Our captor sprang thru the doorway to avoid capture and presumably to lead his men.

With great presence of mind, Abdul slammed the door behind him and piled one of the couches against it. The movement was so quick that it was executed ere our enemies reached it. They recoiled with howls of rage. Evidently this was not what they had expected. A moment later they hurled themselves upon the door. But the door held at the first assault. Before another could be made we had piled the other couch, the chairs, and the two little tables against it. The books, and the food and water we placed in a distant corner.

Upon reaching for his sword, Abdul found that it was missing. All his other weapons were also gone. I found myself in the same condition.

"Nothing but our fists!" groaned my friend.

"We have the tables," I replied, "They're of heavy oak, and about the right size."

"That picture frame," said Abdul, upon casting his eyes around the room, "is made of four rods of brass, joined together at the four corners. It's just what we want."

In a moment he had leaped up and brought down the picture. We tore the canvas out of the frame, pulled the rods apart (they being fastened together by rivets) and in a trice were armed with two clubs apiece. The rods were round, about an inch in thickness, and two feet in length. They felt very comfortable.

Scarcely had this been accomplished, when the men without again threw themselves upon our door. It, however, resisted all their efforts. They retired at last, leaving several men behind to see that we did not escape. The presence of these guards we discovered by their footsteps as they paced to and fro in front of the door.

In about five minutes the besiegers returned, bearing some heavy object with them. This, we rightly conjectured, was a battering-ram.

They drew back a little ways, and then charged. The door cracked in two, and the barricade behind it stirred as if shaken by an earthquake. Again they drew back and charged once more.

The door split from top to bottom, and a portion of it fell away. Thru this gap the foremost of the besiegers leaped. He fell with a broken head. The others were quick to follow him. We killed three of them and wounded another badly. The remainder, of whom there were some half-a-dozen, came in headed by Bikri Mustapha.

We seized a couple of scimitars from the hands of the dead men and leaped to the wall. There we stood and defied our enemies to do their worst. On they came, Bikri at the head. He ran straight at Abdul. Two of his men followed his example. I had all I could do, and more, with the remaining three.

One of my enemies came at me in front and the others attacked at the sides. I had a hard time to beat them off. They then retired to the other side of the room and began to fire at me with their pistols. They wounded me in the left arm and in the right thigh. The latter wound, however, was merely a gash in the side of the leg. It was in no way serious.

As a reply I hurled one of my bars at them. The tallest fell with his forehead completely crushed in. The other end of the missile broke the left arm of his nearest companion. He hurled it back at me with a yell of rage. It crashed into the wall a few inches from my head and dropped harmlessly to the floor.

The man with the broken arm ran from the room and his remaining companion and one of Abdul's assailants attacked me. For several minutes we fought desperately, and with no sound except the heavy breathing of tired men and the clash of steel upon steel.

Looking sideways for a moment I saw that Abdul had been beaten to his knees. I struck desperately at one of his assailants. The blow was luckier than I had expected. The fellow's sword arm was lopped off below the elbow and fell to the floor. The man himself immediately fainted from loss of blood.

But this act gave my two opponents their chance. On they came and before I could turn they had struck me. One blow fell upon the right shoulder and the other I half-fended with my blade. It slipped and inflicted a slight wound in the left shin.

My scimitar fell from my nerveless hand and the two were atop of me. In a trice my hands and feet were bound securely. As my captors bore me out of the room, I turned my head for one brief moment and saw Bikri plunge his blade into Abdul's prostrate body.

I shut my eyes with a deep groan. Slowly but surely I relapsed into unconsciousness. The footsteps of my carriers seemed to grow fainter and fainter, and after that, complete darkness—and *nothing.*

After a while, it may have been minutes, or it may have been hours, I began to awake to a knowledge of the world. My first dim thought was that I was in Paradise. I opened my eyes slowly, and finally concluded that I was not. At any rate, the place I was in was as much unlike Paradise as any place in the universe.

It was a room, somewhat similar to the one I had left. I was reclining on a couch, and several men were standing over me. One I dimly recognized as Bikri Mustapha. The shock of this recognition completely awoke me. I sat up and stared about. Besides Bikri there were five or six other men, two of whom I recognized as my late enemies. The rest I did not know.

One of them, dressed from head to foot in black, and wearing a black mask, stood leaning on a long ax. Near him was a wooden block. He was a tall muscular fellow, and what I could see of his face wore an expression of sadness.

Upon seeing him, Bikri's threat that Abdul and I should die, flashed across my mind. "This fellow then," I said to myself, "is here to kill me. Well, I'd rather die by his hand than by Bikri's."

When the drunkard saw that I was recovered he turned to me and said: "Ali Zagan, you are now to die. Rise from your couch and do so as bravely as you can. I long to kill you by mine own hand, but I have granted you the favor of being beheaded by a public executioner. You cannot then say that you have been murdered. If you have anything to say, say it quickly. We have but little time for fooling with such as you. I must be at the palace by night-fall."

Very slowly, and feeling exceedingly faint, I rose from the couch. My brain was working furiously and fast, to devise some means of escape, or at least of delaying the execution. Ere long, however, my mind hit upon a plan. Judge of its success yourself, dear reader, for if it had not succeeded, I should not now be seated in my dungeon writing these memoirs.

"Bikri," I said slowly. "How many wives have you?"

"I have two," he said slowly, his face paling somewhat.

"And our religion allows four," I said in reply. "But listen to me, my amiable friend. I know that you have more. The exact number I don't know, but in my room at the barracks are papers which prove it, and also a few crimes of yours. I have long intended to hand them over to the Sultan, but I have always forgotten to do so. If you kill me, my comrades will search my room and find those papers. They will, of course, be given to his Majesty. The consequences will be anything but pleasant for you."

When I had finished this discourse I saw that Bikri's face was deadly pale. Of course, all this had been but a guess, which might, or might not, be right. But by one of those vagaries of fate, it had turned out right!

"It is a lie!" shouted Bikri. "It is true that I have several concubines but what matters that! I can have has many as I want."

"They are wives," I said sternly, "and you know it as well as I do. I think it would be best for you to release me immediately. If you do not, the consequences will be severe."

"I shall do no such thing," said Bikri. "How do I know that you are telling the truth. I'll send a messenger to the barracks with the news that you want certain papers relating to me. The agha will, of course, allow him to hunt for the papers. My man will find them, if they are there, and that will be the end of the matter."

"And I am to die now?" I asked, all hope forsaking me.

"No," said Bikri. "You'll have to wait till the messenger returns. If the papers are not there, as I suspect is the truth, you'll die by a worse death than beheading."

For a moment I felt inclined to tell him the truth, preferring being beheaded to some more cruel death, but refrained at the last moment. Anything might happen in the hour it would take the messenger to go to the barracks and return.

A moment afterwards the aforesaid messenger went out and I sat down to wait as patiently as I could, his return, or anything that might occur in the meanwhile.

Chapter X

I lay down on the couch and soon fell asleep from faintness and fatigue. My sleep was troubled with strange dreams, more fantastic than words can tell, and at times I half awoke, and became somewhat conscious of my surroundings.

After ages had passed away (it seemed thus from the apparently long duration of the dreams) I awoke with a start. A man was bending over me with his finger on his lips. It was he who had awakened me. I sat up and stared at him. By the pale twilight streaming into the chamber, I recognized his face. My hair stood on end with horror. Could this be the ghost of my dead friend, Abdul Alcorez!

At that moment it seemed to be so. The features, the expression, the manner, were Abdul's. But how could this be Abdul in the body, when I had seen him stabbed thru and thru? Yes, it must be his ghost. What else could it be? It was clearly impossible for a dead man's body to be moving about like that. It was a totally unheard of thing. This, then, must be the dead man's spirit. But why had it come to me? Presumably to give me comfort, or else to save me from Bikri Mustapha's wrath. Yes, that was the only reasonable solution.

These thoughts, and more, which I have now forgotten, flashed through my brain in rapid succession, with the speed of lightning, while I sat there, on the couch, frozen stiff with terror.

And now the spectre made as if to speak. I covered my face with my hands and shrank back, as if dreading the sound of the voice. Why should I have thus shrunk from the spirit of one who had been so dear to me in life? That is a question for the psychologists to answer. You and I cannot. Therefore we shall not attempt to do so.

Then, with a sudden access of courage, I flung my fears to the four winds and stared straight into the eyes of the apparition. They were burning bright and the face was very pale. Yes, it *must* be a ghost. What else?

And then, oh! horror of horrors! the ghost spoke. I would fain have closed my ears, but I was powerless to do so, enthralled by the chains of the King of Terrors. At that moment I felt the deadly fascination which comes over some men when they find themselves face to face with a snake, whose bite meaneth death.

"Come," said the spirit. "The guards without the door are bound and gagged. They can do nothing. Come, my friend, ere it is too late! Bikri and his villains may enter at any moment. I wonder that they have not already slain you. You can explain that to me afterwards, Ali. There is no time now. The sun has, I think, been down half an hour."

Oh God! Explain my escape to a ghost! Well, it *could* be done. And with the aid of Allah I'd do it— if I escaped from this infernal prison.

At that moment, the apparition touched my arm with its hand. Could this be the hand of a ghost? Ghosts, I had heard, were formed of filmy matter, which could not be felt by a human being. *And the hand, which touched my arm, was of solid human flesh!*

"Abdul," I whispered, "how is it that you were not killed by Bikri's blow?"

"Hurry Ali," said my friend, "I'll tell you that later. Sufficient to say that it did not kill me."

All terror had now left me, and I rose from the couch with a feeling of great joy in my heart. Abdul, then was living, and was here to rescue me.

We tiptoed to the door and opened it silently. Without, all was darkness. We stepped carefully over the bodies of the two guards, and onward into a long corridor. At the end of said corridor we came full tilt against a door. Abdul pushed it gently open and we stepped into a room.

The twilight coming thru the windows showed it to be deserted and gave it an eerie, weird air. In the center was the top of a staircase, and down this we went, very carefully. It seemed interminable, and our footsteps as loud as the report of cannons. I verily believe, had we stopped for a moment, that I could have heard a pin drop. Such was the silence that we had to pass thru. I expected at every moment to be confronted by some horrible apparition.

But no such apparition favored me with a look at itself. Whatever, or whoever the apparitions were in that house, they were singularly unobliging. At the foot of the stairs we found ourselves in utter darkness. Upon groping about, Abdul discovered a door. Taking hold of the handle he pushed it gently open, and then recoiled in astonishment at what he saw.

A room brilliantly lighted by a score of candles, and containing a number of people. These people were seated at tables, eating. Bikri Mustapha was not amongst them, but I recognized the executioner and some more of my old enemies. The rest I did not know. There may have been a dozen altogether.

They had not seen the door open, the movement had been so soft and gentle. Abdul closed it softly ere they perceived it. "Now what shall we do?" he asked.

For answer, I turned to the stairs and began to ascend them. My friend followed close at my heels. But no other staircase could we find, and to the room we had just been in there was no other door save that entering the room in which were our enemies.

The windows were not available, they being barred and rebarred and we having no weapons with which to remove the bars. All at once an idea occurred to me, so simple that I wondered it had not occurred before. Perhaps it was its very simplicity that prevented me from thinking of it.

I confided it to Abdul in a whisper. He nodded assent and we forthwith proceeded to carry it out. We went to the bodies of the sleeping guards in front of the room in which I had so recently been incarcerated. We then quickly secured their weapons, and with these, hacked the bars of the windows into pieces. It was a jump of little more than fifteen feet to the garden below.

Abdul and I alighted without undue noise in the said garden. From it we escaped by leaping over the garden wall, aforesaid wall being some eight feet in height and made of uncut stone.

Once in the street we turned to view the house. A survey of its prominent features assured us against missing it on our return.

At that moment we came full tilt against a man. He swore profusely at us and I recognized his voice as being that of Bikri's messenger. This information I confided in an undertone to my friend Abdul.

We turned and leaped upon the messenger at the very moment he reached the door of the house. He fell silently to the ground and lay quite still. To make sure of him we bound him hand and foot with his turban which we tore in two strips, and carried him into a dark alley nearby. We also gagged him to prevent his yelling for help should he recover consciousness ere we returned.

After having accomplished this we set out for the barracks. The journey was without event, and lasted some twenty minutes. The sentry was somewhat indignant. "This is the second time you've returned late. If it happens again I'll have to report the happening to the agha. He'll know what to do with you."

"Perhaps," we answered, "but we have not stayed away at night because we wanted to, but because we had to. Include that in your report."

The fellow admitted us without more ado, and we went straight to the agha's room. He admitted us and demanded what we wanted.

We related our story, taking turns. "It is a bad affair," said Ismail, when we had finished. "His majesty must hear of it. I'll warrant he won't be pleased with Bikri."

"What are we to do now, agha?" I asked.

"Take twenty men and surround the house in which these men are. Capture them if you can, or if that is too hard, shoot them. It matters little to me."

Abdul and I left the building and went to that occupied by the common soldiers. We selected twenty of the best, for all clamored to go, upon learning of the object of this nocturnal expedition.

With these at our back we left the barracks and proceeded towards the house in which we had been incarcerated. We arrived there, as well as I can remember, somewhere about eight o'clock. The place was quietly surrounded, and then one of our men went up to the door and knocked. It was immediately opened by the executioner, who evidently thought that the messenger was without.

Upon perceiving the janissary he sprang back crying out. "We have been betrayed! The janissaries! The janissaries!"

The soldier immediately shot the executioner thru the heart. He fell at our feet with a wild cry.

There was evidently much confusion within. A pistol shot or two rang out, and someone slammed and bolted the door in our faces. We could hear them piling chairs and tables against it.

"Set the house on fire and form a cordon around it," I commanded. "Shoot all who attempt to escape. If any surrenders, bind him and bring him to me."

This order was immediately carried into effect. The house blazed up and we heard the yells of the inmates. Two of them sought to escape. They were both desperate fellows, and Greek mountaineers.

They issued from the house, firing at our soldiers, and when their weapons were all fired off, flung them in our faces. One was shot down ere he could do any mischief, but the other succeeded in wounding a janissary. He was shot down a moment later and fell, gasping his life out at my very feet. I passed my sword thru his body to make sure of him. His body moved slightly and I perceived the hilt of his sword. I drew it forth, and behold! it was my own. Evidently our weapons had been divided amongst this party.

The fight became more interesting now. Four of the besieged came out at once and charged in my direction, firing as they came. None of the bullets took effect.

Two were immediately shot down by the muskets of the soldiers. The remaining two, tho wounded in many places, succeeded in beginning a hand-to-hand combat. One attacked me, the other Abdul, for they had immediately recognized us.

I quickly cut down my adversary, but Abdul did not have such good luck with his. He was weak and faint from loss of blood, and his antagonist was a good swordsman.

My friend was laid low by a blow on the head, and did not rise again. It was fortunate for him that his enemy's weapon was a very blunt one. Had it been otherwise, Abdul's end should have been assured that night.

A moment later the desperate fellow was shot down by a man from Pera. He fell across Abdul's body.

The house was now thoroughly afire. The noise was awakening the city, and many heads peered forth from windows, and many shouts rang out upon the air.

What we took to be the rest of the besieged now issued from the flaming structure. I counted six of them in all. They rushed us in a body, like their four predecessors. There was some very lively fighting for a little while.

The greater part of our men collected together and surrounded them firing incessantly into their midst. Two dropped at the first volley. Their comrades returned our fire with precision. Three janissaries dropped dead, and a fourth was wounded in the arm.

Again we fired. Three fell, and the third, tho wounded, made a wild rush, firing his two pistols simultaneously. The native of Pera, who had killed Abdul's assailant, dropped, and I felt a red-hot something graze my left side, below the arm.

Wounded in half-a-dozen places, the fellow came on. When almost within striking distance, he fell, pierced thru and thru. A few seconds later we perceived another man come forth. He was an Arab, a veritable giant, and as everyone knows, the Arab hates the Turk violently.

This fellow came on at a terrific pace. His shots did not take effect and he drew his sword. It was a magnificent scimitar, over three feet in length and the blade was at least four inches wide at the broadest. It was a weapon which no one save a giant could wield.

A whole volley was directed at him, for all our men had gathered together. Many of the bullets took effect, but he only staggered and then returned to the attack.

A pistol volley was fired. It did not stop him. Another volley. Still he came on. Our men drew their swords and prepared for a hand-to-hand engagement. The giant struck wildly, killing two men at the blow, and maiming a third, and then with a wild yell, threw up his arms, staggered and then went down in a heap. The death-cry gurgled in his throat and he rolled over and lay still. He was the last man.

At the very moment of his death the house collapsed with a crash. Volumes of smoke went up and then all was comparatively still.

We then went to the dark alley and secured our prisoner, the messenger. The return to the barracks was a short, but sad one, for we had lost six killed and three wounded.

Abdul and I immediately retired, after having had our wounds dressed, and quickly fell asleep.

Chapter XI

At breakfast on the following morning I noticed that a number of the officers were very sulky and silent. They exchanged glances full of meaning, and occasionally winked at one another. That some conspiracy was on foot I had no doubt. I whispered my suspicions to Abdul, and he nodded in compliance.

During the exercises that morning I noticed that the soldiers seemed more discontented than ever. The expressions on their faces showed that something was wrong. There was much whispering in the ranks, but few of the officers took any notice of it. The drill was gone thru very badly, and I found much occasion for reprimanding the men of my company. Many of them murmured openly. Everything seemed to point to a mystery.

During the last few years there had been few insurrections amongst the janissaries. Murad had instilled fear into their hearts during the early years of his reign by executing and punishing great numbers of them. As a natural consequence they had been very obedient. What mutinies there had been were not wholesale, and were caused only by the dissatisfaction of some captain, aching to take revenge upon the Sultan for sundry real or imaginary wrongs.

The agha did not seem to notice the murmurings amongst the men. Possibly he did not, possibly he did. No one knows the truth. All that is certain is that he did not *seem* to.

After the exercises were over, Abdul and I went to him and unfolded our suspicions. He did not seem to regard them in a very serious light. "You may be right, or you may be wrong," he said. "It is most probable that you are wrong. There has been no wholesale mutiny for many years. It is true that there have been small ones, isolated instances. But what matters that? The cause of dissatisfaction, if dissatisfaction there is, has nothing to do with the Sultan. You can impart your suspicions to his Majesty if you wish, but I'm sure that he'll only laugh at you."

In the afternoon we went to the palace. His Majesty had already heard of the affair with Bikri Mustapha, and had reprimanded that person most severely. He had been almost on the point of banishing the fellow from the city, but had at the last moment refrained. But Bikri was under the ban of his Majesty's disfavor, and it would probably be long ere he was restored to his former influence with the padishah.

"Your Majesty," I said, "my friend Abdul and I noticed this morning that the soldiers seemed dissatisfied about something. They murmured at our orders, and many of the officers seem imbued with the same spirit. It seems to me that such actions can spell nothing but mutiny. The agha refuses to think so, and says that such things must be due to another cause."

"Is that the state of affairs at the barracks?" asked his Majesty.

"Yes, your Majesty," I replied.

"It means insurrection. Keep an eye on the men, and let me know if anything of an unusual character happens."

"Your Majesty's commands shall be obeyed to the letter," I replied.

After a short conversation with Fatima, we returned to the barracks. As we neared it I felt a subtle something in the very atmosphere. What it was I cannot tell, but I think it was the spirit of impending trouble. An uneasiness stole over me, that I am at a loss to account for, and Abdul experienced much the same feelings. Such things may seem strange and inexplainable to you, but they are an accomplished fact. The fact remains, and let he who can, divine its meaning.

There are many things in this world and in the next of which mortals know nothing. God alone possesses the key to Universal Knowledge, and to it man has not yet aspired. Yet he moves slowly forward in the path of knowledge,—slowly, it it true, but surely. He stops not, neither does he bound forward at an accelerated pace; but he goes always onward. At some distant period in the future, man will surely be able to explain happenings, which, to us, at this time, seem wholly unexplainable. This is the law of eternal, everlasting progress which goeth onward to the End.

But nothing unusual seemed to have taken place at the barracks. Still, there was around it that subtle something, which always spells trouble.

There was, during the remainder of the day, an ominous stillness in the air,—that stillness which invariably prevails on the eve of a great storm.

But something worse than a storm, infinitely worse, was to break forth that night. Everyone seemed to feel it, and everyone seemed to be prepared for it.

The great majority of the officers answered my greetings with a grunt, a monosyllable, or utter silence. Abeuka whispered as he passed me. "There's something wrong, Ali, and tho I'm not certain what it is, I think it's insurrection. Better look out for yourself."

Before I could answer, he was gone, and some officers nearby who had heard his words, frowned ominously, and glared at me as if I had been their worst enemy. They looked at me, nodded to each other, and moved away, still regarding me, and speaking in low tones among themselves.

While they were thus engaged I managed to slip unobserved, out of the room, and bent my steps towards the agha's apartment.

I reported all that had happened to him. "It certainly does not mean good," I said, at the end.

"No," he replied. "I advise you to keep your eyes open to-night. Go and bring to me all the officers whom you presume to be out of this mutiny. I shall send a messenger to his Majesty to report the matter. It is much more serious than I at first thought."

I proceeded immediately to carry out his orders. Ten minutes later, three captains, besides myself and Abdul, were assembled in the agha's apartment.

One of them was Abeuka, the other was Ahab, and the third, a man from Damascus, named Zamil. He was one of the finest swordsman in the Ottoman army. "Gentlemen," said Ismail Pasha, "I have called you here because of an impending mutiny amongst the soldiers. This mutiny may, or may not take place to-night, but it is best to be prepared for all emergencies. The cause is, of course, a dissatisfaction as to pay. They intend to compel the Sultan to increase it. All we can do is fight till help comes. At present there is no escape. They would know that if we left the barracks it would not be for ordinary reasons. Therefore we should be prevented, and this, doubtless, would bring the matter to a head. Therefore, gentlemen, we must stay here and do our best. If they attack, as they doubtless will do, we will be able to kill a few of them. We shall not be without companions on our journey to the next world."

Chapter XII

This speech was warmly applauded by all five of us. It voiced the sentiments of each, exactly. We were prepared to die, if need be, and take a few of the enemy along with us on our journey to the future world.

The mutineers evidently heard us for the bustle below stopped, and was followed by an ominous silence. Such a silence boded no good to us. A few minutes afterwards we heard the rattle of arms, and loud voices issuing commands. These voices we recognized as belonging to a couple of captains. Their names I have now forgotten, but they were the main ringleaders in this insurrection.

Soon we heard footsteps, and a babble of voices. These footsteps came nearer and nearer, and finally paused at the foot of the staircase.

Someone amongst them stepped out in front and called to us to open the door, swearing that no harm would be done us within—five minutes. The agha flung the door open and stepped out into full view. Abdul and I stood by his side with cocked pistols. The three captains were just behind us.

"What do you want, dogs of mutineers?" roared Ismail Pasha.

"This is our case," said one of the ringleaders, he who had called upon us to open the door. "Our pay is not enough. We presented a petition to his Majesty, begging him to increase it. He refused, saying that it was too much already. As a consequence we have determined to mutiny. We shall not return to our duty until our requests are satisfied. We shall go to the Seraglio and present these terms to the padishah. If he refuses to gratify us, we shall put Istanboul in a tumult, upset the entire city, prevent the sailing of any ships, and, in short, put a stop to all trade until his Majesty sees fit to give us what we ask. You have the choice of joining us or of being killed. Which do you take? I'll give you just three minutes to decide."

"Disobedient dog!" roared Ismail Pasha, "We have already made our choice. It is death, but we shall not die alone!"

Suiting the action to the words he leveled his pistol at the mutineer and fired. The fellow dropped to the floor, stone-dead.

There was silence for a little while, a silence that boded no good. Then the other ringleader spoke. "Shoot them!" he roared.

A hundred pistols cracked, and bullets flew past us by the score. Ahab fell, with a ball in his heart.

We did not wait for another volley, but leaping back into the room, bolted the door and put a heavy table against it.

For the next five minutes the room below was a scene of confusion. Muskets and pistols cracked incessantly, and the door was pierced in more than one place.

Then came order and voices issuing commands. We heard footsteps, as of men leaving the room. Presently they returned, bringing with them some heavy object, which we took to be a battering ram.

A little later came cheers and the sound of men coming up the stairs. There was a dull thud and the door shivered and cracked a little.

The batterers retired a little way and came on again. The door was shivered into many pieces, and fell, leaving only the table as an obstacle.

It, however, the enemy did not choose to batter down. They came on, with drawn swords, and strove to leap over it. Four of them we shot dead in the act. We then fired into the mass on the stair.

Four or five of these were killed or wounded, and fell, carrying many of their comrades with them. The mass struggled and cursed, and fought among itself.

The captains finally restored order, and the air above our heads was filled with flying bullets. We crouched behind the table for protection and fired at the enemy as fast as we could load.

We must have killed and wounded at least ten of them ere they saw fit to charge upon us again. We emptied our pistols amongst them, and then drew our swords.

This volley did not seem to check them much. On the contrary it served to increase their rage. Two or three of the captains had fallen.

Six of them we cut down, as they strove to surmount the barricade; but they shot down Abeuka, and wounded the agha badly.

They then drew back to the room below, and began firing at us. This gave us an opportunity to reload, and we returned the fire briskly. We dared not raise our heads above the table, but we guessed, from the shrieks that followed our shots, that they had taken effect. For three or four minutes this went on, and the table was riddled with lead.

Being of heavy oak, three inches in thickness, the bullets could not penetrate, inasmuch as they were fired from an angle which caused the bullets to enter on a slanted line, thus making the table as effective as a barricade of much greater thickness. The advantage of out position can thus be plainly seen.

Finally the mutineers, tired of firing, seeing that it did us no harm, decided upon another charge. They came leaping up the stairway, firing at every step, waving their swords and yelling like madmen. They were furious, desperately angry, and fully determined to slay all four of us ere much time passed away.

We reserved our fire until they were almost upon us, and then fired our eight pistols almost simultaneously. There was no chance of missing, and one bullet was sufficient to kill and wound two or three. About fifteen were killed and wounded, and they carried many others to the floor below in their fall.

About half of those on the stairs were swept away. The rest charged with wild cries. They were now a band of howling fanatics, bent upon killing. Abdul was wounded by their shots before he could dodge behind the table. He fell backwards, and they, thinking him dead, emitted a wild cheer.

Abdul crawled over to where we were, and drew his sword. His wound was not very serious, being in the left arm, and the bone not having been touched, but it had sufficed to knock him down.

We crouched behind our barricade until they were nearly atop us, then rose to our feet, and cut down three or four of them. This only served to check them for a moment. They came on in large numbers, and leaping over the table, swiftly drove us to the opposite wall. There we turned and faced them. We fought them off several times, but they attacked again. The wall above our heads was splintered and scarred by their bullets, but, and tho it may seem a miracle to you, none of us were wounded seriously.

Zamil, the swordsman from Damascus, covered himself with glory. Five men lay stiff and cold before him ere many minutes had passed, and at least half-a-dozen more wore marks that would stay for a lifetime.

The agha fought well, too, but to tell the truth, he did not fight as well as the rest of us. The severe wound he had received began to tell upon him. Blood streamed down his face, and his shirt turned slowly to a crimson color. He breathed like a man almost spent, and seemed to lift his weapon by sheer force of will. His lips were white and compressed, and his eyes glowed with an unquenchable fire.

Seeing that ere long he would fall, we renewed our struggles, and fighting with the fury of giants, drove the janissaries slowly towards the door. How we did it I know not, but for the moment we seemed endowed with superhuman strength and courage.

Inch by inch we drove them back in spite of all that they could do. Our strokes were like the strokes of demons, and we were animated by anger and hate. Fear had no place in our thoughts, and we exposed ourselves recklessly, well-knowing that it could do no harm to us. For is it not said in the Koran, that the moment of a man's death is written in a book by the Angel of Death? And what force can prolong that moment for the smallest space of time?

Behind and around us we left a trail of blood, and dead and dying men. And before us fell the janissaries like withered leaves from a tree in the autumn.

Covered by a hundred wounds, we struck fearlessly, and Mahomet and God struck with us. Into the heart of the renegade janissaries stole the fiend of fear, and leaping over the table they fled recklessly down the stairway.

And then we followed them. In the room below they turned, with a hundred fresh men to help them, and came at us. For a few moments we held them off.

A native of Mosul struck the agha in the breast with his sword. Zamil cut the man down. The agha half-fell, then staggered to his feet and struck a last wild blow at the enemy. Two of them he killed. A captain, named Al-zim, fired at him with his pistol. The agha tottered, his sword dropped from his nerveless hands, his face turned ashy pale, and he fell at the feet of the mutineers. So died Ismail Pasha, the bravest soldier that ever served a Sultan.

And with him died his slayer. I cut down Alzim and he fell across the agha's body. His comrades, enraged at the death of one of their leaders, attacked us with renewed courage. Step by step they drove us up the stairs, tho we slew many and wounded more. Their rage knew no bounds, and they yelled like wild beasts.

Half-way up the stairs, Abdul fell, shot thru the center of the breast by an Arab. The wound was not mortal, but was very serious. He tottered, and with a shriek, fell from the stairs to the floor below, landing with a dull thud. He did not move. The janissaries took him for dead and left him undisturbed.

Zamil and I were now left to fight the battle alone. And no man may say that we did not fight it as well as we could. Seven or eight janissaries fell before they drove us to the agha's room. How many were wounded I cannot tell; but there were many.

The floor below was covered with dead and dying and over them stood live men, running to and fro, and firing at us when they got a chance. But their fire was more dangerous to their friends than to us.

The staircase grew slippery with blood. Men slid and slipped, and with wild cries, fell to the ground below. Many did not rise again, but lay there with broken arms or legs. It was a long fall, over fifteen feet.

My strength began to fail at last. Such a thing could not go on forever. I slipped in a pool of blood, and before I could regain my feet I was shot down.

Everything went dark, and I seemed to be falling into eternity. I dimly heard the clash of steel upon steel, and then I seemed to stop. A sharp pain ran thru me, and a moment later I knew nothing. I lay amongst the slain on the floor of the barracks, like a dead man.

When consciousness returned to me I found myself lying on a couch. Abdul, with a bandaged arm, and Zamil were leaning over me, pouring water on my face.

I sat up with a clear recollection of all that had happened to me.

"Where am I now?" I said, in a voice that sounded curiously weak and thin.

"You're at the Seraglio," said Abdul. "You have been unconscious for three days. That pistol wound was a very serious one. Any other man but you would be dead now."

"And you?" I asked.

"My wound is almost healed now," replied Abdul, "but I have a very badly cut arm. I landed on someone's sword when I fell from the stairs. It is a wonder that the arm was not broken."

"And you, Zamil?" said I.

"I have a few wounds," answered Zamil, "but none of them are serious. Here is a sabre cut on the head," and he pulled off his fez to show it to me, "and here is a bullet scar in the arm. I have almost fifty little scratches, but none of them are worthy of mention."

"What happened after I fell?" I asked him next. Zamil seated himself on the couch beside me and told the story as follows:

"After they shot you down, Ali, I was the only one left to fight the battle. I fought very well, if I may say so, and I think that many of the rebels can bear testimony to the same. They finally drove me to the barricade at the head of the stairs. I stood there, and vowed that I'd die before I went a step further.

"For two minutes I fought on. At last they beat me to my knees by sheer force of numbers. I struck desperately at them as best I could.

"They would have made short work of me then had not help arrived. Fifty or sixty Bostanjis entered on the run, and the janissaries had to turn their attention to them. That gave me a chance to get to my feet. But I soon fell down again and lay in a swoon for two or three hours. When I came to I found myself in the Seraglio."

"What happened to the mutineers?" I asked.

"The Bostanjis, and the Bashi-Bazouks overpowered them after a bloody fight. Twenty of the ringleaders were shot yesterday. It turned out afterwards that not more than two-thirds of the janissaries were in the mutiny by their own free choice. Their mutinous comrades had forced them to insurrection on pain of death."

And that, my dear reader, was the end of the first mutiny which occurred amongst the janissaries after I became a member of that corps.

Chapter XIII

Several priviledges of the janissaries which had been withdrawn from them a year or two before, were now restored to them. Why this was done, I do not know; perhaps it was to discourage any more mutinies. The priviledges that were restored were as follows: To marry and engage in trades for the support of their families.

The discipline to which they had been subjected, was also withdrawn, and the simple exercises which they had been obliged to perform went with it. The janissaries were now, as they had been of old, a settled colony, without discipline or drill, which was allowed to engage in trades and to marry.

These concessions immediately gained the good-will of the janissaries, and after that there was little prospect of another mutiny. Any man who would have dared to suggest such a thing, would have met with short shrift at the hands of our soldiers.

But no one even thought of suggesting. Everyone was contented and happy. Therefore, why should they think of mutiny. What use would it be to them, anyway? None at all. And therefore, there was no thought of insurrection amongst us. The ringleaders who had been executed were speedily forgotten.

Some ten days after the mutiny, Abdul and I had occasion to go to the Seraglio. I forget the reason, but I think it was a letter from the new agha, Zamil Bey. He was the same person mentioned in the last chapter. Because of his bravery in the fight the padishah had bestowed this rank upon him. Many had considered that Abdul and I had each a better claim to the promotion, but his Majesty thought not. And of course, the Sultan's word was law. Who would dare oppose it? So Abdul and I had to be satisfied with an increase of twenty piastres a month in our pay. And we thought ourselves very lucky to get that.

But to return to the story. As I before stated we found occasion to go to the Seraglio. And, as I also said, we bore a letter from Zamil to the Sultan.

We arrived at the Seraglio without any adventures and presented our message to the padishah. He read it, nodded to us, and we went to seek the princess.

We found her holding an animated discussion with Bikri Mustapha. Bikri was protesting his love for her, and she was answering him in pretty strong language. Several eunuchs were standing near, grinning openly.

Abdul and I stopped in the doorway to listen. No one had perceived us coming. The princess and Bikri were so engaged with each other that they had neither eye nor ear for anything else, and the eunuchs were engrossed in watching them.

"I can never love such a detestable monster as you," said Fatima.

"Princess," said Bikri, getting onto his knees, "you are the light of my eyes, the music of my ears, the delight of my soul, and the most perfect woman on earth. I love but you. Condescend, my sweet, to cast but one smile upon thy loving slave, and you will transport him into the seventh heaven of happiness."

"Begone," said Fatima. "You detestable drunkard! I'd love a pig before I'd love you, tho to confess the truth, there isn't much difference. Still, the pig is preferable."

"Such words are arrows in my heart, O light of love," said Bikri. "Princess, they need not be said."

"Bah!" replied Fatima. "Arrows? Bosh! You speak nonsense."

"You are more perfect than the houris of paradise," replied Bikri.

"Wretch!" said the princess. "Imbecile! Lunatic! Madman! You are the worst fool that ever lived. Eunuchs, remove this imitation of a man from my presence. The very sight of him sickens me."

The eunuchs, grinning still more, if that could be possible, hastened to comply. Bikri offered some resistance, but it was of no use. His captors ejected him from the room with a few parting kicks and then turned to their mistress. She had not yet noticed us.

Bikri turned and saw us. He frowned, and his violent temper broke forth in a raging torrent of words. "You'll repent of this rash act, Fatima," said he to the princess. "I shall speak to your uncle. I have not lost all favor with him yet, and his anger against me has begun to abate. You'll repent of it, my fine lady, when I am your husband. I'll make you love me!"

"You shall do nothing of the kind," said Fatima indignantly. "They may force me thru a mock marriage, but I can never love you. Remember that, my good friend."

"As for these young men," said Bikri, pointing towards Abdul and me, "Your uncle will tend to them some day. I'll not forget to mention them to his Majesty, to be sure. Oh, no, I'm a kind man, and I love to tell him of this kind and what they do. And he always rewards them, you know. Ha! Ha! Ha!"

With a sneer on his lips, Bikri turned to go. Fatima saw us and blushed.

"Not so fast, Bikri," said I, drawing my dagger and following him. "I'd like to speak with you a moment."

Bikri turned, saw the dagger, and drew his sword. His face was a blaze of malice and fury. His whole nature and character stood revealed in it, and no adept was required to read it.

"You'll never get her, you nor your friend Abdul," he hissed walking slowly towards me. "I'll take care of that. His Majesty is somewhat reconciled to me now, and I think that a little talking with him will convince him that I'll make a better husband for Fatima than either of you."

"And I'll take good care that you don't speak to his Majesty again," I replied, hotly, drawing my sword.

Bikri was convulsed with fury. "Rash youth," he cried. "I shall make you swallow your words. 'Tis you, who'll never speak to the padishah again."

He punctuated his words with a rush at me. I parried his stroke and inflicted a slight wound in his arm.

"Stop it! Stop it!" cried the princess. "They'll hurt each other. Stop them, Abdul. If you don't I'll have to call the eunuchs."

Bikri and fought madly for a little while.

Suddenly someone struck my sword from my hand. The same service was done to Bikri. Without stopping to recover our weapons we rushed at each other and grappled wildly.

I sprang like a tiger, straight thru the air at Bikri's chest. I landed fairly, grasped him by the throat, and we went down in a heap, with myself on top. For the next few moments everything was confusion.

The first thing I knew someone was dragging me off my enemy. Bikri rose to his feet, breathing in short gasps. He cast me an evil glance and stumbled out of the room aided by a couple of slaves. "You'll pay for this," he called back, and disappeared.

I turned and found that Abdul was the person that had dragged me to my feet. He was still holding me by the arm. Fatima was standing nearby. We stared at each other in silence.

"There's trouble ahead," said Abdul. "No doubt what that serpent said was true. He's wormed himself into the Sultan's favor in some manner or other. Why else should he speak such words?"

"There *is* trouble," said the princess. "Bikri has told no lie. I've been watching him when he speaks to my uncle, and I've heard what was said. There's no doubt but that that rascal will be restored to his old priviledges and favors. What can we do?"

And that was the question.

Chapter XIV

It was a hard one to answer. For a while no one suggested a solution. Finally the princess spoke.

"Why not go and listen to what he says to the Sultan? It is easily done. There is a small closet back of the audience-room. You can hide in that and listen thru the key-hole. It has two doors, one in each side. Come, I'll lead you to there."

She immediately proceeded to do so. We, having no scruples as to spying, followed readily. We entered the closet on tiptoe. It was square, some twelve feet each way, and, as the princess had remarked, had two doors. One of them entered the audience-room, and the other was the one by which we had come in.

Fatima retired and closed the door softly. Abdul and I went to the keyhole of the opposite one and listened. There were two voices speaking in low tones. One was the Sultan's, the other Bikri's. They were having an animated discussion.

"You will remember, Bikri, that I promised them that you would not wed Fatima," said the padishah.

"I remember that unfortunate event very well, your majesty," replied Bikri, in his softest accent. "Yes, I remember it well; too well, in fact." Murad gave vent to a low laugh.

"I presume you do," he said. "You had good cause to. But now, Bikri I have changed my mind. What you have told me bids me cast off these young serpents. I swear to you on the Koran that neither of them shall wed the girl. That honor shall be yours."

"Your majesty, I must thank you very much for this kindness."

"Not at all. It is no kindness, simply a duty. Six wives a-piece, they?* My niece shall not marry them."

"And that is not all, your majesty," said Bikri. "Abdul, I have heard, has two wives at Damascus. Besides this, they used to lure innocent girls to their homes. What think you of that?"

"My opinion cannot be expressed in words, Bikri."

"When shall I marry the princess?" asked Bikri.

"At any time you please."

"I choose the present."

"Very well."

"And what shall be done with the two captains?"

"I will not allow them to come here again."

"Your majesty is very kind."

"It is nothing."

"I shall send for a muezzin."

"Do so. The sooner you are her husband the better for all concerned."

"That is my opinion, your majesty."

"Where shall the wedding take place?"

"In this room."

Bikri went out, to get a muezzin.

The Sultan followed, as we supposed to speak to the princess.

---

*The Koran allows four wives for each true believer.

"What is to be done?" I asked of Abdul. Abdul thought a moment.
"I know," said he, at last.
"What?"
"We must first speak to the princess."
"Yes."
"Then we must speak to the muezzin."
"What then?"
"You must go to an apothecary's shop and purchase a certain kind of drug. I'll tend to the princess and the muezzin."

He whispered in my ear the name of the particular drug he wanted. I ran immediately from the palace, and towards the city. Five minutes later, I stood in an apothecary's shop.

I told him the name of the drug I wanted. After a little searching he produced a small vial containing an amber liquid, and handed it to me. "The price is ten piastres," he said. I produced the money and ran back to the Seraglio. I found Abdul speaking with the muezzin.

"My son," said that person, a venerable old gray beard, "I believe you. I shall do as you say."

I gave the vial to Abdul. He, in turn, gave it to the muezzin.

"What is the meaning of this?" I asked.

"The meaning is," said Abdul, "that this old man has agreed to give the vial to Fatima, with instructions to swallow what is within."

"Then it is poison," I said, my face blanching.

"No," replied Abdul. "It is not. But it will have pretty much the same effect, apparently. It is a powerful narcotic, mixed with a subtle drug. The drug has the property of apparently suspending the action of the lungs and heart. Therefore, any person swallowing it will immediately fall into a deep sleep. This sleep, owing to the action of the drug, will appear so much like death that even the best of physicians will be unable to detect the difference. Do you see my plan?"

"I understand," said I. "It is a good one. But how long does this sleep last?"

"Two hours," replied my friend.

"And what are we to do in the meanwhile?"

"Hide," was the laconic reply.

"And where?"

"In the closet behind the audience-room."

"And when?"

"Immediately."

Abdul thanked the muezzin for his promised assistance and pressed a piastre into the old man's hand. The man handed it back to Abdul with an injured air. "I accept no pay for doing right," said he.

"If all priests were like him there would be no unjust marriages," observed Abdul.

"You are right," I replied. "And I wish they were all like him. There is too much corruption in this age."

We entered the closet and closed the door behind us.

"There is nothing to do now but wait for the result," said my friend.

"There are chances that she will be prevented from swallowing the drug," I remarked.

"Yes, my friend, but there are chances to everything."

"Truly a wise observation."

"Not wise. Simply the truth."

"I see you are at your philosophy again."

"Of course. There is little else to say during the period of waiting."

"Is it my turn to make an observation?"

"Yes."

"My observation is that Bikri and the Sultan will be very sorry for what they have done. His majesty really loves Fatima, but he is inclined to be rather strict with her at times. Bikri's influence also causes him to be strict and he thinks that this marriage is for her own good."

"That is not philosophy," said Abdul.

"What is it then?"

"Merely the truth."

"It is your turn now, I hope you'll do better."

At that moment we heard footsteps in the audience-room. I looked thru the keyhole, and saw the Sultan, Fatima, Bikri, the muezzin, and the Grand Vizier, enter. The latter I knew, was to be the witness to the marriage.*

"Will you take this woman for your wife?" said the muezzin to Bikri.

"Yes," said Bikri.

"Will you take this man for your husband?" asked the muezzin.

"No," replied Fatima, drawing the vial from her bosom, and swallowing its contents, "and if Bikri weds me he will wed a dead wife!"

She tottered for a moment, her face went deadly white, and she fell in an inert heap at her uncle's feet. There was silence for a moment, a silence as of the grave. Everyone stared with astonished eyes at the corpse.

Bikri stepped back, staggered and fell at her side in a swoon. He did not rise. Everyone in the room began to weep and wail, with the exception of Murad. He stood like a statue, his face as white as marble and his eyes fixed upon Fatima's body.

---

*The Mohammedan religious ceremony is more a civil than a religious one.

It was seven in the evening. The sun had set and a pall of darkness hung over Istanboul. Abdul and I stood in Fatima's room. She lay upon a bier, white, cold and beautiful. We were the only other people in the apartment. "She ought to awake soon," said Abdul anxiously. "The two hours are up now, but we must allow a few minutes."

Five minutes passed away. Still she did not awake. Abdul's face began to pale. "There may have been a mistake," said he. "The apothecary may have given you the wrong bottle."

"Allah grant that he did not," I said, my own face beginning to pale.

"There is a poison of an amber color," said my friend.

"There may have been more of the drug in this vial than in ordinary ones," I suggested.

"It is impossible. The men who manufacture this stuff never make a mistake. It was poison that he gave you."

I sat down on a couch, a dreadful foreboding beginning to overwhelm me.

Ten—fifteen—twenty—twenty-five—thirty minutes passed away, and still the princess showed no signs of recovery. Thirty-five—forty—forty-five—fifty—fifty-five—an hour passed by. At the end Fatima lay precisely as she had done at the beginning. Abdul flung himself down beside me, his hands on his face. "Oh God! Oh God!" he groaned.

There was no doubt about it. The apothecary had made a mistake, given me poison instead of the drug for which I had asked. It was horrible, a grim irony of fate that we, who loved her should have been the means of killing her. Still, I reflected, it was better than a marriage with Bikri Mustapha. I knew that if she had been given the choice, she would have taken the poison.

"There is no use waiting any longer," I said to Abdul. "She is dead now."

"None—none at all," said my friend in a sad voice as he got up from the couch. "We had better go ere the mourners come and find us here. It would look bad if we were discovered in this room, by a dead woman's bier."

"We are not ghouls," I said, with a shudder.

"No, but appearances are against us. We had better go."

We stepped forth from the room, to be met by the Sultan and Bikri Mustapha. The astonishment was mutual.

"What are you doing here?" roared his Majesty.

We had nothing to say for ourselves at the time.

Chapter XV

"I suppose I must repeat the question," said the padishah. "What are you doing here?"

"We came to take a last look at the woman we both loved, your majesty," said Abdul.

"Go," said the Sultan. "Go, and do not return. I'll have no serpents in the palace."

"Your majesty, may I inquire what you mean by serpents?"

"I mean men who marry more wives than the Koran allows—that's what I mean."

"And your majesty insinuates that we did so?"

"Yes."

"Well, your majesty, the only serpent I know of in this palace is the man who stands beside you."

"Do you mean Bikri Mustapha?"

"Yes, your majesty. That's just who I mean. He, I suppose, is the person who told you majesty this lie concerning us."

"He told me no lie that I know of."

"Did he not tell you, your majesty, that we had more than four wives apiece? If he told you that he told you a lie, for, as anyone can tell you, neither of us is married."

"Go," said the Sultan. "Go, and come not back. My eyes ache with the sight of you. Go!"

We went. Outside the Seraglio all was darkness, and when we had passed the Sublime Porte and found ourselves in the streets, we did not know which direction to go to return to the barracks.

In our wanderings we found ourselves before the apothecary's shop. "This is where I purchased the poison," I whispered in a strained tone to Abdul.

"We will enter," said Abdul, "and take revenge upon this perfidious rascal."

"It is a good idea," I replied.

With grim faces, and still grimmer thoughts we pushed open the door and entered.

The apothecary was seated upon a small couch, reading. Upon our entrance he threw aside the book, a leather-bound, silver-clasped Persian volume. I caught sight of the title, and it impressed itself so in mind that I remember it to this day. It was "Nigaristan."*

---

*Literally translated, this means "The Picture Gallery." The book itself is a very famous one, perhaps the most noted book by a Persian author.

The apothecary was a tall, muscular, well-formed man, about thirty years of age. He had a beard and a pair of long, black, very fierce looking mustachios.

His nose was very aquiline, almost a beak, his eyes were large, and his ears somewhat prominent. He had the look of a man possessed of great courage.

"What do you want?" he asked, in a pleasant voice.

"We want you to explain why you gave me a vial of poison, instead of the drug I asked you for," said I.

"I gave you no poison," he said, recognizing me.

"Yes you did. A woman, beloved of us both, lies dead as a result of your carelessness!"

The apothecary's face turned pale. "There must be some mistake," he stammered.

"There is no mistake. The lady is the Sultan's niece. She lies dead at the palace at this very moment."

"This is terrible," said the apothecary, with a groan. "Unhappy man that I am. Would to Allah that I had never been born."

"And what," asked Abdul, "do you think would be a suitable punishment for a man who committed such an unpardonable negligence?"

"Death," said the apothecary, with a still bigger groan.

"Have you pistols?" asked Abdul.

"Yes."

"Then we will fight. I give you this chance for your life."

The apothecary fetched his pistols and loaded them. Abdul did the same with his own.

"We will fire from opposite ends of the room," said Abdul, taking up a position at one end. "My friend Ali will drop his turban as a signal for us to fire."

"If I kill you, will your friend interfere?" asked the apothecary anxiously.

"I swear I will not," said I.

"You must swear it on the Koran," said the man.

He went out and returned a few moments later with a copy of the book. He held it to me, and I, placing my right hand on it, said, "I swear to you, on the Koran, the Holy Book of God that I will do you no harm in any manner if you kill my friend Abdul in this duel."

"It is well," replied the apothecary, as he took up his position at the other end of the apartment.

The two men faced each other in silence, their eyes fixed immovably upon the upraised turban in my hand. "One—two—three," said I very slowly and distinctly. The turban fell with a soft thud.

The duelists fired simultaneously. Both missed. Two bottles of medicine on the shelves which ran around the room, were shivered into atoms. The liquid they contained dripped slowly to the floor. I held up the turban again. "One—two—three." It fell.

Once more they fired simultaneously. Abdul was unhurt, but the apothecary dropped to the floor with a bullet hole in the exact center of his forehead.

"You played with him the first shot," I observed, as Abdul thrust his smoking pistols into his sash.

"I did. It was dangerous, but I could not help it. A spirit of devilment prompted me to do so, I suppose. The fellow is quite dead. I struck him exactly where I wanted to,—the center of the forehead. Serves him right for selling poison in place of something else. I'd like to do the same service to all other careless apothecaries."

Abdul walked over to the body, and taking up the man's pistol from where it had fallen, placed it in his right hand. This gave him the appearance of having committed suicide.

"Come," said I, "let us be going. The people of the neighborhood will have heard these shots. They will enter, find us here, and conclude that we murdered the man."

Even as I spoke we heard the sound of voices without.

"What are we to do?" asked my friend.

For answer I thrust the door open and stepped out into the street. My friend followed at my heels with drawn sword.

On sighting us the crowd without gave vent to a shout of surprise and astonishment.

"What has happened?" they asked.

"Go within and you will find out," I answered, grimly.

Many were for arresting us on the spot, and others were for letting us go. They finally concluded to detain us while some of their number investigated.

"I must ask you to deliver your swords," said one of the party, a stalwart fellow of thirty.

"We shall do no such thing," I answered. "Our swords are our own. We shall keep them. Take them if you dare."

"Deprive them of their weapons," said the stalwart one to his companions. They attempted to comply but met with a dismal failure.

We backed against the wall and wounded two of them. They then retired to a respectful distance, tho still surrounding us in a half circle.

In the meanwhile those who had entered the house to investigate now returned and made a report to the others.

"Just as I thought," said one. "These men are robbers. They entered this house for the purpose of robbing it and meeting with opposition from the owner, killed him. Arrest them!"

The men who had met with our swords were very reluctant to try this. Said one:

"These men will kill many of us before we capture them. They are soldiers and know how to use their swords. We do not."

"Then shoot them," came the sharp order.

Many hands went to the sashes of the owners. But ere a weapon could be leveled at us, Abdul and I had drawn our pistols and had covered the whole party.

"You first four who attack us are dead men," said my friend. Our would be captors edged away slowly. No one dared to shoot, for fear that he would be killed, as had been promised.

"Cowards!" hissed the leader. "Cowards. Arrest these murderers, or I'll shoot some of you."

He dashed forward, pointed his pistol at Abdul and fired. At the same time I fired at him. He staggered back, shot thru the shoulder. Abdul was unharmed.

"Come," I whispered to him. "Make a dash for it. We can cut our way thru."

I reloaded my pistol, and we dashed at the crowd, which was now greatly reinforced, firing into its midst as we went. We then flung our pistols amongst them and drew our swords. They drew back a little, and we hurled ourselves upon them, cutting down many. It was rank butchery, massacre. They made scarcely resistance at all after the first onslaught. The ground grew red with blood, and the gutters were filled with it. We slipped in it, our clothes were covered with it, and our eyes were almost blinded by it.

The air was filled with shrieks and groans, and men ran by us. We cut them down and dashed upon the main body. The lust of battle was upon us, and the lust of blood. We knew not what we did.

Till the end of my life I shall always be ashamed of what I did upon that night. But I scarcely think that I was responsible for myself. Neither was Abdul.

But this, like all other things, came to an end. There was a volley of shots, and I saw in the darkness behind me, by the pistol flashes, the forms a half-a-dozen men. They were police, who, hearing the sounds of the fight, had come to the scene.

Everything went red before my eyes, there was a pain in my back as of hot iron searing it, and I ran foreward a few yards and fell into darkness and something wet. A cool feeling came over me, and I lay back and became unconscious.

When I came to I found that I was lying in the Bosphorus, half my body in the water. The upper part lay on the bank. Looking up I saw the stars and moon and the gates of Istanbul. I was perhaps a half dozen yards from the gate itself. There was a pain in my back, and when I rose I was very stiff and faint.

I looked about me and saw a huddled form on the bank a few yards away. I walked over to it and found that it was Abdul. He was lying stiff and cold, his pale face turned towards the heavens, and apparently dead.

"Abdul," I cried. "Wake up! Wake up!"

Abdul did not awake. I leant over him anxiously, and placed my hand upon his heart. Thank God, it still beat faintly, tho very faintly. I picked him up in my arms and bore him towards the gate. Here an obstacle intervened. The gate was closed, and in spite of my pounding and yelling I could not awaken the watchman. I could hear him snoring loudly.

I walked back the water's edge and hailed a passing boat. The occupants did not, or did not want to, hear me. At any rate they passed by in silence, without acknowledging my hail.

There was nothing for it now but to wait until morning, or the coming of another boat, unless I passed over the bridge to the other side of the Bosphorus. I finally decided to do the former.

I sat down and soon fell asleep. When I awoke the sun was just rising. Abdul had already awakened and was standing, looking at the river. I arose and intimated to him that I was ready to enter the city.

"Then come," said he, walking towards the gate. It was already open and a few people were passing in and out. We entered, and found ourselves on the scene of the tragedy of the night before.

"When the police shot us," I said, "we must have been near this gate. We turned, staggered thru it, and fell into the water. The police, thinking us dead, did not search for us. The heard the splashing when we went into the Bosphorus, and concluded that we would speedily be drowned. They were very careless, but their carelessness was lucky for us. Had it been otherwise we should be dead now, or in a prison.

"Yes," replied Abdul, but I noticed that his voice was strained and unnatural. I looked at his face. It was very pale, and the brow was covered with fine lines.

"That was a bad affair last night," he remarked. "I did quite right in killing the apothecary, but I think we should have surrendered to those people instead of fighting and killing so many of them."

"And been torn into pieces by a mob before we could explain?" I asked.

"What we did was not entirely justified," he said. "It will be a blot on my soul till the last day of my life."

And in my innermost soul I acknowledged that he was right. I still think so.

We walked on, conversing of various subjects. We studiously avoided what had happened the night before, and strove to banish it from our minds. But, like some ancient monster it stayed, tormenting us forever.

Finally we reached the barracks, and entered. On the exercising grounds near the building, we saw the Sultan standing. Beside him was the agha, and the Grand Vizier, and a veiled lady. They were attended by half-a-dozen eunuchs. Our comrades stood around in groups, whispering among themselves. Evidently something had happened in our absence.

"What can be the matter?" I whispered to Abdul.

"Don't ask me," he retorted; "but there's something afoot. It's strange to see his Majesty here. Wonder who that lady is?"

"We'll soon find out," I answered.

We drew near to them and they advanced to meet us. I could see the Sultan's face wore an expression of happiness. There seemed to me to be something familiar about the veiled lady. This puzzled me, for I had known few women, and scarcely any of them very intimately. She lifted her veil and I saw the eyes and the brow. I staggered backward in astonishment.

"Can I be dreaming?" I shrieked aloud, and fell to the ground. The veiled lady was Fatima!

Chapter XVI

When I came to I found the Grand Vizier and Abdul bending over me, throwing water on my face. Abdul's face wore an expression of happiness, which made me wonder what had occurred.

I sat up and looked about me. The Sultan and Fatima were standing at some little distance, watching us.

When Abdul saw that I was recovered, he walked over towards them and took Fatima in his arms and kissed her. I rose to my feet with a jarred feeling. The day seemed to have suddenly darkened. I turned my eyes away from them and addressed some remark to the Grand Vizier.

A feeling of nausea, of disgust with the world in general began to pervade me. I drew my pistol and looked at it. It suggested an idea to me.

At first it was an idea of abhorrence to me, for it was directly in defiance of the Koran.* Then, after a little while it seemed sweet, and productive of comfort. Life lost all attractiveness for me. I felt that I had nothing more to live for.

---

*The Koran forbids the taking of one's own life.

I became conscious that the Grand Vizier was watching me closely. I directed his attention to something else, and with a quick movement, raised the muzzle of the pistol to my forehead, and pressed the trigger. There was a dull click, and that was all!

Before he turned I slipped the weapon back into my sash, and composing my face as well as I could, walked over the his Majesty the Sultan.

"Well, Ali," said he, "I hope you're feeling well."

"As to that, your majesty," I replied, "I am not quite certain. But, tell me, how comes it that the princess is not dead?"

"That is easily told," he answered. "The drug you gave her was very powerful. Therefore, she slept all the longer. She awoke half-an-hour after I so angrily dismissed you. She told me what had happened.

"Afterwards I investigated what Bikri had told me concerning you, and soon found it to be false. He could produce no proof that either of you was married, especially to six wives apiece. Therefore, I discredited his tale. I will still retain him at court, but I shall never again allow him to gain the influence over me that he has recently exercised. I owe the fellow a debt of gratitude for having introduced wine to me,* so I cannot throw him off entirely. The princess has told me of her love for Abdul and the wedding is to take place immediately."

His last words did not surprise me, for when Abdul had taken the princess in his arms, I had guessed that such was the case. But I was cast down by this, and walked away feeling very unhappy.

A dull gray feeling gnawed at my heart, and I fain would have made another attempt to commit suicide. But this, I reflected, was the act of a coward and strictly against the laws of the Alkoran.

My comrades perceived what was the matter with me and openly pitied me. Some of them even evinced hostility towards Abdul, saying that I deserved Fatima far more than he.

---

*Amurath's love of the bottle has been attributed to a nocturnal adventure. He had, in the early part of his reign, promulgated strict laws against the use of wine; one night, when making his rounds, he met a drunken fellow who ordered the Sultan to give place to him, and when Amurath, astonished, said he was the padishah, the drunkard only professed his indifference to padishahs in his ability to buy up Constantinople and all that was in it. The monarch ordered that he should be taken to the palace, and interrogated him the next morning as to his meaning. With increasing sobriety, Bikri Mustapha had not lost his courage, for pulling a bottle from beneath his coat, he vaunted its quality and told the Sultan that here was that which could give him more than all the world. The Sultan was persuaded to try the liquor, and was so much charmed with its effects, that he made Bikri Mustapha his boon companion, and ever after evinced the deepest devotion to the wine cup — *New American Cyclopaedia.*

"Abdul is my friend," I said angrily. "I will do nothing against him, and I will allow no one to say anything in my presence which detracts from his merit."

I slapped the face of one of them. He grew angry and told me to mind my own business.

At this my anger flamed up. I seized him by the beard (he was over thirty years of age) and spat on it.*

There was a strained silence. I drew my sword and glared at he whom I had insulted. He glared back a little while, and then seeming to lose courage turned and ran, followed by a volley of jeers and laughter.

I was not present at the wedding. I was too miserable for that. Abdul wished me to come, but I refused, very sulkily. He understood, and said nothing, but pressed my hand in silence.

I went out and attempted to solace myself by a walk about the city. That, however, did no good. So I returned to the barracks. Abdul, who had now taken up his abode in the married men's quarter, came over to see me. We talked for awhile, I making a desperate attempt to appear cheerful. I was not jealous, only very miserable and sick at heart. The whole world seemed to have gone away and left me stranded in a burning-hot desert of despair.

After about an hour, Abdul left, leaving me to my misery. This, perhaps, was the best thing that could be done under the circumstances, for it is much harder to keep up false appearances, than to be honest with the world and one's self.

That evening, finding myself still much depressed, I determined to abandon myself to a spirit of revelry. Therefore, the other officers and I, who were very sympathetic, purchased some wine and had an entertainment in the dining room. After it was over we drank the wine and told stories till midnight. Two of these stories, the best of them, I must say, are worth repeating. Tho they have no part in this tale, I think it will do no harm to relate them, as they may seem to divert the reader's attention and thoughts from the recital of my woes, recently given.

And this is the first of the stories:

The Tale of the Two Merchants and the Brass Bottle.

A hundred years ago there lived in Persia, in the city of Ispahan, two brothers, one named Ayoub, and the other Yusuf. Yusuf was the oldest, and the handsomest of the two. He was twenty-seven years of age at the

---

*In Mohammedan countries this is a terrible insult, perhaps the worst in the eyes of the followers of Islam that any man can perpetuate upon another.

time of the tale. Ayoub was twenty-three, and not as tall nor as strong as his brother.

Their father had died some years before and left them all his property. They had no relations in the world. They were grown somewhat wealthy, were merchants, and unmarried.

Yusuf proposed going to Bagdad for the purpose of trading with the merchants of that city. Ayoub agreed, and they set out for the city of Teheran to buy certain articles required, which were not procurable in Ispahan.

The two brothers accomplished their journey safely, and after buying what they wished, set out to return home. Their goods were on two camels, and they, themselves rode on two additional ones. They were attended by several slaves who led the camels carrying the merchandise.

A quarter of a mile from the gate of Ispahan, the two brothers caught up with a merchant who had come from the direction of the Persian Gulf. He was a middle-aged man, pleasant to look upon, and rode on a camel. Behind him were two more, loaded with bales of cloth, led by a tall, muscular African. The merchant was well-dressed, apparently opulent, and a well-educated man, which appeared from his polished conversation.

"I have here," said the merchant, "a brass bottle, which was sold to me by a fisherman. He had not opened it and did not know what it contained. Neither do I know. I am certain, however, that it is empty. Perhaps you would like to buy it?"

He opened one of the bales and brought forth a brass bottle, of the size of a water jar and showed it to the brothers. It was fastened with a stopper, on which was engraved sundry characters of an unknown language.

"I will give you twenty dinars* for it," said Yusuf, gladly. He recognized the bottle as one of those in which Solomon sealed the Genii.

"Done!" cried the merchant. He handed the bottle to Yusuf, who immediately paid him the promised price. They rode on the Ispahan, conversing pleasantly, and once within the gates, parted, the brothers going one way and the merchant another.

Ayoub and Yusuf went to their home, and Yusuf told his brother what the bottle contained. Ayoub was inclined to be skeptical, but the other finally convinced him of the truth of his statement.

As soon as they arrived at their home they retired to one of the upper rooms, taking the bottle with them, and bolting the door. Yusuf then proceeded to open the bottle. The result was very surprising, and not exactly as they had expected.

A thick black smoke rolled forth, filling the room from top to bottom.

---

*A small coin.

The brothers fell over in their astonishment, and when they had regained their feet, saw that the smoke had begun to materialize into a tall, indistinct figure. This figure steadily decreased, becoming more distinct all the while, till it was the size of an ordinary man. The genie, for such it was, was clad in antique robes of priceless silk, and wore a long beard. The eyes were very piercing, and the countenance not unpleasant to look upon. Upon the whole, the genie differed from an ordinary man only in his robes and clothing.

"Beneficent mortals," said he to the brothers, who had now recovered their composure and courage, "I thank thee for the great service thou hast rendered me. Know that I am of the genii whom Solomon Gian Ben Giasi imprisoned in bottles of brass countless ages ago and had cast into the seas. For these countless ages have I waited, waiting to be delivered. And praise be to Allah, my deliverance hath come at last. Name thy reward, O mortals, and I will bring it to thee. Nothing is too costly, nothing too precious, but that I can obtain it for thee. Thou hast but to name it, and I will fetch it."

"Bring me," said Ayoub, "twenty chests of precious jewels, and twenty of gold."

"Bring me," said Yusuf, "that which is best and most to be desired of all things on earth!"

The genii bowed in compliance and disappeared. In a few minutes he returned, bearing upon his shoulders the forty chests called for by Ayoub. Ayoub opened them one by one, and gazed in delight at what was within. Millions of gold coins there were in twenty of them, and in the other twenty jewels of all kinds, none smaller than the egg of a hen.

Priceless pearls, rubies, diamonds, sapphires, turquoise, garnets, emeralds, and opals were jumbled together in confusion. And all shown with a lustre which it is beyond the power of words to describe.

"Your request," the genie said to Yusuf, "is harder to comply with. I may have to hunt longer for it than the other. But never fear, I will find it if it is to be found."

He came back, after awhile, bringing on his shoulders, a maiden more beautiful than the houris, attired in priceless garments. She smiled upon Yusuf, and leaping from the genie's shoulders, ran to his arms. And at that moment love entered into Yusuf's heart and he was happy.

"I am the Goddess of Happiness," said the maiden. "Without me, the world would be miserable. I have come, at the genie's bidding, to make you happy. Then I must return to the world."

She implanted on his lips a kiss, and disappeared, leaving nothing behind her.

And after that, Yusuf was always happy. His sorrows were few, and his years many. His brother and he married and lived in opulence and comfort till the coming of the Separator of Companions and Terminator of Delights.

And this is the other story:

The Camel's Tale.

A camel, without a rider, came in from the desert. A merchant took possession of it and put it with his other animals of the same kind. These camels desired the newcomer to tell them his story, which he did somewhat as follows.

"I was born in the city of Mosul, upon the banks of the Tigris, and was the property of a certain merchant named Yacoub. When I was full-grown this merchant took me and some other camels with him to Bagdad. We carried bales of cloth and were led by African slaves. Our master rode ahead on a larger camel.

"Far out in the desert the slaves set upon Yacoub with their swords, and killed him. One of them then took command of the caravan, and we went towards Damascus, that being the destination intended by the slaves.

"The next adventure happened in the Arabian desert. A band of robbers set upon the caravan, killed the slaves and took possession of us and what we carried. The bales they kept themselves, but the camels they gave as a present to a certain sheikh, named Abdullam.

"This master was so cruel to us that I and another camel, proposed running away. We endeavored to incite our comrades to do the same, but they were afraid, and would not listen to the proposition.

"So I and the other camel had to escape by ourselves. We slipped away into the desert at midnight, and walked all night. In the morning we rested in the shade of a solitary palm and then went onward.

"For a week we wandered, finding no food or water. The sun was hot, and sands were burning. A sandstorm came upon us, and when it passed away we were almost dead.

"We staggered desperately on and at last came to an oasis. Here we rested for a week. At the end of this week, as we were about to push on, a large caravan came up. We soon discovered that Sheikh Abdullam, our late master, was at the head of it.

"As a consequence we hid away behind some bushes. But they found our footprints and tracked us. Abdullam recognized us and again took possession of us.

"Our old comrades, who were in the caravan, laughed and told us that running away was not such great fun. We agreed with them, and secretly resolved not to do so again.

"But we soon broke our resolution. Abdullam was more cruel than ever, and one dark night we slipped away. The next day we fell in with another caravan, which took possession of us. The master was more kind than Abdullam, and we were inclined to stay with him. We did so until the coming of our next adventure.

"A week after we joined the caravan, we met with Abdullam. The two leaders exchanged courtesies and rode along together very amicably. I was in a passion of fear that my old owner would spy us.

" 'You have a fine lot of camels, friend,' said the sheikh, looking at us.

" 'Yes,' said our owner, 'there is no doubt but that I have. Take a good look at them.'

"Abdullam immediately proceeded to do so, and soon spied my friend and I.

" 'These two,' he said, 'are camels that once belonged to me. They ran away, and until now I have not seen them. I trust you will return them to me.'

" 'Indeed, I shall do no such thing,' said the other. 'They are my camels, and belong to no one else. I bought them from a dealer at Damascus.'

" 'Give me my camels!' shrieked Abdullam.

" 'Liar! They are mine.'

" 'They are not.'

"My new owner drew his pistol and shot Abdullam. Abdullam, who was only wounded fired back and killed him.

"A battle between the two caravans followed. During the fight my friend and I slipped away. For many weeks we wandered across the desert. My friend was killed by a lion, but I escaped, and last reached this city and was taken possession of by my present master."

All the camels agreed that this was a very interesting tale, and congratulated their new comrade on having come unscathed thru so many exciting adventures.

Chapter XVII

For six months everything went along quietly. There was no outward sign of another insurrection. Everyone was apparently contented, and there was no obvious reason for one.

Little did I think of what was soon to happen, and littler still did I think that I was to be one of the rebels, one of their leaders.

It came about in this wise. There was a woman at the bottom of it, and that woman was *Fatima*, yes, Fatima, and no one else.

I went many times to visit her husband, and Abdul allowed me to speak to her freely, she apparently considering me in the light of an old friend.

At first she was somewhat cold and distant, and then she warmed, till we were as good friends as we had ever been. There were little smiles, of course when her husband was not looking, and gentle pressings of the hand.

At first I was inclined to be angry, and thought it my duty to tell Abdul of this, so that it might be stopped. Would to Allah that I had carried out this resolution ere all was too late!

But my old love for the princess, which I had partially smothered, began to return, fanned into flame by Fatima's little attentions. Struggle against it as I could, I was unable to vanquish it. I know, of course, that such love was sinful, but I could do nothing. My only excuse is that I was in the grip of the most relentless and powerful of passions,—love. And with love came a passion that I had not felt before. That passion was jealousy, the green-eyed monster that has wrecked so many lives.

I grew jealous of my friend, whom I had never hated before, and to whom I had always been a friend. He—unsuspecting, allowed such things to take place before his very eyes, so good a friend was he to me. And I,— I hated him.

Fatima grew bolder day by day, and my love grew in proportion. At last she asked me, with a winning smile, to meet her at night. And I, mad with passion, complied. It was fortunate that Abdul was not in the room, for had he seen my face at that moment he could not but have understood.

Well, to make a long story short, I met her. I strode up and down back of the married men's quarters, consumed with impatience. My heart was burning with flame, and I could scarcely refrain from calling to her. She came at last, at the stroke of midnight—the time we had agreed upon. She was attired in a beautiful dress, which enhanced her beauty wonderfully, and was unveiled.

She came to me with a happy smile upon her lips. She ran to my outstretched arms, and I embraced her. I smothered her with kisses, upon the cheeks and lips, and eyes and forehead, until her face was burning with the marks of my fervent love.

And she, she returned them. I was mad—mad, and my passion was a living, breathing thing, which pushed me ever on and on to the end of things.

It is utterly impossible to describe love. He who has felt it, like I have, will know something of it. But he who has felt a weak, puny passion, like most men feel, can know nothing of it. The love that is love, is a burning, all-consuming desire, which naught but death can check. He who feels it is perfectly willing to sacrifice honor, glory, the world, and everything, to gain the object of his desire.

And that was the love I felt—a burning, palpitating, living thing, which consumes the lover in flames fiercer than those of Hades; yea, much fiercer. The few moments in which I held Fatima in my arms were the happiest in all my life. When I was done, and my passion was somewhat abated, I released my hold and poured out my love in incoherent, jerky sentences, spoken in the voice of one who is intoxicated with strong wine, intoxicated to the last stage. And intoxicated, drunk, was I with the wine of sinful happiness and the gratification of a still more sinful desire.

"I love you—I love you—my princess, my love—my star of happiness—the most desired of all on earth. Say—Say—only that you love me—a little—only a little—and I will be the happiest one on this planet. Say that little word—my love, my heart's desire, and I will be lifted to the seventh heaven of bliss—there to stay for all eternity!"

"I love you, Ali, I love you," sobbed Fatima. I again took her in my arms and smothered her with kisses. Ah! the sweetness of them! Warm and burning, and sweeter than all the sweetmeats of the Orient! Never, O never again, in this gray, unhappy world, will I feel them. They are gone, gone forever, never to return again! And she who gave them, sinful woman that she was, is in Hades, and I, sinful man that I am, am soon to follow her!

In Hades I shall meet her, and in my arms I shall press her, and once more shall I be happy, glorying in sin, in that place of flames, from which no one who enters, shall emerge again. Tormented by the fiends, I shall still be happy, and all the torments and tortures of the pit, shall not be able to tear love from my heart! For love is immortal, and shall survive the grave. The love that is holy shall not die, and neither, I swear, shall that that is sinful. My heart is in flames even as I write, and I yearn for that death, disgraceful tho it be, that shall unite me once more to she whom I love, and shall always love, for all eternity!

And now to return to the recital of this sorry narrative.

When my passion had somewhat cooled down, I was able to talk more coherently, able to utter sentences which could be understood. But my brain and heart were afire, and I spoke in the tone of one who is drunk—as I had spoken before.

"Sweet-heart—love!" I said. "What of Abdul, your husband, what will we do with him?"

"Leave him to me, Ali—my love!" she said, softly. "I'll tend to him, you may be sure."

"And what will you do with him?" I asked, very curious to learn of her method.

"Leave that to me, Ali, leave that to me."

"Yes, darling," said I, satisfied with her reply.

We spoke for perhaps fifteen minutes. Finally Fatima said, "Ali, I have a strong dislike for my uncle the Sultan. While I was at the palace, he generally treated me cruelly, especially in his fits of drunken rage. It is my desire to take revenge upon him for this, and I think that you might help me."

"I'll do anything you say," I cried in my madness. "I'll lay down my life for you if need be, or kill his Majesty."

"I do not think it necessary for you to the the former, and the latter I do not wish done. What I want you to do is create an insurrection amongst the janissaries!"

At this I almost wavered, but remembered my promise. The next moment my passion killed all thought of loyalty to the Sultan.

"I'll do it, Fatima," I said; and those words sealed my fate forever. From that time on I was doomed. We parted, after many tender words, and I returned to my room feeling happy, in spite of the dastardly task I had undertaken.

I began immediately to plan as to how to carry out this task. The janissaries, I know, were contented, and a more than ordinary purpose would be needed to incite them to rebellion. This purpose I taxed my brain to find. At last I hit upon it. Why not arouse their anger by forging false letters from the Sultan, to some other person, speaking slightingly of the janissaries, and pretend I found these letters in the street where they had been dropped by the carrier.

No sooner thought than done. I produced a letter from my pocket which his Majesty had written to the agha, and which the agha had allowed me to keep after he had read it.

I practiced at the handwriting till I found myself fairly able to imitate it, and then set about writing the forged letter. In a couple of hours I had this done to suit myself. The letter I addressed to my father. It was somewhat as follows:

"To his excellency, Alzim Zagan, Pasha of Room-Elee, I, Murad IV, Sultan of Turkey, do hereby send my most heartfelt greetings:

"I speak to you of the noble conduct of your son in the mutiny six months ago. If all of his corps were as noble as he, Turkey would be the greatest of all nations. But they are not. Satiated by their many priviledges, they are bold and insolent, and have often been disrespectful to me. I intend, before another year has gone by, to take their priviledges away from them, on some pretext or other, because of their misuse.

"Besides this, the janissaries, with the exception of two or three amongst whom I include your noble son, are nothing but a pack of cowardly cattle. I may even disband the corps if they do not behave themselves. I do not trust them in battle, and fear that they will run if once they catch a sight of the enemy.

"Such a pack of cowardly dogs is a menace rather than a protection to Istanboul. I really think that I will have to disband them, and send them to raise pigs in the country, tho I don't think there's much difference."

"Murad IV,

"Sultan of Turkey."

And that was the letter I wrote. It was well-calculated to rouse the feelings of the janissaries, and incline them towards insurrection. I knew that loyal tho they were, their priviledges had made them arrogant, and therefore more ready to resent an insult, even from the padishah, without much fear of the consequences. I had a few qualms of conscience upon reviewing the deception, but threw them to the four winds and prepared myself to show the letter to my comrades.

On the evening of the next day, after the agha had left the room, I produced the letter, which was simply a folded piece of paper, unsealed. My heart was beating lest my plan should fail, or the deception be detected.

"What's that, Ali?" asked one, "a love letter that you're going to read us?"

"It's not much of a love letter, as you'll soon find," I said grimly, opening the paper. "I found this lying in the street this afternoon. As the seal had been broken off, I read it, and at the finish, concluded that you'd like to see it. It is addressed to my father, from the Sultan. The carrier evidently lost it in some manner, and the seal was evidently broken during the fall, as I found it near."

With a beating heart, I handed them the letter. They read it from start to finish, their cheeks reddening with anger as they progressed. The letter was handed about till all had read it, and then returned to me.

The officers began to talk in low, but angry tones. His majesty's name was mentioned many times, and always with anger in the speaker's voice. I saw at once that the forged letter was taking effect, and had but little doubt but that my plan would succeed. For about an hour they talked, I with them.

"Such an insult ought to be resented," said one.

"But how?" I asked.

"That's the question," returned the speaker.

"Why not mutiny?" suggested a third, and bolder one.

"March to the Seraglio, and refuse to return to our duty till he took back the insult."

"That's right!" broke in a dozen voices.

"We'll do it," said a dozen more.

"Are you with us, Ali?" said another, putting a pistol to my head. "If you are not, I'll blow your brains out."

"Of course I am," I said, stoutly. "I'd trouble you to lower that pistol. It might go off accidentally and hit you."

This sarcasm on the fellow's marksmanship evoked shouts of laughter, and the butt of it slunk away, eyeing me angrily.

The plot was soon formed. Certain of the officers, a dozen or so, were told off to incite the anger of the common soldiers, so that we might have their aid in our enterprise. I gave them the letter, so they might use it as proof of the Sultan's insult. They went out and did not return for a long time. When they did so, they brought news of a complete success.

"Every janissary is with us," said one. "They're as angry as a lot of scorpions. This mutiny will be a very serious one, and all the troops in the city won't be able to put us down. His majesty will have to admit that we're not such a 'pack of cowardly cattle', after all."

"He will," we agreed, and retired after a space of time to our rooms to think the matter over, and to sleep.

But for me there was no sleep. I was in a fever till midnight, and when that time came, stole forth to meet Fatima. I had not been waiting long, when she came forth, still more beautifully dressed, and unveiled.

We met and embraced once more, and I covered her face with my fervent kisses. When the first ardor of our meeting was over, I told her of the success of my plan.

"Ali, my love," she said, "you are a genius. I cannot love you too much."

"Nor I you," I cried, pressing her to my bosom.

After awhile we parted most tenderly, with many protestations of mutual love, and retired, I to dream sweet dreams of her till the morning.

Chapter XVIII

Saturday was the day set for the mutiny tho I would fain have had it soon being most impatient to have the matter over and done with. Never once did it occur to me that our plan would fail, so mad with love was I, and neither did it once occur to the other officers.

Abdul was let into our plan on promise that he would not reveal it, and joined. He, like the others, was angry at the Sultan. The agha also joined, and all of the married officers, of whom there were some half-dozen. To make a long story short, every janissary at Istanboul was in the mutiny. I was somewhat ashamed of the deception I had carried out, but feared the consequences if I should reveal it. I therefore determined to see the matter to its end, and trust that it would end well.

I met Fatima every night. Abdul suspected nothing, and I was apparently as much his friend as I had ever been. True, I avoided him a good deal, and spoke but little when we were together, yet he set this down on account of the coming mutiny, and rallied me, asking if I was afraid and if I intended to back out at the last moment. My only answer was, "No!"

At last the day of the mutiny came. We quietly assembled in the exercising-ground early in the morning, and set out toward the Seraglio. The journey was brief, but created great excitement in the city. Everyone saw at once that a mutiny was taking place.

Our troops cut down all who got in the way, and as a consequence we were little bothered. Many heads appeared at windows, for fifteen thousand janissaries, led by their agha, in full revolt, was not a sight to be seen every day of the year.

We made a great deal of noise, and at the Seraglio, found the Bostanjis drawn up in full force to oppose us. We charged them and drove them, after a brief struggle, within the walls. The agha then caused us to retreat to some distance and called for the Sultan to come out, promising that no harm should befall him.

The Sultan delayed about half an hour, and then appeared on the wall, attended by the Bostanji Bashi, and the Grand Vizier.

"Rascals of rebels, what do you want?" he yelled.

"We want you to take back the insult you gave us in your letter to the Pasha of Room-Elee."

"I wrote no insult," said the Sultan, "there must be some mistake. Get you back to your duty, dogs of rebels, ere I come forth to slay you with my own hand. Go back, I say, or I'll hang every one of you."

One of the janissaries laughed and dared him to do it. The Sultan raised his pistol and fired. Abdul, my old friend, threw up his arms and fell without a sound!

"That's one traitor less," said the Sultan, as he disappeared.

"Tell your master," said the agha to the Bostanji Bashi, "that we won't return to our duty till he take back his insult."

The Bostanji Bashi and the Grand Vizier disappeared without giving the slightest sign that they had heard him.

We waited for fifteen minutes. No one came forth and all was silent within the Seraglio.

The agha was about to give the order to scatter in small parties and terrorize the city, when we heard the tramp of many thousand feet.

The next moment the Bostanjis came forth thru the Sublime Porte and the Bashi-Bazouks, the Cossacks, and the infantry burst upon us from the other three sides. We were entirely surrounded.

The Sultan raised his pistol and fired . . .

The janissaries fought well and hard, but there was no escape. The battle lasted perhaps an hour, and at the end the ground was strewn with dead and dying. Most of the officers died fighting but some half-dozen, I amongst them were taken prisoner.

Zamil, the agha, fell with a ring of dead around him, and his sword broken at the hilt. He was covered with a hundred wounds, anyone of which would have been fatal to an ordinary man.

We were taken to separate cells below the Seraglio. At my special request they furnished me with pen, paper, and ink with which to write these memoirs.

My dungeon was about fifteen feet long by ten feet in width. The walls were of heavy stone and there was but one window, that very small, and close to the top of the wall.

The furniture consisted of a small table, a wooden couch, and a couple of chairs. It was very luxurious for a Turkish prison, and was given me because of my high rank.

Two days after my imprisonment came the news that my father was dead. He had died the day before the mutiny. I abandoned myself to much weeping, but still could not refrain from thinking that it was well that he had not lived to hear of my disgrace. I well know that it would have broken his heart.

Four days after that came my trial. It was a very simple trial. The Sultan himself acted as judge. My comrades were tried with me.

There was little need of evidence. What was needed was soon produced, and after making a very stern speech the Sultan sentenced us to death. My comrades were sentenced to be hanged, and I, in consideration of my high rank, to be beheaded.

We were then taken back to our prison. The time at which we were to suffer death was not told us. I have at the present time been here nearly a year. I was told yesterday that I am to be killed within ten days at the most.

But to return to the main tale.

Some two weeks after the trial, a couple of officers entered my cell.

"The Sultan has requested that you be brought before him," they said. "We will be greatly obliged if you will come with us immediately."

"What's the matter?" I asked.

"That I don't know," replied one of them, "but it has something to do with his niece and a forged letter found in your room at the barracks."

"So they found that letter?" I said to myself. "I wonder what Fatima has to do with it?" All the same my heart beat violently at the prospect of again meeting she whom I loved above all others.

I was conducted thru the Seraglio to his Majesty's audience-room. The Sultan was seated, and by him stood Bikri and the Grand Vizier. Before him was a man whom I did not know. I saw that he was a janissary. Near him was Fatima, very pale, between two stern-looking guards. Bikri grinned malevolently at me as I entered, as if to say: "Now you're getting it." I returned the grin with interest and a little more.

"Ali Zagan," said the Sultan, looking up, "did you write this forged letter?" He held up the identical one which I had written to fool my comrades and incite them to insurrection.

"Yes, your majesty," I said without a tremor. There was quite a stir in the room. Apparently, no one had expected me to tell the truth.

"That is one point in your favor," said his Majesty, "you've told the truth. For what purpose was it written?" he went on.

"To incite the janissaries to insurrection," I replied boldly.

"Your purpose succeeded admirably, but brought you no gain."

"Your majesty is right," I replied.

"And at whose instigation was it written?" he went on, ignoring my remark.

"At your niece's," I replied, my voice trembling, but I was determined to tell the whole truth cost what it might.

"Is this true, Fatima?" said the Sultan.

"Yes, your majesty," quavered Fatima.

"And why did she wish you to do this?"

"Because she bore your majesty a spite."

"What was this spite?"

"Your cruelty towards her."

"And why did you do what she wished you to?"

"Because I loved her."

"Ah! I see. She asked you as an instrument to vent her spite against me."

"I love him!" said Fatima indignantly.

"Is all that he has said, true?"

"Yes, your majesty."

"This is a most amazing revelation," said the Sultan gravely. "I find after all, that Ali is not so much to blame! 'Tis you, Fatima, that has caused all this trouble and suffering."

"May I ask, your majesty," said I, "how you knew that Fatima had anything to do with this affair?"

"I did not know till after this officer found the letter in your room," said his Majesty, indicating the janissary. "After that I began to suspect that there was a woman at the bottom of it. I made inquiries, and discovered you had been very friendly with my niece. I therefore had her arrested on the mere suspicion."

"It is all very strange," was my only comment.

"You have good cause to think so," said his Majesty, grimly.

"Yes, I have."

"Now Fatima," said his Majesty, "what have you to say for yourself? You see the consequences of your wickedness: three or four hundred janissaries and other soldiers slain in a fight and many others condemned to death; and all because of a spite you bore me."

"I have nothing to say," sobbed Fatima.

"What do you think a fitting punishment for this woman?" asked the Sultan of those around him.

"Death! Death!" replied every voice.

"Then death it shall be," said the Sultan.

There was a grim silence.

"Ali, you may embrace her, and for the last time," said his Majesty to me.

I walked over to Fatima and took her in my arms and pressed her silently to my bosom. I kissed her many times, and the color came back to her cheeks. It was the embrace of death, the embrace of two people condemned to die, but it was none the less sweet. They looked on in silence and no man dared to laugh.

I released her at last and went back to my guards. The Sultan drew his scimitar, walked over to Fatima, motioned the officers to stand aside, and before she had comprehended the meaning of this action, struck off her head! So died Fatima, the only woman that I ever loved, and one of the most wicked that ever lived.

I was taken back to my cell ere I had time to recover from the shock. I spent the rest of that day in great depression and sorrow.

There is only one more incident with which I will weary the reader. That is the death of the five officers who had been among the ringleaders in the mutiny.

Three months after Fatima's death I was again called forth by my jailors. I was conducted to a certain room in the Seraglio. There I found my five comrades, the Sultan, Bikri Mustapha, the Grand Vizier, and half-a-dozen guards armed with long spears. Besides this there was an executioner, in black, with a large ax and a block.

"I have determined that these men shall be beheaded," said his Majesty, "and I have called you here to witness their death."

I had hoped at first that I was to die with them, but these words dashed all my hopes to the ground.

Ismail, the tallest of the five advanced towards the block. In his face there was no sign of fear, and he wore a bold, defiant look. The executioner motioned him to kneel. Instead, the fellow drew a pistol, pressed it to his head, and blew out his brains.

The next advanced. At the block, he snatched a dagger from his bosom and stabbed himself to the heart. He reeled and fell atop his comrade's body. Almost at the same moment, two of the others drew daggers and stabbed themselves. They fell in a heap, close to their comrades.

"Where did they get these weapons?" questioned the Sultan of the fifth.

"The jailors furnished them," was the reply.

The speaker walked forward to the block, knelt, and laid his head upon it. The next moment the executioner struck, and it rolled across the floor to my feet.

They led me back to my cell and left me alone. The scene, in spite of the fact that I have as strong nerves as anybody, had unnerved me and I was sick for several days.

And now, my dear reader, I must bring this tale to an end. In ten days, or less, I am to die as my comrades did. I have little more to say except to warn the reader against doing as I did. But the punishment that befell my comrades in guilt, and the penalty that I must pay, are sufficient to warn you.

The End

Epilogue

The sequel to the above tale was told to me by my friend Manning some ten days after he presented me with the manuscript. I was at his home at the time. "By the way, Travers," said he, "do you remember that Oriental manuscript I gave you?"

"Yes," I replied, "but what of it?"

"Yesterday I was examining a report of the siege of Bazdas which was made by the agha of the janissaries. In it I found this passage:

"About the middle of the day a man rode into our camp. He inquired for me, and I was pointed out to him. He came to me and said:

"I am Ali Zagan, who, perhaps you will remember, was one the ring-leaders in the mutiny at Constantinople last year. Ten days ago, I escaped from my prison. The jailor, it seems, was heavily bribed by friends of mine, to release me. He did so, and I came here, hearing that the Turkish army was before Bagdad. I pray you sir, to give me a company and allow me to die in my country's defense in the attack on Bagdad."

"After some thinking, I complied with his request. He thanked me joyfully and went to take command of the company I assigned to him.

"The next day, when we delivered the assault, he was foremost amongst the soldiers. He fought like a lion and I well knew that it was to expiate his offense.

"When the assault was over and we had carried the city, I found his body lying in the breach. His sword was broken, and his death wound was in the center of the chest.

"Around him lay the bodies of a dozen Persians, testifying to his prowess. He was ever a great fighter and a brave man, and as such he died. Glory to him!"

"That's the end of Ali Zagan!" said Manning.

"It was a fine end," I remarked.

"Most glorious," said my friend.

"It was really a remarkable story—the story of his life."

"It was."

"After all, he wasn't such a bad fellow. He might have done better in his life, but he was only human. He was no worse than Adam."

"Not a bit. And his death atones for all the wrong he ever did."

"Certainly it does."

I was much impressed by the sequel to Ali Zagan's memoirs. It was so tragic, dramatic, and his death so glorious. Therefore I deem it worthy of a place in this tale.

The story of Zagan is a strange one and one of the strangest ever penned by he to whom it happened. I do not doubt its veracity, and tho people will say it is a work of the imagination, I, for one, assert that it is true.

Poems

Editor's Note: The following poems are organized in a sequence roughly reflecting the author's age at the time of composition: most likely from age 10 or 11, to his middle 30s. The finished poem, "Rêve Parisien," a translation from Baudelaire, was first published in *Sandalwood* (1925). It is included here in the "first draft" form from my collection of Smith manuscripts.

Three poems occur on one page of manuscript: "The River of Life," "The Departed City," and "The World." They differ greatly in quality, and were obviously copied from a note-book onto this manuscript, possibly to produce a final draft of each.

The River of Life

Winding—winding to the sea,
Ever on, goeth the river free.
Here he bends, and there he goes,
Here he stops, and there he flows.
Onward—to the sea
Goeth the stream so blithe and free.

And so floweth the River of life,
Onward thru peace and strife,
Here it turns and there it goes,
Here it stops, and there it flows.
Onward—to the ocean of eternity,
Goeth the river of life so blithe and free.

The World

The world is world of ups and downs,
A world of smiles and frowns.
The sunshine followed the rain,
And pleasures cometh in the tracks of pain.
There's joy that succeeded sorrow,
Tho cloudy today 'twill be sunny tomorrow.

Spring cometh in the path of Winter,
And spring into summer doth enter.
Dawn cometh after night,
And darkness gives place to light.
So don't worry my dear,
If thy life be drear,
For 'tis a long lane that hath no turning:
Thy grief is only a school for learning,

To appreciate the joy that cometh after pain,
And value more greatly the sunshine after rain.

And all the grief and all the sorrow
We shall forget in the bright tomorrow.
We shall wonder why we cried
And laugh where once we sighed.
When cometh the happy day
When grief and pain shall pass away.

Editor's Note: I would judge this to be probably the earliest poem saved by Clark from his youthful works. In any other context, one would subscribe it to Hallmark or Robert Schuler. It is possible that his mother encouraged him to emulate at a very young age some of the verse common in the ladies' magazines she sold in order to support the family.

The Departed City

I stood 'mid the ruins of a city great,
And mused on the vagaries of destiny and fate.
Here, where I stand a city once stood,
With all its mingled bad and good.
Here dwelt man in all his glory,
Here men were born, and here men grew hoary.
In this empty hall wherein I stand
A king did issue his command.
There stood a palace stately, and tall,
Yonder, once was the city wall.
Yet where are all these now?
Where is all the glittering pomp and show?
All—all in the dust is laid low.

Bedouin Song

Across the hot sands, towards fertile lands
On our swinging camels we forward fly
On a heaven of lead, on the sands of red
Shines the sun, as it goes on high.

O camels go, to waters that flow,
Where the green palms wave in the breeze.
Forward, forward fly, passing swiftly by,
Till we see the waters and trees.

Sing, sing, each step shall bring
Us nearer to our journey's end.
Across hot sands, towards fertile lands,
Till red into green doth blend.
Brothers, brothers sing as we go, towards waters that flow,
And palms whose branches wave on high.
Camels trotting, camels swaying, each step bringing
Us to our haven of rest more nigh.

They gleam, they gleam, 'neath the sun's bright beam,
And the waters like silver glow.
And green branches move in the fronded grove
With the zephyrs that come and go.
The journey is done, our course is run,
And we lie 'neath the grateful shade.
Brothers sleep, in slumbers deep,
And dream of some faithful Arab maid.

Editor's Note: This poem is as close as you will come to reading doggerel by Clark Ashton Smith—or so it seems. Yet it is likely that this was written to seem to be a piece by the lost travelers in "The Black Abbott of Put-huum." If the former is the case, it is very early indeed. There are five lines that do not scan; therefore, either the poet is very new to his art, or it is deliberate doggerel to fit the characters presumed to be singing it.

Zuleika: An Oriental Song

The last red rays of the sun are glowing
On minaret and wall,
Slowly they sink, so slowly going,
And the shadows spread o'er all.
And loudly thru the gleaming rings
The muezzin's call to prayer.
I smile, and think of other things,
Of heaven, and all that is there.

Yet into my brain there steals
Slowly, sweet thoughts of thee.
While my knee to Allah kneels,
My heart, in secret, kneels to thee.
My brain is a chamber haunted
By the image of thy face.

'Tis a holy shrine, enchanted,
By thy lingering, sensuous grace.

But welcome the ghost that haunts me,
The image of my sweet.
Dear is the face that enchants me,
And the eyes have brought me to thy feet.
Where are the waters that can quench
My quenchless love for thee?
For there is no earthly power or strength
That can separate thou and me.

Editor's Note: The manuscript is difficult to read; however, after some struggles and debates, I am confident of this text.

Benares

1

I stood by the Ganges and watch'd the pilgrim's come and go
Forth from the city's streets and lanes, and all of India's land
Stood in the ghats and saw them coming, going, fast and slow.
Out of the streets and plains and jungles and hot desert sand.

11

All races and peoples and castes, they came to the stream,
From all lands of the East and some of the faraway West,
There by the Ganges I saw them under the burning beam
Of India's sun king and beggar, the worst and the best.

111

And lo! I saw the blind jacquer stand by the Rajah's side;
Each one stood, judged not by rank and power, but acts and deeds,
All men came with their sins, to stand the Ganges stream beside
To bathe in its holy waters—his and his brother's needs.

IV

Down by the ghats I saw them come out from the tribes of man,
Out of the cities and jungles, and deserts of the East.
Turban of red and turban of white, as the river ran
I beheld each by his brother's side—the greatest and the least.

V

The temples of sandstone shimmered in the haze of sultry heat,
The river gleamed as gleams a glittering Orient blade.
Out on the ghat the people came the holy stream to meet.
I saw the Rajah's palankeen, the priest within his shade.

Editor's Note: The themes of teeming mankind, a brotherhood in sin, honored seers, and (telling line) the priest in subservience to the ruler, occur often in Smith's stories and poetry. Additional stanzas to this poem exist in a manuscript in the Clark Ashton Smith Papers at the John Hay Library, Brown University.

Rubaiyat of Satyed

1

I stood in the forsaken market-place
Of an old and long-forgotten ancient race;
Before the palace of some great Sultan
As the pale moon was seeking his lost face.

II

But think ye, that tomorrow I may be
As much forgotten an unmourned as he.
I, myself, in this mighty universe,
Am but a pebble in a boundless sea!

III

Editor's Note: A fragment? The theme of the insignificance of the individual is typical in Clark's poems. The use of the "a-a-b-a" rhyme scheme is rather rare. Probably a youthful experiment in verse that he abandoned, although since the third stanza is labeled in pencil, it could be that the poet discovered to his surprise that the poem was actually finished. The first stanza clearly recalls Omar Khayyam. Once, Clark and I recited the whole of Khayyam's *Rubaiyat,* alternating until we had done all 101 of the FitzGerald translations.

The Isle of Saturn

"In one of these (islands) the barbarians feign that Saturn is held prisoner by Zeus."
—Plutarch

1

Say, what seer, what poet had beheld Saturnia?
Clio or Euterpe, tell, if this ye know:
Zones of guardian storm unslackening, sempiternal
Doldrums of the flat untraversible foam,
Drive the encroaching keels to leeward,
So no mariner glimpses it, no chart includes.
Never yet has man profaned it, never printed
Xanthic roads whereover duskier flames the blue.
For tall marble cliffs whereon the hippogriffin
Lifts his head and gazes seaward.
Unalarmed and all replete with grainy grasses,
Slant with wind, and drenched by spindrift, walls of cypress
Closely ward untended crofts where mellowed apples
Fall not from the bough to break their cyclic release.
Of a mightly myth that slumbers.

There, in Calamus and the lush hemlock matted,
By the hidden windings of unmurmurous streams,
Black gigantic swans that summer in strange planets,
Make these rents, and age to age returning rear
Shadowy broods that no one numbers.
There the dragon-mother, couched among the boulders,
On the rugged fells that rim the muted main,
Hatches out her blotched and horny young, with folded
Wings that open soon in fluttered, brief essays—
Tumbling on on downs and tors.
Darkly, in the gaunt and gleamless mountain-sides,
Drowse the metals for the mail of gods reawakened;
And the trees of savage forests hold on high
Still-unshapen hafts of Titan battle-maces
To be wielded in vast wars.
Stretched between two peaks, within a lea-wide valley,
Saturn, slumbering, heals his wounds through halcyon cycles:
Rains and dews like balm anoint him; wild grapes clamber
Over him with repairing clusters; and black ivy
Plaits his golden beard uncombed.

                    *   *   *   *   *

Others there are sleeping . . . Will they haply waken—
Monstrous phantoms striding down from fell and highland
Crawling like to rivered lava through the dale-beds?—
Gods who rose and reigned and died before the Titans
Lying in topless tombs undomed.

Editor's Note: Ms. Inscribed "For Bill Farmer." The poem was written in two pens—the first five stanzas in a spreading ink, very difficult to decipher, the last two in a thinner yet black ink. The signature and dedication are in modern ink. I would place this poem in the 1920s, probably the latter half. The poem was first published in *The Dark Chateau* (1951).

Temporality

Minutes and hours and days and months and years,
As life-blood flowing from a wound!
Let knee to knee and breast to breast be bound,
And still awhile the tremors of our fears.

Ah! deep is love's oblivion withdrawn,
As in some far and faery place to dwell,
Nor hear the sinister metallic knell
Of tolling pendulum clocks at moonset or at dawn!

Though time runs on, and star nor sun may stay,
Thy bosom is the maze of my delight,
Where I can lose the minutes in their flight,
And know not when to-day is yesterday.

April 13th, 1928

Shapes in the Sunset

Daylong was my slumber. At the sunset
Waking, I beheld the clouds, a hundred
Shapes of antic gods and beasts of wonder
Gathered on the horizon.

Vulcanus, his forge behind him, towered,
Greaved with aureate fire, against the boundless
Concave west, and purple Scylla mounted,
Warring with Poseidon.

There, with gaping mouth, the Mantichora
Showed his teeth and uttered silent roarings;
Light and silky as thistle-down, the Astomians
Came from lands of marvel,

Wafted on their ether; and the headless
People followed after them, the Blemmies,
Bearing on humped shoulders through the heavens
Their enormous fardels.

There, across dismembered Titans crawling,
Python rolled his volumes; there the Gorgon,
Eyed with blinding gold, through rack amorphous
Trailed her sinuous ringlets.

There, with skyward soles, with head inverted,
Hung the Sciapod, torn from his earthly
Plot remote; and swam the cod-tailed mermaid,
From the surges riven.

While the sunset, deepening and rubious,
Limned the bestiary shapes in lurid
Salamandrine hues, and robed with murex
Gods from myths forgotten,

I, the watcher, cried: "O clouds of wonder,
Fables, carry me, where an age-long sunset
Arches your lost Thule, by no sullen
Earth-born shadows blotted!"

Editor's Note: Ms. Inscribed "For Bill Farmer." A frequent theme in Clark's poetry is a longing for the lost age of Myth, as a place where the mind is unbound by "facts" and "science." This poem also appeared in *The Dark Chateau.*

Epitaph for the Earth

Somewhere in Space the disunited dust
That formed a visible comparted world,
Floats in unnoticed formlessness, nor mars
With stain of fleck the ethereal claritude
Of vacancy; nor with its monads driven,
Separate, irrelevant, athwart the suns,
Impedes the tangled multidudinous passage

Of rays that cross each other like the thrust
Of unrelenting swords.
                        The tombs that tooth
With granite mouths successive glut of Life
At last are not distinguished from the lips
Of earlier-crumbled earth. And man himself—
An evanescent peak of foam that pointed
One wave, subsided now, of matter's tide
Leaves but bequest of stories that he took
From forms long antecedent, that were not
As he; that shall not thus combine again
In all the future sequences of Change.

With hope of some far-off, supernal goal,
Changeless, and independent of the years
He strove on low and shifting ways, and sent
Commissioned dreams ethereal-wing'd before,
On summits that achievement's laggard feet
Scarcely approached, till on one lesser peak
He knew his own futility at last—
Himself an immaterial trick of Chance.

Editor's Note: This poem was inside the cover of copy #48 of the original
250 printed by the *Auburn Journal* of *Sandalwood*—signed and edited by CAS
at the time of printing.

Night

Twilight dim and gray,
        The last, red rays of the sun;
And slowly dieth the day,
        Its work is done.
Darkness cometh on apace,
        The shadows into darkness merge;
All is black before thy face,
        All things the night doth purge.

Darkness—and the stillness of the tomb:
        Thou canst feel an oppressing weight.
Suddenly the yellow moon doth loom,
        Like the impending hand of fate.
The second day hath come,
        The night in silver light

Is bathed. Nature, sticken dumb,
    Is silent all the night.

Blacker seem the shadows dark,
    In contrast with the silver gleam;
The trees stand gaunt and stark,
    Like spectres in a dream.
And over all the silver pall,
    The bright and silent beam,
Shining on illuminating all,
    The hills, the woods the silent stream.

The yellow ball on the water shines,
    The shadows dance in a sudden breeze;

Editor's Note: Incomplete—the paper has two holes at the top and a curious arc cut out at the bottom, the same as found on "The Guardian of the Temple" and other fragments.

Rêve Parisien

The memory of this dread demesne
Unknown, unsought by mortal eyes,
That morning, like some glad surprise,
Returns insistent, dimly seen.

What marvels fill the gulf of sleep
By some bizarre caprice
From all my dream the grass, the trees,
Are banished in the oblivious deep!

And I, tho' sculptor of a world
Of superbly tasteful monotone
Of metal, water, metal, flame, and stone
At mine enchanted will unfurled!

Babel of stairs and of arcades,
There stands a palace infinite,
Where fountains fall in chrysolite
On the dull gold of long estrades;

And from the ramparts far and high,
Enormous cataracts have sprung,
Like heavy crystal curtains hung
On the huge walls within the sky.

No blooms nor bower, but pools enchanted
Where lies the columns' mirrored frieze—
By the titanic naiades
Of pale and marble haunted.

Blue waters endlessly are whirled
Between the quays of malachite,
And quays of rose that stretch for light
A thousand leagues athwart the world—

A world of magic mineral;
And magic billow! Shore and sea
In dazzling cold immensity,
Redoubling and reflecting all!

An architect of Faëry
I make, with runes softly murmured,
A cavern wrought of rubacelle
That passes neath the conquered sea.

And all things, pale or sable, shine
Like furbished armour; flaming spaces
Of land a flaming gulf enchases,
Immured in splendour crystalline.

No star has passed, no sun has flown
To climb the adamantine skies,
Illuming these prodigies
That burn with lazy beams all their own!

And on this form of grammerie
In even beat lies (O! dread demesne
Where naught is heard, and all is seen!)
The silence of eternity.

In silence frozen the vault beyond
Great rivers negligently turn
The treasure of teeming urn
Adown the gulfs of diamond,

With funereal slow, the pendulum
Brutally sounds the hour of noon,
And heaven pours the night too soon
On the sad world forlorn and numb,

Opening eyes replete with fire,
Once in my sunless room again,

And feel re-entering in my brain
The fang of cares accursed and dire.

Editor's Note: Ms. inscribed "For Bill Farmer"; also "From Baudelaire."
This is a first draft of the translation that appears in finished form in *Sandalwood* (1925).

Averiogne

In Averiogne the enchantress weaves
Weird spells that cast a changeling sun,
From the sepulchral regions dark,
To abide on ivy blackened towers
Whose fungi mottled castles have
Time's phantoms for their seneschal.
There are the tyrannous monarchies
That walk with thunder-echoing shoon
In iron castles past the moon—
Close moated with eternities

Where the cathedral satyrs make,
From mouths of sullen sombre stone,
Unending silent moan
Wherein is writ the secret of our dole
Of mortal woes immortalized by thee
And wisdom, through time's olden perfidy
Draws back to life from some Lethean shoal.

Editor's Note: The above is clearly the germinal work that eventually became the complete poem as found recently reissued in Hippocampus Press' *The Last Oblivion* (2002). As such, and written as it is on an envelope received most likely from a publisher in Uxbridge, England in 1949, it is of inestimable importance to researchers seeking to explore the working of the poet's mind. Only the opening, the seminal concept or launching pad for the whole work, and a few other lines remain in the revised poem.

Short Stories

The Emir's Captive

The sun was setting in the Syrian Desert. Already the fiery ball was concealed behind mass of glowing, red clouds, which mantled the distant horizon with crimson. The sand of the desert shone bright yellow in the fleeting light.

For a moment the clouds parted, and a long, fiery beam of light pierced through the gap and was reflected upon the untarnished shield of a desert horseman. His mount, a steed of the Kochlani blood, the horses which are said to be descended from the steeds of King Solomon, stood silent and impassive, sharply [limned] against the horizon. His master seemed for the moment a part of him, and the two a statue carved from solid stone. The Arab was watching the sunset, but his eyes roved constantly on the distant horizon as tho he were expecting something.

He was a tall impressive man, long-bearded, and clothed in a flowing caftan. A curved sabre of Damascus steel was at his side. In his right hand was a long spear, and on his left arm a small buckler of rhinoceros hide, with a sharp spike in the centre. His face was grave, yet handsome. He was a man in the prime of life, and his cheeks were dark with the fierce heat of the Eastern sun.

Some distance to his right rose a group of date palms, from amongst which burbled a crystal spring which stream ran some distance, and was lost in the sand. Amongst these palms stood a number of black tents, and near them were camels and horses. White-robed figures hastened about, and a low hum of voices was audible. At a distance from the encampment, several silent figures, bearing long spears, sat on horse-back. They were the outposts.

The Emir, Yusuf ben Omar, to whom we have just been introduced, gave a sudden start. His sharp eye had detected something—a black speck moving slowly, far out on the sea of molten sand. The setting sun drew gradually nearer, and soon it revealed itself as a horseman. On, on he came, the camp of the Arabs seeming to be his destination.

The sun was poised a moment above the red horizon and was gone. The darkness fell like a blanket over the desert, and the stars shone out. The moon was peeping from the East.

As its first rays shone over the desert, making all things white and silvery, the horseman galloped up to the Emir, and flung himself from the back of his panting steed.

He reeled a moment, as a drunken man, then stood up and faced the Emir. He was young, tall and handsome, and dressed in much the same manner as Yusuf ben Omar.

"Father, I have escaped," he gasped. "For seven days they held me prisoner in the Camp of the Infidels—I, who went to them as an envoy. It was treachery, for I came to them with a flag of truce, and their Chief guaranteed my safety.

"Today they would have sent me to the Camp of King Richard, but I escaped, and on my own horse. For [forty?] miles they pursued me, but their steeds were not as fleet as mine. And now I am with thee—safe!" As he spoke the last word he staggered and fell, almost at his father's feet.

"I am wounded—in the breast," he gasped. "Their bows are strong, and their arrows reach far. The curse of Allah be upon them—the infidels!" Here the speaker relapsed into unconsciousness.

The Emir, with a dark look upon his face, stepped forward and lifted the limp body in his arms. The caftan at the breast was stiff with blood, and there was a gaping wound in the lad's right side, where the arrow had been wrenched forth. It was not necessarily fatal, but would require skill and time to heal.

Yusuf bore his son to the camp, and called a dark faced, wizened little man before him.

"See that he be well ere long," said the Emir, addressing this person, "else thy head, Jew, shall pay the price." He withdrew, leaving Molochi, the Jewish physician, in sole possession of the apartment.

"Now for revenge," muttered Yusuf as he passed out of the great tent. Many of his warriors, who had seen him bring in the body of his son, had gathered in a group. They knew at once that Ali, the Emir's son, who had been sent as an envoy to the camp of Robert, one of King Richard's knights, had met with treachery.

Here a few words of explanation may be necessary. Robert de Montrevel, with a band of men-at-arms, had detached himself from the English King's army, and had set out to find Yusuf ben Omar, who was an old enemy of his against whom he had fought in the Second Crusade. He had been badly beaten, and now was longing for revenge. So, with Richard's permission, he had set off to find his old foe.

Yusuf, hearing of his coming, had sent to his camp his son Ali, as an envoy, it being the Emir's purpose to arrange a place of combat, in which he and his enemy could settle their quarrel once and forever. It was to be a single combat, the side whose Chief was beaten to leave the field in possession of the victor. And they were to fight to the death.

Robert, in spite of his given word that no harm should befall Ali, had immediately imprisoned him. Ali, as he was taken out to be sent to the camp of King Richard, had espied his horse. He called to it, and the obedient steed came galloping up. Before the soldiers could recover from their momentary confusion, the young Arab, who was unbound, leaped onto his horse and was off like a flash.

A portion of the band, returning from a foray, attempted to intercept him. One sent an arrow into his breast ere he was out of bowshot. They pursued him for many a mile, but at last he outdistanced them, and arrived as before related, at his father's camp.

The Emir called his chiefs before him, and gave them a brief account of what had happened. "Now for revenge," he said. "Tonight, by moon light, we will swoop down upon the infidels, and take their chief captive. We will kill his men without mercy, so they may not escape with tales to Richard. Here in the desert will I deal with my prisoner. If my son dies, his head shall pay the penalty. If not, we will hold him for a ransom. Now to your horses, for though the night is yet young, the way is long. We will attack in the hours before dawn, when men sleep the heaviest, and sentinels are drowsy from their long night."

In half an hour all was ready. A few men, perhaps a score in all, were left to guard the camp. Three hundred horsemen with long spears and flowing caftans, with the Emir at their head, at a given word swept away into the desert, and like white spectres soon faded from sight. The stillness of the night fell upon the encampment, as the beating hoofs grew fainter and fainter, and naught was heard save the weird and melancholy cry of the jackal in the distance.

11

In the tent of the Emir lay Ali, still unconscious and breathing heavily. He was laid on a silken couch. Several dim lamps, suspended from the roof of the tent, burned dimly, and threw a golden radiance on the rich rugs with which the ground was covered. The Jewish physician, Molochi, stood over him, feeling his pulse. It beat rapidly, for Ali was consumed with fever. A couple of negro slaves darted about the apartment at the doctor's orders, and every now and them a swarthy face peered through the curtains, and a low voice asked for the health of Ali, the son of Yusuf bin Omar.

The young man stirred uneasily in his sleep. He muttered for a moment, and seemed to speak. The Jew bent down to catch his words. But they were inaudible, and Molochi again rose to his feet.

Again Ali stirred, his eyes opened, and he awoke. He stared about for several moments before realizing where he was. His lips moved again, and the physician heard the muttered words, "Water, water, for the love of Allah!"

Cooling drinks were brought and administered to Ali. Into one of the cups, unobserved, Molochi dropped a lozenge of bhang.

Ali lay back on the cushions. His eyes closed slowly as the influence of the narcotic made itself felt. In a little while he had fallen into a deep and peaceful sleep. The worst of the fever was over.

III

It was night in the camp of Robert de Montrevel. The knight, a burly man of about forty, and renowned for his love of wine, as well as his prowess, lay in a drunken stupor. Without, in the long watches of the night, the sentinels stood guard. In the tents his men lay, snoring heavily. The sentinels were drowsy, for they had not been relieved at Midnight, as was the custom, for their comrades, having indulged freely in liquor, had forgotten all about them.

One by one they nodded at their posts and fell asleep upon the sand. The night wore on till morning was but a few hours distant.

Suddenly the desert resounded to the Moslem battle-cry, and the clatter of galloping horses. The drowsy sentinels, as they arose to their feet, rubbing the sleep from their eyes, were cut down, and the Arabs swept on towards the tents.

"Allahu-akbar!" went up the cry from three hundred throats. Spearheads waved in the moonlight, and where a few moments before all had been silence, all was now tumult. Tents were overturned upon their inmates. The drunken soldiers, entangled in the folds, were unable to rise. Before they had time to become fully aware of the situation, they were pinned to the ground by long spears.

A few gathered in a group and contested the advance of the Emir's followers. The Moslems, being at close quarters, drew their swords, and the little band was quickly cut to pieces. The ground was slippery with blood, and the camp resounded with the clash of steel, the yells of the living, and the groans of the wounded and dying.

In the short space of ten minutes, some two hundred men lay dead or wounded upon the sand. Those who were maimed, were shown no quarter, but speedily dispatched by the swords of their assailants.

The Emir had lost very few men. Half a score of his warriors lay dead, and a few had been wounded. But in opposition to this most or all of Robert de Montrevel's soldiers had been slain, and he himself, still asleep, was a prisoner.

Ere noon of the following day the Emir and his men were back in camp. The spoil taken from the Crusaders was divided amongst them.

IV

When Robert de Montrevel awoke he found himself amongst strange and unfamiliar surroundings. He was in a large and spacious apartment, part, in fact, of the Emir's tent.

He was lying on a couch of silk, at which he marvelled greatly. Rugs from the looms of Smyrna and Ispahan covered the floor. The rough black cloth of the walls was concealed by silken draperions, and golden lamps hung from the ceiling.

A tabouret with a tray of fruit and cups of sherbet stood at his side. In the door stood the figure of a follower of the Prophet, leaning upon his long spear and surveying the captive with some measure of curiosity. Without there was a hum of voices, and the stamping of horses and cries of camels.

De Montrevel stared about stupidly, taking in the surroundings with great wonder.

"Where am I?" he muttered. "Surely I am dreaming." His eye fell upon the sentinel in the doorway. "Who art thou?" he asked in the Lingua Franca, the common medium of intercourse between Europeans and Saracens.

"A warrior of the Emir Yusuf ben Omar," was the reply of the turbanned Moslem.

Robert started violently. "I am, then, his prisoner?" he asked.

"So it seems," answered the guard, with a grin.

De Montrevel's hand went to his sword. It was gone. He stared gloomily at the wall, and then, feeling hungry, stretched out his hand to the tabouret. He ate ravenously of the fruit, and drank the sherbet. He had scarcely finished when the Emir himself entered. He told his prisoner what had occurred, and then explained his situation to him.

"If my son dies, you die," he said. "His condition is very critical. The physician is doing his best, even though he is a Jew, but the wound is worse than we expected. The arrowhead must have been rusty, for gangrene has set in, and a terrible fever has seized him. Curse you!" he cried, stepping closer, and shaking his fist in Robert's face. "If he dies, your fate is certain."

Robert paled, but said nothing. Yusuf ben Omar withdrew soon afterwards, leaving him to his own gloomy thoughts.

Ali's condition, as the Emir had said, was indeed critical. Molochi, who had come to love the lad, wrung his hands. Blood poisoning had set in, and blood had collected around the lungs. The bleeding, indeed, had been mostly internal. Hemorrhages were frequent, and the young man was on fire with a terrible fever. His pulse beat like a hammer, and his face was drawn with pain.

As night approached, matters grew worse. Ali breathed fitfully, and was entirely unconscious. Molochi, in despair, announced that nothing more could be done. Yusuf, with a stern set face, strode about the room, muttering. There was a constant hum of voices and patter of feet.

About midnight the end came. Molochi had done everything he could, and the Emir realized that it would not be the doctor's fault if his son died. He spoke to the Jew. "You can do nothing more," he said, "so you had best retire." But Molochi would not go.

Soon the word went through the camp that Ali was dying. The chiefs clustered in the tent, behind the Emir, who stood close beside his son.

It was midnight. Suddenly Ali's eyes opened, and he gazed about the room. Then he looked up, stretched out his arms, with a wild cry to Allah, and fell back dead.

The chiefs filed out of the tent. Molochi wept and wrung his hands, and the Emir, with a stern and set face strode up and down. The lamps burned low as the night advanced, and ere they knew it, morning was upon them, and sorrow reigned.

V

Three days later Yusuf ben Omar stood before his captive. "I have altered your fate," he said. "I shall fight you with my own hand, and slay you, if such be the will of Allah."

So he and Robert de Montrevel went out into the sunshine. The Arabs clustered about them, and formed a ring. Three swords were laid before him, and he was given his choice. He selected the largest. The Emir picked up another, and they attacked fiercely.

But the Knight of King Richard, strong though he was, was not as lithe and skilfull as his adversary. He fought clumsily, and at every stroke he was driven back. His enemy's blade seemed everywhere. The flash blinded his eyes, and he could scarce defend himself.

The Emir had scarcely begun to fight. He was merely playing with his clumsy foe. Soon the knight was out of breath, and his strokes went wild. The Arab, darting at him from nearly every side at once, was too much. He could not turn in time to ward off the blows.

Still Yusuf continued to play with him. There was a fiendish smile on his face. A dozen times he could have driven his blade home through armor and all, but he refrained.

De Montrevel's head drooped forward, and he staggered for a moment. The Emir stopped and watched him. When he had regained his balance he was at him again.

The knight's breath came in pants. The hot sun and his adversary's agility began to tell upon him. The Emir was cool and crafty, and breathing as easily as if he were at ease in his harem.

Round and round they went, stabbing, striking, and guarding, the one cool, the other furious. De Montrevel grew weaker and weaker. At last the Emir was ready. As his foe dropped his guard for a moment, his keen blade drove home, and Robert de Montrevel fell dead on the sand.

Fakhreddin

Fakhreddin, Grand Vizier to Abdallah Harun Al-Raschid, seventh Caliph of the race of the Abassids, was a tall, handsome man, well versed in all the known sciences. He was well-beloved of his master, but in his secret heart, cherished that malignant monster, Jealousy. Yes, he was envious of the Caliph's great wealth and position. He was a cousin of Harun Al-Raschid.

Being of a secretive disposition, however, he had kept his envy strictly to himself, except on certain occasions when it had broken out in great fury.

A certain rich merchant of whom Fakreddin was purchasing a turban, extolled to him the praises of the Caliph.

"Our good Prince, Harun Al-Raschid," he said, in a sonorous voice which was meant to be impressive and was not, "is superior to all princes of this earth, living or dead, with the exception of Mahomet. He is wiser, kinder, wealthier, and more holy than any living ruler. He is richer than any of the emperors of Cathay, wiser than the wise men of China, and more holy than any of his predecessors, except the prophet himself."

"Perfidious liar! Dolt! Thou knowest not what thou sayest," cried Fahreddin, siezing the unlucky merchant by the throat and throwing him to the ground. Drawing his poignard he would have stabbed him (the merchant) dead, had not some people who had been standing nearby, interfered. They held back the furious Vizier, while the merchant, his face livid, staggered to his feet.

"Is it meet for the Grand Vizier of the Caliph to thus abuse his master?" he asked, still gasping for breath.

"I did not abuse the Caliph," said Fakhreddin, "I merely called you a liar and a dolt, and told you that you knew not what you said."

"You did, I'll admit that," said the merchant. "But all the same you meant that the qualities which I ascribed to the Caliph were not his. Everyone knows, who knows anything, that what I spoke was the truth."

"I'll say one thing for the Caliph," sneered Fakhreddin, "he's much better that Mahomet ever was!"

At this sacreligious utterance, coming from the lips of so illustrious a person as the Grand Vizier of the Vice-regent of God, the people who had collected in the bazaar drew back in horror and astonishment.

Finding that his captors had relinquished their hold upon him in their amazement, Fakhreddin drew his poignard and with a swift movement, stabbed the unhappy merchant to the heart.

The merchant fell without a sound, and the Grand Vizier made his escape during the confusion that followed. He reached the palace out of breath and immediately retired to his room.

Luckily for Fakhreddin, the Caliph was absent from Bagdad at the time and on his return, heard nothing of what had happened. Had it been otherwise than this the Vizier would assuredly have lost his head. But this, rest assured, was not the only occasion in which the malignant Fakhreddin displayed his hatred for the Caliph. It is not my purpose to weary the reader with an account of all that the Vizier did. I do not applaud his actions, for Harun Al-Raschid was the best of all the Caliphs, from Mahomet to the present Sultan of Turkey, who, tho he asserts himself to be vice-regent of Allah, is not regarded in that light by the Arabians, and other Mohammedan peoples outside his own dominions.

It is sufficient for my purpose to recite one more of the Vizier's acts of jealously, if by doing so I give the reader a better comprehension of his (Fakhreddin's) feelings towards the Caliph. This I hope I shall do, but the final issue is left to the good judgment of the reader.

It happened, that one night, the Caliph, who made it his custom to pass thru the city every night to see that all was well, was taken sick with a slight illness, brought on by needless exposure. Fakhreddin, who always accompanied him on these nightly rambles, had this time to go alone.

The task was not at all to his taste, he having been wearied by a long day of hard and incessant work. The divan had been assembled several times and some hard thinking had been done.

The last of these councils had been assembled for the purpose of judging the Caliph's illness and what should be done about it. As no opinion was arrived at, the divan was broken up, and the Grand Vizier and the lesser viziers retired, much vexed by the gloomy disposition of the Caliph, who had ever been bright and happy.

And now, to return to Fakhreddin's journey. About ten o'clock that night he sallied forth from the palace disguised as a common eunuch. After traversing the city from end to end he hastened homeward, spurred on by the thought of a warm supper.

He passed by a large house thru the windows of which a light could be seen burning. This was strange, it seemed to the Vizier, so he ventured nearer for the purpose of making closer observations.

He walked noiselessly up to the door and listened. From within came the sound of music and singing, the latter decidedly feminine voices. The Vizier, curious to know the reason of this, stopped to think for a moment. As he was perfectly aware that the Caliph had forbidden entertainments later than ten at night, this particular one needed some investigation.

The Vizier knocked loudly upon the door, first making sure that his scimitar was ready for use. As he knew not what might happen as a result of his intrusion, he determined to be ready to meet all emergencies. The first result was that the music and singing immediately stopped, and that the light was blown out. The second was that no one came to admit him. Both were highly suspicious, inasmuch as they admitted that something was happening within, which the participants did not think it best to reveal to people whose intention they did not know.

Finding that the inmates entertained no intention of admitting him, Fakhreddin bestowed upon the door a heavy kick. The door was equally as heavy and was barred into the bargain. It was of mahogany, and evidently very thick.

Fakhreddin, who was a strong man, put his shoulder to the offending door. It cracked slightly. Fakhreddin pushed again, this time with all his strength. The obstacle collapsed with a crash, the Grand Vizier collapsing with it. He was on his feet in a moment, and with his sword in his hand he rushed into the room.

Aforesaid house was as dark and as still as the tomb. As a consequence, Fakhreddin collided with a wall. His scimitar was broken during the operation. The Grand Vizier got up, cursing heartily. He cursed all the inmates, their personal property, going much into detail, then fathers, mothers, aunts, cousins, nieces and nephews, sons and daughters, wives, slaves, and concubines, and all their ancestors back to Adam. This occupied him at least five minutes and was done in a whole-hearted manner, intended to convince those who heard of the speaker's veracity and sincerity. And very undoubtedly those who heard were fully convinced. Fakhreddin was an adept in the art of cursing, and the aforesaid performance fully sustained his reputation. When Fakhreddin was finished he began to grope around for the door. He found it. The he tried to open it. But the door would not open. Fakhreddin cursed again. This time he did it a little more thoroughly. Then he applied his shoulder to the obstacle. It collapsed instantly and the unlucky Vizier executed a double somersault, coming down on his back. At the same moment he heard the sound of laughing nearby. He sought to rise and find the laugher, but he sought in vain. Then someone precipitated himself upon Fakhreddin from out of the darkness. Fakhreddin sat down very suddenly and the next moment was neatly trussed.

Someone lighted a lamp. The Vizier's captor suffered him to sit up. Fakhreddin blinked a little and then looked at the man who had captured him.

This person was to all intents a rich merchant. He was well dressed, and his garments were of expensive silks. He might have been forty years of age. His face wore a young expression, and his beard was of a rich black color. He had long hair, and a fierce looking mustache, about six inches in length. His great height exceeded that of Fakhreddin and he was correspondingly broad. Besides him there were two youths, who in their appearance the Vizier took to be the sons of the man. It was one of them who had lighted the lamp.

He approached and held it over Fakhreddin, so that his father might examine that person more closely.

"What do you mean by breaking into our house like this?" he asked angrily. "I see that you are one of the Calph's eunuchs."

"I am the Grand Vizier, Fakhreddin," replied that person. "Know you not that the Caliph has forbidden any entertainments to be held after ten at night!"

"I beg your pardon," said the merchant, cutting Fakhreddin's bonds, "I did not recognize you. If I had known that the Caliph had forbidden entertainments after a certain time I would not have held one. You must present my humble apologies to Harun Al-Raschid, whose equal for beneficence and generosity has never been known."

These last words, spoken in a loud voice, aroused the slumbering jealousy of the Vizier. With a quick movement, he drew his dagger and stabbed the merchant to the heart.

The two sons, with loud cries drew their sword and rushed upon Fakhreddin. The Vizier parried their furious blows and after a little while disposed of both of them. Hearing voices, he then rushed from the house and continued his homeward journey. Of course he did not relate this story to the Caliph, but was forced to devise a falsehood to account for the loss of his scimitar. The scimitar had been given to Fakhreddin by the Caliph and the hilt was encrusted with diamonds. The Vizier's story was that it had been stolen while he was passing through a dark street. The broken scimitar was discovered the next morning by the wife of the man who had been cruelly murdered. Recognizing it she took the hilt to the palace, and accused Fakhreddin of the murder.

"You are mad," said Fakhreddin. It was stolen from me last night, long before the time of the deed. If you can find the thief, you will find him who killed your husband and sons. Besides, what reason could I have for murdering them?" The woman acknowledged that there was none and went home perfectly well satisfied with this explanation.

A search was made for the thief, but he of course, not existing, was not found.

Editor's Note: So much of the final page is marred by stains, dirt, and water that a full half is illegible entirely; this, plus bleed-through from the ink on the other side, makes it almost beyond reading. However, enough is there to indicate that the scene shifts to the illness of the Caliph, which seems to be worsening; he is consulting the stars for a remedy; this seems to be fitting into Fakhreddin's ambitions. My guess is that the denouement will involve finding that Fakhreddin has either been slowly poisoning the Caliph, or has consulted with a sorcerer to enchant him; if the latter, then the sorcerer will have been done in by Fakhreddin after he attained his desire, and the spirits which served the sorcerer will wreak vengeance on

Fakhreddin. If the former, at some point his jealous rage will erupt at some inopportune moment and lead to the discovery of his plot and crimes, and some desperate last attempt to take over will countervene the mercy which the Caliph would have shown.

Prince Alcorez and the Magician

The following is translated from an old manuscript of the time of Limour the Lame. The author's identity is unknown.

Takoob Khan, the Sultan of Balkh, had but one son named Alcorez. This son, of a fierce disposition by nature, was not improved by the luxury and power surrounding him. He became cruel, licentious, and over-bearing, and made himself universally unpopular. In this he was exactly the opposite of his father, who was a wise and just Sultan, and who had endeared himself to the people. In contrast with him, the faults of his sons were doubly accentuated.

Prince Alcorez spent his days in sports and pleasure and his nights in reprehensible dissipation. He soon became noted for his love of wine, and for the number of his concubines. His father's remonstrances were of no avail. In spite of all that was said he continued in his course.

At this time there came to Balkh from Hindustan a noted magician, Amaro by name. He was skilled in the art of foretelling the future, and his fame throughout the land soon became great. To this dark-skinned man of an alien race and religion came all afflicted with trouble, or who sought to tear aside the veil of coming events. His patrons were of all ranks and station in life, for trouble is the lot of all, and curiosity a universal attribute.

Prince Alcorez, actuated by the common impulse, entered the presence of the magician. Amaro, a small man with gleaming eyes, and clad in flowing robes, arose from the cushions whereon he had sat wrapt in meditation, and saluted his royal visitor.

"O Prince," he said, "Comest thou to thy humble servant that he may read for thee the hidden and inscrutable decrees of fate?"

"Aye," said Alcorez.

"In so far as lies my ability I will serve thee," replied the Hindoo. He motioned his visitor to be seated, and then proceeded with his preparations.

As if at a word of command the room became darkened. Amaro took various perfumed woods and cast them into a brazier of heated coals. A thick black smoke arose, and standing in this, his figure seemingly grown taller and more impressive, and half-veiled in the curling vapor, the magician recited incantations in some strange and unknown tongue.

Alcorez sat spell bound, and saw the smoke form itself into various fantastic shapes. The room seemed to widen out indefinitely, and with it the black vapor. Soon the fantastic shapes became the semblance of human forms in which Alcorez beheld himself and many whom he knew.

They were in the throne room of the royal palace. Alcorez, seated on the throne of Sultans, was crowned ruler of Balkh, and his courtiers did him homage. For many minutes the scene was maintained, and then the shapes seemed to dissolve once more into black smoke.

The magician stood at Alcorez's side. "Thou hast beheld," said he, "the shadow of a coming event. That which thou hast seen shall in time come to pass. And now thou shalt look upon another scene."

Again the magician stood in the whirling smoke and chanted incantations in a strange and unknown tongue. And again the room seemed to widen out, and the vapor to form itself into a familiar scene and human shapes.

Alcorez beheld the Hall of Audience, in which the Sultans of Balkh dispensed justice to their subjects. And he, himself, sat on the throne. Before him came many stating grievances and demanding justice. And Alcorez gave his decisions.

Then Amaro, the Hindoo magician, entered. Straight he came to the royal throne, and presented his petition. The Sultan was about to make some reply, when the Hindoo drew a knife from his bosom, and stabbed him.

At the same moment, he who sat watching this spell-bound, gave a cry of horror and fell dead, stabbed to the heart by Amaro.

Editor's Note: Alcorez is a name used elsewhere in Clark's work. This little gem shows a very early attempt at the sudden and unexpected denouement. I think it works rather well, though one is not quite sure of the motivation of Amaro. Perhaps it was just good old Texas justice where "he needed killin'" is a valid defense in court.

The Haunted Gong

Among the many queer shops in San Francisco's Chinatown is that of a Japanese dealer in antiques—Takamoto Satsuma. Satsuma himself is a puzzle, but his place of business is, above all others, one of the strangest collections of the odd, the weird, and the unexpected that I have ever run across. Satsuma is brown and wrinkled—an epitome of his native land—of all that is mysterious, incomprehensible and exclusively Japanese, and his shop is likewise. There you may see all the gods of the East, deities of Buddhist and Shinto theology, squat images that look at you with the accumulated wisdom of long years and of a land and people essentially foreign. There, too, are swords and weapons of which I do not know the names, painted fans, lacquer work, Japanese armor, and a thousand and one other articles all resplendent of Japan.

Satsuma, who is invariably smiling and polite, as condescending if you leave without making a purchase as if you had bought twenty dollars worth, showed me about, exhibiting his treasures and extolling them in English which appeared peculiarly his own.

"You buy Matsuma sword?" he said, "I assure you most exceedingly ancient, and razor-blade keen. Matsuma mighty sword maker—forge devil-blades." The dealer was about to enlarge on the diabolical qualities of Matsuma when I espied a Japanese gong, decorated with figures of gods, half-human, half-animal, which lay on a counter between a miniature Kurannon and the "getting up little god" Daruma. "How much?" I inquired. I was informed that the price was two dollars, which, considering

the age of the gong, made out by Matsuma to be three hundred years, was not exorbitant. The money being produced, I soon departed, much delighted with my purchase, and followed by many thanks from the dealer in antiques.

The gong was hung near my writing desk, ~~and added, I thought, greatly to ornamentation of the room. I am by nature a collector of the odd, the picturesque, and particularly the Oriental, and my apartments show unmistakable traces of this predilection. Few have fairer Turkish rugs than mine or a more extensive collection of miscellaneous Oriental articles~~

I was seated at my desk several weeks later, engaged, if I recollect rightly, in an article [on] the Chinese Immigration Question. ~~Anyway, it was of a practical every-day nature.~~ Just as I had got well-started, I was suddenly interrupted by the sound of the gong striking. The sound, I may remark, was strangely deep and mellow, and different in tone from the ordinary gong. Five strokes followed each other in rapid succession, and when, much startled, I turned about, the instrument was still vibrating. My first thought was that some friend, wishing to play a joke, had stolen into the room and struck the gong. Great was my surprise to find myself absolutely alone. To my knowledge, no one was in the house. The sound having ceased, it was followed by unbroken silence. ~~broken only by the beating of my heart~~

Much puzzled and perturbed, I examined the instrument closely, wondering if there was any internal ~~arrangement~~ mechanism which could have been responsible. ~~This being without result, I looked about for some external agency, such as the proximity of some other articl~~ My search was fruitless; I could find no agency which could have produced the sound.

The affair was so mysterious and perplexing that had it happened other than in broad daylight in the very heart of bustling, matter-of-fact San Francisco, I should surely have put it down to supernatural agency.

But that was impossible. However, the more I thought of it, the ~~greater~~ more inexplicable the mystery grew. ~~But everything has its solution.~~ Determined to solve ~~the mystery~~ it, I went to Satsuma and told him the story. The dealer thereupon told a tale, which in plain English, runs thus:

Several centuries ago the ~~feudal~~ Lord Takamura Jiro ruled over a ~~great~~ portion of Kyoto. Jiro, ~~had raised himself to that position~~ beginning life as a common soldier under a former ruler, had, by a combination of circumstances, and his genuine abilities, raised himself to this high position, ~~and displaced his displacing~~ supplanting his master. Juster and more humane than his predecessor, whose cruelty had been instrumental in ~~displacing~~ dethroning him, he was beloved of his people, and ~~ruled over them~~ ruled in peace and prosperity.

Over another and larger portion of Kyoto, the Prince Umetsu Hakone held sway. Between Jiro and Hakone there had been smothered enmity originating many years before in the sheltering by Jiro of certain fugitives of justice from his neighbor. Though not resenting it at the time, Hakone had ~~long~~ nursed this grudge against Jiro, patiently awaiting the time when some excuse should arise for paying it off.

Seven years passed, and during these years ~~the prosperity wealth~~ prosperity abode in all Kyoto, the ~~crops~~ seasons being propitious and the crops abundant. Then, when least expected, there came a drouth, and after it a famine. Seven years had nature lavished her gifts over-generously, and now, as if in the balance of things, she withheld ~~those gifts~~ them.

The famine fell heaviest in that part ruled by Jiro, visiting but lightly the realm of Hakone. And Hakone, more far sighted than his neighbor, ~~foreseeing~~ perceiving that ~~these~~ this time must arrive, had stored up an abundance of ~~food~~ grain in preparation. During the famine he sold this to his people at an enormous profit, being both humanitarian and financier!

Seven years passed before his opportunity came. Jiro, then becoming engaged in a war with a neighboring prince, Hakone took advantage of the absence of his army to advance at the head of his troops into Jiro's territory. Jiro, having been wounded, was at that time abiding in his castle surrounded by a few soldiers, while his army was perhaps fifty miles away engaged in carrying on the war.

Hakone, advancing by forced marches found himself at nightfall near Jiro's castle. So swiftly and stealthily had he come that Jiro was ~~not~~ unaware of his presence in the neighborhood.

Knowing this, and also that the castle was practically ungarrisoned, Hakone, in the dead of night, attacked, carrying the outer gates and meeting with little resistance. Jiro's men, astonished and confused, were driven into the castle.

Jiro made preparations for a determined resistance. At first he thought that the prince whom he was fighting had stolen a march on him, but he soon became ~~apprised~~ aware that it was his old foe, Hakone.

With but twenty men he held the castle until dawn. Hakone's force, numbering many hundreds, strove vainly to effect an entrance. Each attack resulted in their retreating with great loss, only to advance once more. Jiro's soldiers, all samurai, fought with the courage of trapped rats, and when morning broke the men of Hakone advanced on an incline formed of dead bodies.

In spite of his wound, Jiro stood foremost to resist the enemy. He was a noble swordsman, and his blades, which rose and fell as regularly as trip-hammers, wrought terrific carnage.

But twenty men against many hundred could not hope for victory. At dawn but half that number remained to Jiro, and they were driven back, very slowly, into the castle. Every step, however, lost Hakone several lives.

In the great hall of the castle, Jiro, with two soldiers left, refused to retreat further. Here he would die gloriously, as befitted a samurai and the son of a samurai, and so, shouting the war-cry of his clan, he faced his enemies.

Close at hand was a gong. When Jiro fell, several minutes later, covered with wounds, and surrounded by a ring of dead, his sword struck it, and the sound, echoing strangely, seemed to those who heard it to toll the death of Jiro.

Hakone, having conquered his ancient enemy, now ruled over his realm. A year later, on the anniversary of Jiro's death, while standing near the spot where he fell, Hakone heard the gong strike five times though no agency was visible. And each year on that day, and at the hour when Jiro died, the phenomenon has occurred. Men say that it is the sword of Jiro striking the hour of his death.

Such was Satsuma's tale. Is it true, or is it a legend of old Japan, that land of many fictions and multitudinous folk-lore? But a year later, on the ~~sam~~ anniversary of that day, the gong was struck, tho no one stood near, and no agency was visible. It is very strange and most incomprehensible. Was it the sword of Jiro striking the hour of his death? Who knows? Who knows?

Editor's Note: In this transcription, I have chosen to leave the crossed-out portions as an example of Clark's reworking of the story. The hills of Auburn, where Clark grew up, were filled with ghostly mining lore. As recently as my own childhood, I heard stories of ghost miners, and strange sounds around jumped claims, and so on. Who knows?

The Malay Creese

"Sahib," said Hir Mohammed, "this weapon has not its equal in all Delhi. From far Singapore it came—from the land of the Malays, and its deeds are well worth relating." The sword-dealer held up the blade for my inspection. It was a long creese, or Malay knife, with a razor edge and a curious boat-shaped handle.

"Yea", continued Hir Mohammed, "strange have been its adventures. I bought it of Sidi Hassan, a Singapore dealer into whose possession it passed at the capture of Sultan Sujah Ali by the British. Hast heard the tale, sahib? No? It runs thus:

"Sujah Ali was a pirate, the younger son of a famous Sultan, who set out to carve for himself a name and an empire. In the space of a few years he became noted throughout the peninsula for the number of his ships, the ferocity of his men, and the quantity of his plunder.

"Sujah was not a common river-pirate. In the days before the coming of the English, his ships ran upon the sea, and were held in fear and respect by every tossing Chinese junk whose square sails loomed above the waters of the Strait.

"From Sengora to Malacca they went, preying upon all ships. And as the years passed, Sujah Ali became bolder, and sent his *prahus* out into the China sea. Inland, he became a great Sultan, and his dominions extended many leagues. The shadow of his name reached far and lay upon many peoples.

"When the English came, Sujah Ali ceased not, but dispatched more ships to prey upon the Feringhee vessels. In this he succeeded until ships bearing many guns and armed men came and sank his *prahus.*

"It was a disastrous day for Sujah Ali. When the red sun sank into the sea, fully fifty of his best *prahus*, and thousands of men, among whom he mourned several of his most noted captains, lay beneath the waters.

"The Feringhees resolved that Sujah Ali must be crushed decisively, sent many boats up the rivers which flowed through his dominions. In numerous hard-fought battles they sank his *prahus*, and cleared land and water of the infesting pirates.

"Sujah Ali himself they sought in vain. He had fled to a well-nigh inaccessible hiding place—a small village deep in a network of creeks, river and jungle. Here he remained, guarded by his best fighting men and *prahus,* while the English sought vainly the narrow and winding entrance which was its key.

"His capture came about, as all things come, through a woman. He had allowed his favorite wife, Amina, to accompany him. She loved Sujah Ali, and refused to be left behind.

"Jealousy is one of the most portent factors in life, and its resolution often far-reaching. It was the jealousy of Amina that brought Sujah Ali into the hands of the English.

"In the village where he had sought refuge was a beautiful girl with whom the Sultan chanced to fall in love. She became one of his wives, and exercised such an influence over him that Amina who had hither to considered herself first in his estimation, became jealous.

"As time passed, and she beheld more clearly the Sultan's complete infatuation, her jealousy increased. Among the Malays, Sahib, passion in any form is most violent and intense. Amina's jealousy finally prompted her to leave the village secretly, and seek out the captain of a Feringhee vessel which had been cruising up and down the river for weeks. It is probable that her desire was more for revenge upon her rival than upon Sujah Ali. But who knows the heart of a woman? At any rate, the secret of the Sultan's hiding-place was revealed to one Rankling Sahib, who, at midnight guided by Amina, passed through the network of creeks and jungle, to the village wherein lay Sujah Ali. The crews of two boats landed, in the hours before dawn, and entered the village. The Malays, taken completely by surprise, made little or no resistance. Many awoke only to find themselves confronted by loaded rifles, and surrendered without opposition.

"Sujah Ali, who had lain awake all evening wondering as to the cause of Amina's absence, made a futile attempt at escape. Accompanied by half-a-score of trusted men, he dashed out into the open and was secured only after a hard fight. In this he used his creese. The same which you see before you, with deadly effect. Two Feringhees he stretched dead, and a third he wounded severely.

"Rankling Sahib had given orders that he was to be taken alive if possible. Finally, surrounded on all sides, he was made prisoner, and still glaring defiance at his captors, was in the early morning taken aboard a ship for Singapore.

"This creese, with other weapons, was purchased by Sidi Hassan of that city, and the knife eventually came into my possession."

Editor's Note: The tale is an early version of "The Malay Krise" (*Overland Monthly,* October 1910), Smith's first publishesd story. The "creese," or "krise" figures in a number of his tales. "Chercher la femme" is also the crux of the juvenile stories. My guess for this one is about age fourteen, or 1907/8.

The Shah's Messenger

The Shah sealed the letter and summoned a servant from another room. The servant entered, and salaamed till his long beard touched the floor.

"Ahmet," said the Shah, "you are to take this message with all speed to Amurath, Sultan of Turkey, and bring his answer to me. By all means you must be back within a month. If you are not—well, you know as well as I do," he added significantly.

Ahmet understood. Genghis, Shah of Persia, was a man whose slightest command must be obeyed to the letter, otherwise, trouble for the disobedient one would surely ensue. And the punishment would be no slight one—a sound bastinadoing at the least, and death by the cruellest tortures at the most. Ahmet had no desire to incur either. Besides, he loved his master.

He left the presence of Genghis, after salaaming three times in his profoundest manner. He went first to the stables to make his preparations for the long journey. He selected a horse, but not the swiftest he could find. The one he did take was a small, wiry, impatient beast, not over twelve hands high, of a deep, black color. This steed was noted for its endurance, and tho many a horse could easily have outstripped it, none could hold out as long. The beast could run a hundred miles on a little water and a handful of dates. It was of the purest Arabian breed.

Ahmet told the grooms to have it ready for him within an hour and then returned to the palace to make his other preparations.

Going to his room he took a large quantity of money from a box and placed it in a leathern wallet. The wallet he securely attached to his belt.

In another and smaller wallet he placed the King's letter. Then he stowed the wallet in an inner pocket of his jacket and proceeded to sew the pocket up with strong pack-thread.

This done he went again to the Shah, took his farewells, went to the stables, leaped into the saddle of his horse which the grooms held waiting for him, and was off at a gallop.

The walls of Ispahan were soon left behind. He put up in a Khan by the roadside for the night, and then proceeded on his journey again.

In due time he reached Istanboul, the capital of the Turks, and delivered his letter to the Sultan.

After reading it the Sultan wrote a somewhat lengthy reply and handed it to Ahmet.

"Do not read it!" cautioned Amurath. "If you do, trouble will come of it for you, myself, and your imperial master the Shah."

"Your command is sacred to me, and shall be obeyed," replied Ahmet, and he withdrew with a great curiosity gnawing at his heart.

Two hours later, Istanbul and the Bosphorus were out of sight behind the hills of Room-Elee, and Ahmet was galloping swiftly on the homeward journey.

"What can it be that disaster will ensue if I read it?" thought Ahmet. "Surely there will be no harm in that. No one will be the wiser, save I."

But his promise to the Sultan kept him from opening the packet. Nothing else could have done so. But strive against it as he might, curiosity still gnawed at his heart, and at last he determined to satisfy it. "There can be no harm," he said to his troubled conscience. "No one, save I, will be the wiser."

He drew the letter from his pocket, but knew not how to break the seal and replace it so that the opening would not be detected. Then he put it back and thought awhile.

"Why not duplicate it?" he said, at last.

At Bagdad, on the next day, he secured wax, exactly alike as to the color, to that of which the seal was formed. Then, with his knife, he removed the seal which was on the letter. This was of a round shape, and no design was stamped upon it.

He unfolded the sheets of fine parchment, which were closely written in the Arabic character. The language was Persian. First, before reading them, he counted the sheets. They were two in number and written only on one side.

This done, he began at the beginning and read the letter. It was somewhat as follows, but I have shortened it by half to accommodate it to the length of this story:

"To thee Genghis, Shah in Shah of Persia, I, Amurath the Fourth, the prince of all true Believers, Shadow of God on Earth, King of the Two Worlds, Lord of the Two Seas, thru whose existence life hath been ennobled, send greeting:

"On this very day, thy messenger, Ahmet, arrived at our palace, and presented thy letter to us. I have no objection to telling thee where the treasure is hidden. It seemeth strange to me that thou didst not before ask me this question. The treasure, which is lawfully yours, is situated on the main road between Bagdad and Ispahan, exactly ten miles east of the former, in a large cave which you cannot help seeing, it being the only one within twenty miles, and in the first hillside you come to after leaving Bagdad. As a reward for this information, I think it not unreasonable that you send me one twentieth part of what you find.

> "Thy faithful Friend,
> "Amurath the Fourth,
> "Sultan of Turkey"

Ahmet folded the letter again and sealed it with the wax. He viewed his work with great satisfaction, for to *his* eye there was absolutely no difference between its present appearance, and the appearance in which it had been. "That was well-done," he said, with a sigh of satisfaction as he replaced the whole in the wallet, and the wallet in its hiding place.

Then he went on, thinking of the treasure and keeping a sharp outlook for the cave in which it was hidden. At last he saw it.

"What harm can there be in taking a look at the treasure itself?" He said. His curiosity overcame him, and he dismounted and tied his horse to a tree. Then he entered the cave.

It was large enough for him to stand upright [inside, but at] a distance of twenty feet from the mouth it grew smaller and he was compelled to crawl on his hands and knees. The floor was dry and no reptiles were visible. That, he reflected, was one advantage. Everything was dark and he could no longer see. He stopped for a moment, drew a taper from under his caftan, and lit it.

Then he went on and at last reached the end of the passage. It was a small chamber, seemingly cut out in the solid rock, and perfectly square as to shape.

Ahmet stood up and examined it. It was evidently the end of the cave. In the corner opposite to him, he perceived ten great earthenware jars, each large enough to hold three or four gallons.

Concluding that these contained the treasure, he crossed to them and removed the lid from the first that met his hand. It was full to the top with golden coins. Ahmet hastily replaced the cover and opened the next. It was full to the brim with silver.

The third was half-full of diamonds and rubies, and all manner of jewels. One particularly large one caught his eye, and he picked it up to examine it more closely.

"Why should I not keep it?" he exclaimed half-aloud. "Who should be the wiser?"

"I would," said a deep and well-known voice from behind him. Turning, he beheld the Shah standing in the entrance and regarding him fixedly.

"Ahmet," he said, coldly, "what are you doing here?"

Ahmet turned pale and stammered out some excuse.

"Come with me," replied Genghis shortly, and he led the way out of the cave. In the road without, the unhappy messenger saw the Shah's escort, all mounted and evidently waiting for them.

"Ahmet," said Genghis, "give me Amurath's letter." Ahmet, trembling with fear, produced it and gave it to his master. The Shah broke the seal and read the contents. "It was a remarkable coincidence that you happened to enter this cave," he said, suspiciously. Then he examined the seal.

"This wax was made in Bagdad." He announced. "The Sultan's wax is always made in Istanbul, and by a man employed especially for this purpose. It has a much different smell from the wax that forms this seal. It seems to me, Ahmet, that you are guilty of disobeying the Sultan's orders, for I am sure that he enjoined you not to open this letter. Besides, it is a serious crime to open any letter sent to me. In addition to this you were about to steal part of the treasure, and would undoubtedly have done so, had I not caught you in the act. It is very plain that you deserve either death or banishment from Persia. I give you the choice. Which?"

"Death, your Majesty!" said Ahmet, his face full of shame and fear.

"Bring the treasure to me," said Genghis to some of his retinue. They dismounted and hastened to execute his orders.

"Now, Ahmet," said the Shah, "perhaps you would like to know how I found you here. I grew impatient for your return and set out with a number of my servants to meet you. When we came to this hill we espied your horse tied to a tree and knew that you were somewhere near. I perceived the cave, and instantly divined that you had entered it for something or other, what, I did not then know. I followed, and found you about to remove a diamond from the treasure. That is all."

"Your Majesty," said Ahmet, "I beg your forgiveness. If the Sultan had not told me *not* to open the letter, all these unpleasant things could never have happened. Morally, all the fault lies with him. My *curiosity* did the rest, not *me*. I was helpless under its influence."

"Your reasoning is all very pretty, but it would never do before a cadi," replied the Shah, with an amused smile.

Ahmet bowed his head in resignation to his fate, and said: "Very well, your Majesty. If you say so, it must be so."

"Seek not to soften my verdict by flattery," said Genghis, "If you do so it will be all the worse for you."

The mental torture that Ahmet underwent during the next week is entirely beyond my powers to describe. It is sufficient to say that by the time he and his captors entered Ispaham, he had lost many pounds of flesh.

The Shah watched him closely and began to pity the poor fellow. On the day set for Ahmet's death, he called the man before him.

The headsman and his block were in the room. Two guards stood on either side of the prisoner. Otherwise, the apartment was empty. Silence prevailed for a moment, and then the Shah spoke.

"Ahmet," he said, "I think you have died a thousand deaths during the last few days, from fear. I said that you should die but once. Is that not true?"

"Yes, your Majesty," said Ahmet, seeing a thread of hope and grasping it eagerly.

"I do not think that you will be inclined to break the law again," spoke Genghis, "after all that you have suffered. Remember, my dear Ahmet, that a mental death is much worse than a material one. You may go free."
Editor's Note: This nice little tale is clearly a very early work, and rather tidily done. Since it is written with a very specific "moral," it is easy to identify as coming from Clark's very early work, perhaps age eleven or twelve. His family, though poor exemplified the high standards of Victorian morality in their instruction to their son "by precept and example."

The Bronze Image

It was a small bronze image of the God Ganesha, the elephant-headed, who is the [Hindu] deity of wisdom, and it stood on my writing desk. I had picked it up at an auction, it having formed part of a large collection which the owner, owing to financial embarrassment, had been compelled to sell. (The price was ridiculously low, there being no competitor, and I left thinking that I had made a bargain.)

The image was of Benares workmanship, and Allah alone knew how old. Also it was just the size for a paper-weight, and quite appropriate.

Holden dropped in about a week later. He is an old friend of mine—a grave, reticent sort of man. We had conversed for some time, when he suddenly caught sight of the image, and starting violently, cried out in amazement.

"Where did you get the Ganesha, Lane?" he asked. I told him.

"The last time I saw that image," he said, "was in Benares."

"I was not aware of your previous acquaintance with my paper-weight," said I. Looking at him, I saw that he was deeply absorbed in thought.

"Well," he said finally, "I see that you are anxiously awaiting the story." He then proceeded to tell it as follows . . .

While at Calcutta, two years ago, I was employed by a certain firm, whose name I would prefer not to mention. I was sent up to Benares to negotiate with a Bengali merchant, one Lalji Chatterji. It was important that these negotiations be kept secret, at least for some time, and because of my previous experience with natives, and my general knowledge of India, I was chosen for the work.

So I went up to Benares, with full instructions and certain papers hidden securely in an inner pocket which were to be handed over to Lalji Chatterji.

My identity I deemed it best to conceal. So it was not in the person of Albert Holden that I reached Benares, but I stepped off the train as Fulsi Lal, and to all outward appearances a baboo of the deepest dye.

A baboo is an indigenous production; he belongs exclusively to India and there is nothing resembling him in all the world. From his spectacles to his English, which last is truly marvelous, he is individual.

How the son of Shaitan, who was representing a Central Indian Rajah, a gentleman much interested in my negotiations with Lalji Chatterji, discovered my identity I do not pretend to know. But it is a fact that he did.

When I arrived at Benares, and stepped out of a third class carriage into the teeming, seething station, I discovered a blue-turbaned, side whiskered, Rajput at my elbow, whose general description tallied essentially with that of a man whom I had been warned to avoid; namely, the agent of Baghwan Deos, the Central India Rajah.

Endeavors to lose this man in the crowd were in vain; it was not until I had traversed half the city of Benares and ended up eventually in the Monkey Temple, that I lost sight of the blue Turban and the side whiskers. I thanked Allah devoutly, emerged at the rear entrance, followed by all the monkeys in the neighborhood who evinced a most sociable disposition, and set off toward the Ganges.

Near the Burning-Ghats I again met Baghwan Deos's representative. We exchanged glances of mutual distrust. Once more I tried to shake my tenacious follower.

It was his mission I know, to keep the papers which I carried from reaching Lalji Chatterji. For certain reasons, into which I cannot here enter, Baghwan Deos did not wish this, and to this end had sent his agent to Benares. This man, I was aware, would not scruple at anything; he would kill me if necessary to gain possession of the papers.

About midday he was joined by another Rajput, and intuition told me that several more of these gentry probably lurked in the neighborhood of Lalji Chatterji's house, with instructions to prevent a certain specified baboo from entering. So, for a time, I abandoned hope of reaching the Bengali, and, entering a Khan, sat down to think.

The outcome of this was that Lalji Chatterji shortly afterwards received a letter instructing him to be at the Golden Temple at nine precisely the following morning. There he would receive some important papers from a Moslem horse-merchant.

At the appointed time he arrived. I had been waiting in the person of the aforesaid merchant about half-an-hour, and the local priests were getting suspicious. I had begun to fear that he had not received my letter, or that some accident had occurred, when Lalji Chatterji, a sleek, smiling, clean-shaven Bengali, entered, and looking about him sharply, at length perceived me. He came over, and we exchanged greetings.

"What a disguise, sahib," he said, "You are a perfect horse-trader; the very odor of the serai seems to emanate from you. Truly, I should never have suspected. And you have the papers? Ah, that is good. Now Baghwan Deos's emissaries can wait in vain. They have been hanging about my house for the last three days, following me everywhere, and making great nuisances of themselves. It was with the utmost difficulty that I this morning evaded their surveillance. But I know Benares like a book: her tangled streets are an open page and somewhere near Manikaranika Ghat two Rajputs are doubtless, at this moment, calling down curses on all Bengalis."

He laughed heartily, and I was about to pull the papers from my inner pocket when three men entered hastily, and seeing us, stopped. In one of them I recognized Baghwan Deos's agent. The other two I had not heretofore seen.

They looked at us keenly, and then about the temple in a furtive manner. The priests had disappeared. We were alone, and I felt a bit uneasy as to what would happen. The Rajputs were looking ugly, and I saw that they were armed. I had unfortunately left my revolver at the Khan, and was without weapons. Lalji Chatterji was also unarmed.

The three men began to edge towards us, in a casual manner, and sought, though they doubtless knew that we were aware of their identity, to appear oblivious of our presence, and totally without intentions toward us.

At last the Rajah's agent drew a revolver, and advancing to within a few steps, leveled it in my direction. His two companions stood just behind him in case he should need assistance.

"Sahib," he said, "you have in your possession certain documents which I have been ordered to secure. I request that you hand them over to me. If you do not—"

Here his words were interrupted by the entrance of a priest. He dropped the revolver for a moment and hesitated. In that moment I looked about for some weapon, and perceiving a small bronze image of Ganesha in a niche in the temple wall, snatched it up, and hurled it straight at the Rajput's head. There was a dull impact, a shriek, and image and Rajput struck the ground together, the latter with a crushed skull.

There is very little more to tell. The other Rajputs upon perceiving the fall of their leader, rushed from the temple, and Lalji Chatterji and myself followed close upon their heels. In the resultant confusion we made our escape, and did not pause until we had reached the Ghats. There, after a hasty consultation, we parted, Lalji Chatterji and the papers leaving shortly for Cawnpore, where it was in intention to hide for some time, and myself, having reassumed the baboo disguise, for Calcutta.

Baghwan Deos, I believe, used all his influence to keep the affair quiet. The death of his agent set down officially as an accident, and attracted but little attention. The bronze image which you possess is the same that crushed the skull of the Rajah's agent.

The Fulfilled Prophecy

You may set this story down as a case of coincidence. Indeed, you may not believe it at all. But the facts are well authenticated, and to my mind are far too remarkable to be accounted for by the coincidence theory.

I found the first part in an old Telegu manuscript, written perhaps seven centuries ago, and which today is in a private library in Madras. If fate or curiosity should ever take you to that city, and you obtain access to this library, you will discover this manuscript, and may read it for yourself.

The thing purported to have been written by one Vikram Roo, a priest, who in his time was of much importance in Rajahpur, a Kingdom of the Deccan, which ceased to exist, politically speaking, about three centuries ago.

Skipping a considerable amount of literature pertaining to himself, and the virtues of Natha Singh, the then Rajah of Rajahpur, the manuscript ran somewhat as follows:

It was during the reign of this most beneficent ruler (Natha Singh) that the strange event which I am about to relate, occurred.

It happened in the order of things set down by the fate that the omniscient Natha Singh, on a Wednesday, called his viziers about him and sat on his throne in the Hall of Audience to dispense justice to his subjects.

And it came to pass that many cases were judged by the omnipotent ruler, whose decisions were wise and just to all.

At length there entered the Audience Hall a wandering *Jacquer.* Upon his face were the marks of years, and his long locks were as the snows of the eternal Himalayas.

Natha Singh leaned towards him expectantly, and all present awaited his complaint in silence. For a space he spoke not, his eyes, which glowed strangely, as one who sees many things, fixed upon the Rajah's countenance. At length he spoke, and his words fell heavily upon the ears of the hearers.

"Know ye Natha Singh" he said, "that thy Kingdom shall come to an end. This shall not happen in thy days, or in the days of thy sons. But many years hence when thou and many that shall follow thee are but memories of yesterday, then shall come from the North a great army. And at the head shall ride a warrior on a white horse, whose birth was in a far land. He is a mighty general, and his men are as the sands of the sea. And before them the warriors of the Rajah shall melt as even as snow in the desert. And on that day shall Rajahpur fall, and those dwelling therein be given over to the sword. And before the sun has set, the reigning Rajah shall die, and his Kingdom pass to his conquerors. And after him there shall be no more of thy race, and Rajahpur shall be but a province of a mighty empire. And upon thy throne he of the White Horse shall rule, as a governor holding office under an emperor."

The *Jacquer* ceased. For a space he stood silently, and then he turned to go. Slowly he passed from the Audience Hall and into the streets of Rajahpur. For a time there seemed a presage of gloom within the Hall, and the Rajah wondered if indeed, this strange prophecy should ever be fulfilled.

But the *Jacquer* had passed from Rajahpur, and no man might say whither he had gone. In his eyes was the look of one who has seen many things.

Several months later, while at Hyderabad I came across the sequel. A friend to whom I related the story contained in Vikram Roo's manuscript, supplied me with a history of the wars of Akbar. Opening one of the volumes, he pointed out a passage describing the fall of Rajahpur. The book was by a native historian, little known, even in India, nowadays, and was authentic in every particular. The author, who lived during the reign of Shah Jihan, had taken great pains to make his work complete and accurate. The passage pointed out by my friend was as follows:

"Abd-ul-Marrash, the famous general, after his conquests in Rajputana, was sent by Akbar to conduct a war in the Deccan. His extensive and successful services had earned him the entire confidence of his Master, and, in this new campaign he more than fulfilled Akbar's expectations. Abd-ul-Marrash carried all before him. Several minor states he crushed at one blow—— At length he came to Rajahpur, a large and important Kingdom situated in a fertile plain of the Southern Deccan, and ruled over by a prince named Nasir Singh. Nasir's army, which he led in person, met Abd-ul-Marrash on the plains without the walls. The great general, mounted on a white horse, headed the charge, and carried his foes before him like reeds in a storm. Soon all was over, and Nasir Singh's army, in which was the flower of Rajahpur, lay dead upon the field, or was captive to the conqueror. Nasir himself escaped and reached the city in safety.

"Rajahpur was taken the same day; Abd-ul-Marrash, too impatient to await the following day, pressed on, and ordered an immediate attack. All was carried, Rajahpur sacked, and Nasir Singh slain in a vain attempt at escape, before sunset.

"As a reward for his distinguished services, Abd-ul-Marrash was created subadar, or governor, of this new province."

Editor's Note: Asia Minor and the Orient were, in Clark's youth, "The Mysterious East"—an area little known and to Western eyes filled with arcane religions and dark and ancient knowledge of forbidden things. This vignette is an early example of Clark's experimenting with "strange prophecies" and "ancient manuscripts" containing hidden knowledge of the past. These devices occur in much of his writing. It is doubtful that he had publication in mind for this story; he seemed instead to be trying his hand at a technique. As with many of the vignettes contained in this collection, a sense of being part of a larger story is conveyed, leaving the reader strangely dissatisfied and wanting to know more. Not bad for one who was probably a pre-teen at this point.

The Haunted Chamber

Several years ago, I shall not give the exact date, I received an invitation from a second cousin of mine, one Charles Burleigh, to visit him at his home near London for a few weeks in the winter. As Charles and I are stout friends, and I had no business at the time to detain me, I made haste to answer the note in the affirmative.

Three days later found me at the railway station of my cousin's native town. The village, tho it can scarce be called one, of X. Some snow has already fallen, and when I stepped from the train I found the ground to be white with it. The weather was bitterly cold, so I found it expedient to don a heavy overcoat.

I stood for some time on the platform, gazing about for the man who, I had been informed, would be there to meet me. At last I perceived him-an old servant of my cousin's, bronzed with the hue of a tropic clime. As I knew that he had served in the great mutiny, this was not perplexing to me. But I had cause, in the light of later events, to remember he fact.

Charles' house was on the very outskirts of the [village,] at distance of about a half a mile from the station. It was a stately old building, dating from the time of King James the First. The walls [were] ivy-grown in many places. There was an isin-garden, in which the house was buried, enclosed by a high stonewall.

The place had originally, before our family came into possessing it, belonged to a certain family, whose names are well-known to my readers, but which, I shall not, for certain reasons of my own, mention.

Charles I found anxiously awaiting me. He is a man about thirty-five years of age. His countenance is pleasant, but there is on it a tinge of sadness, as of a man who has known trouble.

His early days were soured by certain events; these, however, I cannot tell now, as they have little or no bearing on this story.

The greetings over, we went within. Dinner was served in a great hall, a few hours after my arrival. It was a lonely-looking apartment, lonely because of its vastness and a certain air about it, as of sadness. It affected me in much the same manner as the [tone?] of the house, that is, with a melancholy feeling, synonymous with that described by an American poet in the following manner:

—A feeling of sadness and longing,
That is not akin to pain,
And resembles sorrow only
As the mist resembles rain.

We sat after dinner for several hours, talking of various subjects. Most of them have escaped my memory, but there is one that will stick in my mind as long as I live. I shall never forget it.

We had reached the subject of ghosts and spirits, and were exchanging opinions and reminiscences. I pooh-poohed the idea of the supernatural from the very moment that we took it up.

"There is no such thing as a ghost," I said.

"How can you know that?" he said.

"Because men have always been able to explain satisfactorily to themselves and others how their only foundation is some optical illusion or else there is a human agency behind it all."

"I don't know anything about the 'human agency' in this case" said my cousin in reply, "but I know that I have seen and heard things in this house with my own eyes and ears that cannot be explained under such a heading."

"How long past have you seen them?" I asked, my curiosity leaping up within me on the moment.

"For three months", said Charles, "On every occasion that I have slept in a certain room in this house I have seen and heard strange things."

"For only three months?" I asked.

"Yes, before that there was nothing the matter with the chamber. It was as good and comfortable an apartment as any man might wish. I keep it open even now, except at night, there is nothing there that seems out of the ordinary. It is my private bed-chamber and I am loath to give it up on account of the things that take place there. Up to a few days ago I had used it but was, on account of what occurred unable to sleep. Last week I abandoned it and keep it locked."

"What have you seen", I asked.

"Stranger things than you think. I am loath to tell you of them."

"And why?" I asked, "Should you not impart the secret to me?"

He hesitated—"You are so incredulous," was his answer.

"I would like to occupy this haunted chamber for a few nights," said I. "I am curious to see for myself the things that you have beheld. Therefore, you need not tell me now. I like to be surprised."

"I know your nature well, Robert," said he, "but I do not wish you to expose yourself to unnecessary danger. Strong as my nerves are, they have been shaken by the strange occurrences within that triply accursed room. I firmly believe that it is haunted by something."

I sternly pooh-poohed this idea, and after more persuading, wrung from my cousin a reluctant promise to allow me to occupy the haunted chamber for the night at least.

By now his fear had worked on me a little so I announced my intention of retiring for the night. I provided myself with a stout Irish shillelagh, picked up during my residence a few years ago in the Emerald Isle. As I was well skilled in its use, I held myself to be a match for any ghost or spirit that might choose to disturb me.

We ascended a long oaken staircase to the upper floor of the building. There are two stories to this house, and a large attic in the very top. It was on the upper floor that the haunted chamber was situated. We went thru two rooms, and found ourselves before a heavy oaken door. My cousin unlocked it and we entered. The apartment was little different from any other, save that it was furnished with rare and antique furniture. There was a large tapestried bedstead of the time of Charles the first, and a few heavy chairs of the same kind, with a large bureau, and various other articles.

There was but one window to the room—a lattice of the Queen Anne style. The moonlight strained, dim shining made a streak of white light on the floor, and a slight breeze entering, cold and frosty, made the tapestries on the walls of the apartment waft slightly. I made haste to close the window, as it was very cold with the breeze coming in. My cousin then bade me farewell, after giving me some words of advice, and then went out, locking the door behind him as I had requested.

There was a strange, eerie feeling in the cold air, by no means pleasant. I presently found my teeth chattering and my eyes roving about in a nervous manner. I laughed at myself and made haste to disrobe. Once within the bed my feelings changed. I drew the curtains together, clutched my cudgel, and prepared myself for sleep.

But sleep would not come to me. I lay for a long time with my ears strained for the slightest sound. My eyes vainly trying to pierce the Stygian darkness. I finally cursed myself for a fool, turned about, shut my eyes and began to count the sheep leaping over the stone wall. But my sheep were singularly unusual. No sooner were they thru than they began again and soon were so numerous I lost all count of them. I should have given up as the effort caused me to strain every sense and nerve.

The hours dragged by like aeons. There was apparently no end to them. Half-past ten, eleven, half past eleven—then came the deep strokes of twelve. I sat up, startled at the sound, but finding out what it was, was about to lay down again.

Suddenly, as I sat there, every muscle rigid, the curtains slowly parted, seemingly by no human agency. With sickly swiftness they swept back, letting in a broad band of moonlight across the bed. And in the very centre of that band, its hands upon the bed—shall I ever forget the horror of that sight!—a ghostly figure, the figure, apparently of a Hindu, clothed in white. It was very distinct, tho to my disordered mind it seemed to be misty in outline. It was a dark, scarce human face that peered down upon me with fanatic eyes, and wild, leering, demoniac expression. The figure was clothed in white, close-clinging trousers and Indian jacket, with a white turban on the head. The figure seemed to me at the moment, to be beyond nature. I sat frozen with horror for a few moments, possibly fascinated by the baleful eyes of the apparition. Then my skepticism on the question of the existence of ghosts stirred and I swung my cudgel at the unlucky apparition.

Whack! Whack! Whack! went the shillelagh, landing on something more substantial than air. The erstwhile spirit yelled and shrieked, and begged for mercy in a voice that I seemed sometime to have heard before.

I soon secured my prisoner, and tearing off his Oriental guise, disclosed the features of my cousin's old servant, the Indian soldier of whom I spoke in an earlier part of this story.

Hardly had I unmasked the captive when the door opened and my Charles rushed in with a lighted taper in his hand. He found me standing over the ghost with shillelagh in hand, delivering a lecture punctuated by sundry flourishes of the stick, on the subject of deceiving.

Burleigh's astonishment was beyond bounds when he saw his servant. He scarcely knew what to say. At last he managed to stammer out, addressing the ghost.

"What does this mean, Ruggles?"

He was silent, and though threatened, sat there refusing to answer, eyeing us sullenly. Neither would he afterwards explain, tho we pestered him with questions the remainder of the night.

"What do you think of it?" I asked my cousin.

"I am greatly puzzled," replied Charles. "What reason could the man possibly have for playing such a trick on me."

I could only shrug my shoulders.

In the morning the servant was gone. He had been confined by his master in one of the upper rooms of the house; a bruised and broken ivy vine testified to the manner of his escape.

On the table was found a badly written note, which, stripped of bad spelling and phrasing, was substantially as follows:

"Mr. Burleigh:

"I have cherished a grudge against you for many years, but showed no sign of it. Within the last few months I have endeavored to be revenged by trying to drive the people from this house by playing ghost at night in your bed-chamber. I have failed. You shall never see nor hear of me again.

"Sampson Ruggles"

Fragments

Editor's Note: The following documents consist of incomplete short stories, a fragment of an essay, and a letter to a publisher. It is hoped that those who are interested in these matters will search the archives at the various repositories of Smith's manuscripts and turn up the end (or the beginning) of these pieces.

When the Earth Trembled

Bernice and I, Harry Travis, have followed our trade, or what was our trade, many lands and with varying success. When we came to San Francisco as passengers in a boxcar, we were what is called "old offenders." San Francisco, as the metropolis of the west, appealed to our lucrative instincts, and on that account and because of sundry designs on our liberty by the Chicago police, we arrived via boxcar. The boxcar was owing to our straitened circumstances. These circumstances it was our purpose to better.

Our first point of view, upon arriving, was the habitation of an old friend of mine, situated on what is known locally as the Barbary Coast, where we obtained shelter, food, professional advice and information.

Editor's Note: This seems to me to be far advanced of the "Oriental" stuff, and has the slant of humor common to W. C. Fields—particularly his Dickens characters; e.g., the elevated vocabulary of the "con" artist type. The handwriting appears also to be the more mature standard.

Oriental Tales: The Yogi's Ring

Cairo was for several years my abiding place. During that time I met with a number of queer adventures. The queerest of which is the one I am about to relate. Cairo is a pretty good place to meet with adventures, and they are generally somewhat *queer*. Believing the above statement this tale may not surprise you.

My abiding place was a house situated near Ezbekiyah road, a large, white affair, with a general air of Oriental mystery. The owner was a wizened little Arab who rented it to me at an exhorbitant price, and tried to get more.

The greater part of six hours was occupied in haggling before a compromise was agreed upon, ~~and I got the house, the Arab the~~
[Remainder of the page is blank.]

Editor's Note: The spelling of "exorbitant" is an archaic usage, and as Clark preferred that usage, I have left it. This is one of several fragments in my possession set in Cairo. All of Clark's experience with "bustling cities" filled with noise, dark alleys, dangerous quarters, and swarthy folk oozing greed and venality was entirely vicarious in the early 1900s.

The Opal of Delhi [1]

Whence it came originally no one knows, although there are many tales current about it. One legend says that the stone came from Persia about the time of Noushirnan Khosrou, having been given by that monarch to one of the Ranas of Meywar. It remained in the possession of this family until the taking of Cheltore by the great Moghul, Akbar, when it was stolen from the palace by a Moslem soldier. This man lost it in Delhi, and the stone was picked up by a jeweler, from whom a neighbor stole it. This man was robbed shortly afterwards, and the thieves took the jewel to Akbar. Akbar discovered their crime, appropriated the opal, and clapped the thieves into prison. Next it was stolen by a eunuch of the palace, who lost it. It was then found by a poor tailor, who sold it, and received a considerable sum. The opal remained in the possession of the purchaser's family down to 1880.

There are other tales, of course, but the one given above is perhaps the most authentic. At any rate, the stone was deemed lucky, and greatly valued by the family of Udai Chand, its owner.

In March 1880, the opal was stolen, and in such a clever manner that no trace of the thief or thieves was found. Udai Chand immediately sent for the chief of the Delhi police, at that time Mir Adbul Ali, and communicated the case to him. As I have helped the Sirdar on more than one occasion, Mir Abdul Ali, who was much puzzled, called upon me one evening, and told me the tale.

"Have you any theory?" I asked.

"Not as yet," replied the Sirdar, "but I am thinking a great deal about this case. I am much puzzled as to who the thief, or thieves, could have been, and have sent detectives all over the city, who have visited every jewelry shop, but they report that no trace of the opal has been found.

"It is a large stone, too, fully as large as a pigeon's egg, and such are not to be disposed of without exciting remark. My opinion is that it was stolen at the instigation of some private individual of means, or else was sold to such a man by the thieves. Or, failing this, it has been taken from the city, which is more likely. At any rate, I am determined to find it."

About a month later Mir Abdul Ali dropped in. He is a rather small and quiet man, and his face is generally impassive. On this occasion, however, he was beaming from the tip of his blue turban to his heels.

"I have found the opal," he said, "and the thieves are in jail."

"How did you do it?" I asked. Mir Abdul seated himself, and after a few preliminary remarks, related the following tale:

"Soon after I learned of the theft, I made inquiries of Udai Chand as to whom he suspected of being the thief. He had no suspicions, it seems, but nevertheless I demanded of him the names of all his intimate friends and relatives. These he gave with some reluctance, and I immediately began to investigate the persons named, and learned as much of their characters and habits as possible. All but two I dismissed as innocent.

The first of these was Fulsi Dass, a cousin of Udai Chand and an impecunious young man. He often visited Udai Chand, and, as I soon learned, was generally in need of money. However, he had a good reputation, and was said to be honorable. Well—knowing that the most honest of men may commit crimes on the spur of necessity, or from some unexplained cause or motive, I put little faith in the man's reputation, but placed spies to watch him day and night. In this way I hoped to learn of any attempt on his part to dispose of the opal, unless he had already sold it.

The second person on my list was Krishna Mal, a high-caste gentleman of Rajpoot blood, but one who was not above suspicion. He, too, often visited Udai Chand. Krishna was known to be in need of funds at the time of the theft, but immediately afterwards paid off his debts, and displayed a surprising affluence. Him I suspected most.

So much for the two men who fell under my suspicion. About a week passed without anything unusual developing, and then I learned that Krishna Mal had been paying visits to the house of a Bengali, a very oily and suspicious individual, suave like all of his class, and as slippery as an eel. This man was a native of Calcutta, who had taken up his residency in Delhi. His source of income was not known, but he always seemed well-provided with money.

The reason for Krishna Mal's visit was not known. I caused inquiries to be made and soon learned that a previous visit had been made to the Bengali's house, and this on the day following the disappearance of the opal. I therefore became satisfied in my mind that Krishna Mal was the thief, and that the stone had been sold to the Bengali. But to prove this was another matter. I soon hit upon a plan.

As you well know I am able to disguise myself in many ways, and am, if I may say so, rather an adept in the art. On this occasion, after completing my plans, I dressed as a wandering *facquir* and made my way to the neighborhood of the Baboo's house, accompanied by two assistants disguised in the same manner.

We arrived before the house, which was situated on a busy street not far from the Afmir Gate, and after loitering about some time requested admission, saying that we would perform some marvelous feats.

We were shortly admitted and found ourselves in a large courtyard. The servants hastened to summon their master, who soon appeared upon the scene, and asked us what we wanted.

I have never before, in all my wide experience, seen a man whom I more disliked on first sight, than Ramchander Mukirjee, the Bengali. He had Baboo written all over him, and politeness and suavity issued from every pore, but still I disliked him. The truth was that he was *too* suave, *too* smooth, *too* polite, altogether. Therefore, I was suspicious.

He was short, fat, and had constantly shifting eyes. His features were not ugly, but their expression was too supercilious, too polite, for any man to retain unless it were to hide some sinister purpose. *That* I saw at once.

I replied to his question in a whining tone, such as is used by *facquirs,* and asked his permission to perform some feats of magic.

The Baboo, like all of his kind, was intensely superstitious, though they always affect an air of skepticism in the presence of Englishmen. However, when they are amongst their own people, they are not so particular. So Ramchander Mukirjee told us to go ahead and seated himself where he could obtain a full view of the performance.

The first feat that I performed was the mango trick, which, as you know, is merely sleight-of-hand. Mukirjee knew this and he took pains to explain to us most fully the exact manner in which the trick had been done.

I managed to look extremely pained at this, and offered to perform the feat in a different manner. This I did, but Mukirjee was still skeptical.

I was fully determined to make Mukirjee believe that I was a genuine magician, and as such, possessed of supernatural power. Therefore I resorted to a third, and very different method of performing the mango trick, a method which few yogis use, but which is very effective. Even the most skeptical of Europeans has been convinced by it.

"Ramchander Mukirjee," said I, "I am much pained at thy doubting. Therefore, to fully convince thee of my powers I will grow before you a mango tree forty feet in height."

I could plainly see that Mukirjee was startled at this, but he told me to go ahead.

Therefore, for the next twenty minutes I whirled about, much in the same manner as the Whirling Dervishes of Arabia and Egypt, and sang incantations in Sanskrit, until I judged that the desired effect had been obtained. Then, stopping, I drew myself up and said, commandingly:

"Behold a full-grown mango tree!" Mukirjee gasped, and several of his servants, who were clustered about the courtyard, shrieked. Evidently they saw the tree, as I had intended them to do, and they stared with wide-open eyes at a space immediately before me.

Of course, sahib, there was no tree in sight, but my incantations, and the whirling about, had so dazzled the sight of the beholders that they really thought the tree, when I commanded them to see it, to be before them. This is hypnotism, and it is a most difficult and exhausting feat. Most facquirs cannot perform it. I learned it in Agra once, when I was seeking a murderer, and was wandering about disguised. It is well to know such things, and I do not forget easily.

The trick (for it was little else) made a great impression on my audience, and I then proceeded to do a little fortune-telling, which I intended should startle the Baboo very much indeed. I saw that he believed me possessed of powers beyond those of ordinary mortals, and therefore I had little fear of his suspecting my true identity.

I pretended to be wrapt in meditation for some time, seated cross-legged, arms folded, eyes closed, and breathing regularly. Then I got up, approached the Bengali, and told him that I intended to inform him of some events of his past life, which none save himself knew, and also some things which were to happen to him in the future.

I saw him tremble a little at this, but he immediately recovered his self-composure and asked me to go on. I watched him closely and then continued.

"O most beneficent one," said I, "Siva has given me power to see all things, past, present, and future, and by such means I am enabled to tell thee those things which have before now occurred to thee, and which have yet to occur. The veil of the future has been flung back, and peering within I see all that is hidden to thee and to other men. Attend thou.

"Baboo, a week ago thou came into possession of a valuable stone, I think an opal, in size approaching a pigeon's egg, which was sold to thee by a Rajpoot gentleman. Beware of this opal, for it bringeth naught but evil to thee, and I see many dark things in the future."

Here I observed that the Baboo was much agitated. He was trembling violently, and speaking in a voice somewhat different from his recent accents implored me by all the Gods of Hindustan to stop.

"Baboo," said I, slowly, "What is to be, will be. The opal will surely bring thee bad luck." He whimpered at this, and again implored me to stop. All his suavity was gone. He had not the least suspicion of my true identity. So well had I played upon his latent superstition, that he fully believed me to be a magician, gifted by the God Siva with marvelous powers.

"Unfortunate man that I am," he cried, as I continued to prophesy in detail the kind of bad luck that was to fall upon him.

Editor's Note: Oddly enough, a separate page with the same title as the above exists:

The Opal of Delhi [11]

Back in the old days, before India ever heard of the Feringhees, when the great Akbar sat on is throne in Delhi, and ruled Hindustan from Kashmere to Comrin, there dwelt in that city a certain Mussulmani butcher. This butcher's place of business was situated near the Ajmir gate.

On a certain day it came about that he went into the country to buy cattle, and was absent a good part of the day. Near evening he returned, driving his purchases before him, and at the same time addressing derisive remarks to some passing Hindoos on what he intended to do to the sacred cattle. As he was laughing at their horror, he suddenly observed something lying in he deep mud at his feet; something which shone and glittered with blue flame in the rays of the evening sun. The butcher picked up the object which was about the size of a pigeon's egg, and saw immediately as he was a good judge of jewels that it was a very large, and certainly most valuable opal. The Mussulman came to the conclusion that some soldier had lost it while passing along the road. As a matter of fact, the stone had originally been the property of a rich and powerful Rajpoot Prince from whose palace it had been stolen by one of Akbar's soldiers, who, as he neared the Ajmere gate on his return to Delhi, had lost his treasure in the mud. Here, as before related it was found by the Mussulmani butcher. This person, after secreting the jewel in the folds of his cummerbund returned home, forebearing, by the . . .

[end of page—nothing further of this version]

Editor's Note: I find it interesting that Clark approached this story in such radically different ways. Both show advances in skill, and the glimmerings of that subtlety which became so polished in his later works, of slipping in an inference that sets up an entire scenario—as the interchange between the butcher and the natives indicates in the second version. It is not unlikely that the second version is later than the first; certain elements strike me as more accomplished.

The Guardian of the Temple

Panjore is a little native state in India, not big enough to be of any political consequence, but still large enough to have a walled capitol, two or three palaces, two-score square miles of barren desert and perhaps half as much cultivatable land, and a lot of jungle. There are no rivers large enough to float a row-boat, and the climate is notoriously hot. There are a few hills, most of which are near the capitol, and all the rest is made up of the aforesaid desert, and the cultivatable land. The population, (if you except the tigers, snakes, and wild boar) is sparse.

It was on a summer's day in 1890, with the thermometer registering 95° in the shade that I drifted into the city of Panjore, via bullock-cart, and accompanied by two native bearers and my baggage. Said baggage was very light, consisting mostly of *shikar-kit,* a revolver, an eight bore, and .450 Winchester Express.

Presently we came in sight of Panjore, a town lying on a plain with hills rising at its back. On one of those hills, or rather I may say rocks, above the palace of the Rajah, a great mass of red sandstone, gleaming dully through the haze. At its foot stretched the city of Panjore, surrounded by four walls, and about a mile and a quarter in circuit. Outside these walls was the barren plain over which we were traveling, and the hills, some of which were capped with jungle.

Three inches of white dust lay upon the road, and our bullocks seemed fully-determined to raise every bit of it. I may say without exaggeration that they succeeded. I was covered with it from head to foot by the time we had reached our journey's end.

There was a dark-bungalow just outside the city walls, for which I thanked Allah, and immediately appropriated. I was the only white man there the Khansamah told me, and also related that it was full three months since the last sahib had left.

"Too jolly damn hot," said the Khansamah, in his best English. "Panjore all dead and buried." Later I found that this last remark was the truest thing that a Khansamah had ever been heard to say.

After resting up for a day of two at the *dak*—being alone I set out to pay my respects to the Rajah in his great red palace on the rock. I ascended the almost red-hot steps leading up the face of the rock with a broiling sun beating down from above, and finally found myself in one of the outer-courtyards. Here I discovered the Rajah, busily inspecting a consignment of European clothes, just received from Bombay.

He was a tall, rather well-built man, very quick and intelligent, and not at all of the usual type of extinct, burnt-out volcano Rajput to which I was accustomed. He was, I judged, about thirty four years of age, well-educated, and spoke excellent English.

I earnestly believe that the Rajah if left to himself and the British Resident, would have adopted some form of progress for his state. But he was under the thumb of a most conservative wife, and a prime minister of the old reform-hating type. Between these two Uluar Singh was kept down and his reform-tendencies restrained. Occasionally they showed themselves in a preferency for European clothes, Calcutta rifles, bicycles, and similar toys. These, however were regarded as harmless eccentricities, and so long as his Highness made no changes in the government, lowered no taxes, and made no reforms the Ranee and Prime Minister did not interfere. But the moment he proposed any reform the two were upon him with arguments, telling him the harm that would be done, the people who would be alienated from him, and even a possible rebellion. Such was the tale told wherever men spoke of Panjore and its Rajah.

Uluar Singh greeted me very effusively, asked me a hundred questions about myself; how many tigers I had shot, and how I liked his country.

"You have come here to hunt, have you not?" said the Rajah. "There is no better place for tigers than the jungles of Panjore. Near the village of Shaitangurh, ten miles to the east, there is said to be a magnificent man-eater. Would you like to hunt him?" I signified my perfect willingness to do so. "This tiger has already slain seven people, two in broad daylight," went on his highness. "He is very bold, over bold, perhaps. I shall be very glad if the sahib kills him."

I had had some experience with man-eaters before, and assured the Rajah that if I got the chance at the iniquitous animal in question, I would do my best to rid the earth of his presence.

"May Indur grant you success," said Uluar Singh

"When do you want to start?"

"At any time," said I.

"In that case," continued his highness, "if you leave, say three hours from present time, you should be at Shaitangurh by night. The road," he swept his hand toward the east, "runs rather erratically amongst the hills, and although it is but ten miles, the distance traveling by bullock cart would be about twelve. I will send two of my best Shikari's with you, who are acquainted with habits of the tiger, and sahib will find them of some assistance. Also, my elephants are at your service."

I thanked the Rajah for his kind offer, but said that I did not think that I would need the animals in question.

"I shall shoot from Machan," said I.

"Very well," replied his highness, "But you will find sahib that the tiger in question is most cunning animal. Three nights, sahib, I waited for him, but he did not come. On the fourth, when I was not there, a man was killed and part of his body found only yards from the Machan."

Twelve miles by bullock east along a winding road, now over hills and across ravines, now through dense jungle, and past patches of cultivated land, brought me to Shaitangurh, a small mud walled village of perhaps five hundred inhabitants.

For the period of my stay there, I and the Rajah's shikaris were given lodging in the village temple, a large building of sandstone, containing a good sized image of Siva. Besides the aforesaid image and ourselves, the place was tenanted by several sacred cobras, who evinced too much familiarity to be pleasant. However, as they showed no hostility toward us, we left them alone.

Indra Singh and Dertab Ras, my two shikaris, immediately upon our arrival, went around paying visits in the village, and incidentally impressed the people of Shaitanguhr with my great importance, telling them that I was an intimate friend of the Rajah's, and an all-round burra sahib. They also related that I had slain 79 tigers in my time and seven of them with no other weapon than a sword; this, of course, greatly increased the respect of the villagers for me, and incidentally, it may be said, elevated the two shikaris, as being my representatives, to a rather higher rank in popular estimation.

In the course of the evening the two men returned and related all that they had learned. On that day it seemed, his highness, the tiger, had slain two men, eating one, and leaving the other. They had last been seen near some old cave temples in a jungle-covered hillside about a mile to the northwest. In one of these temples, it was popularly thought, stripes had his den, but no men dared enter for besides the tiger, the cave was believed by the people to be inhabited by evil devils and all manner of bhuts ("spirits"). The Mohammedans, of whom there were many in the village, claimed these as being sons of Ublis, while the Hindoos set them down as *shaitans* and demons, spirits of departed priests.

"Stripes is a bold tiger," I laughed, "to make his abode in such a place. Do not devils ride him by moonlight?"

"There are many tales, sahib," said Indra, "but no man knows the truth. Men say that on moonlit nights the spirit of Vikram Singh, who was Rajah of Panjore five hundred years ago, rides forth on the tiger. And others say that the tiger himself is possessed of a devil. Who knows? There is truth and falsehood in all. But never yet, sahib, have I seen a tiger who did not die when a bullet entered his heart or brain. Though Bahadur Shah, as the people call him, be possessed of a thousand Shaitans, one bullet from the sahib's gun will slay him."

After a while the shikari went on to tell me about the cave-temples. "Long ago, sahib, a famine came upon the land of Panjore, and endured for seven years—and during that time many men died of hunger, the rivers dried up, and the plague walked abroad through the land. At the end of the seventh year, when the rains were afar off, and all the land lay waste, the Rajah called before him all the priests of Panjore, and bade them find the offended god, for by no other means, said the people, could such a thing have come about. So all the priests of Panjore prayed and offered incense and sacrifice; all the time praying that the offended one would be revealed to them. And at the end of seven days, they announced Indra, the god of the heavens as the offended one. So, to appease him, the cave-temples of Vickram Singh were built, and dedicated to Indra. And when the work was completed, the rains came and all men knew that the anger of Indra was appeased."

On the following morning word of further depredations on the part of Stripes was brought in. Two natives with horror stricken faces told the tale. They, with another man, had been cutting wood in the jungle, when Bahadur Shah, the tiger, broke from the thicket and carried off this other man in his jaws. They described the animal as being five feet in height and three times that in length. This, however, was manifestly an exaggeration. Yet from his numerous depredations, and general bad reputation amongst the natives, it was quite apparent that his highness, Bahadur Shah, was no ordinary tiger.

An hour later, who should appear at the gates of the village, but Uluar Singh, with two choice elephants of considerable size, several shikaris, and a varied and wonderful assortment of rifles, ranging from 6mm Mannlicher to a double-barrelled elephant gun, carrying explosive bullets. Evidently his highness was bent on the destruction of the tiger, and with a view on this had provided himself with a sufficiency of weapons. Uluar Singh, it seemed, had feared that myself, and the two shikaris, with such assistance as we might procure in the neighborhood, would prove inadequate to the task of exterminating stripes. Therefore the elephants, the arsenal, and Uluar Singh and several shikaris, had come to our assistance. Upon hearing of Bahadur Shah's latest indiscretion, Uluar Singh gave orders that we should at once proceed to the scene thereof. Thereupon we joined forces, myself, my two shikaris, the arsenal, and the Rajah occupy the howdah of one elephant, and Uluar Singh's own shikaris, and one of the woodsmen, the other.

A mile from Shaitanguhr, we came to the place. Stains of blood were upon the grass, and a trail of the same ran into the thick jungle. All about us were trees, and high grass, and upon the trees were thick creepers. Some rain had fallen the previous night, and the grass and trees were not yet dry. Further on, as we followed the trail, there was the loud chattering of monkeys recently disturbed.

"He has been here lately," said Uluar Singh, and said no more. Following his eyes, I saw the unfortunate native, or what remained of him, lying in the grass some distance away. Part of the body remained, but the head was not there.

A moment afterwards, I caught the gleam of a striped body in the jungle. Thirty feet from where we sat on the elephant, there was a shower of rain-drops from the tall grass where the tiger had stirred. Following through the high grass, and amongst the tangled jungle we again saw him for one half moment in an open space. Then he was gone.

Gripping our rifles more tensely we followed. A hundred yards further, and the elephants came to a deep [gulley]. As they ascended the opposite bank, the one upon which I rode trumpeted loudly. Looking up I saw Bahadur Shah, the tiger, on a lift of rising ground. It was the first time that I beheld him distinctly—he was indeed of great size, and beautifully marked. He stood regarding us with a malevolent expression, and switched his tail lazily. Even as I raised my rifle, he turned, and disappeared.

Editor's Note: This document ends here. The ink and handwriting change dramatically at the paragraph beginning "On the following morning . . ."— this seems to indicate that a story begun some time, perhaps years, before was taken up again, perhaps in the hope of knocking something out quickly to make a few dollars. But the story became muddied and convoluted and I suspect Clark saw no easy way to reconcile inconsistencies that had been built in from the beginning and just gave it up.

The Emerald Eye

Colonel Manners, though some twenty years my senior, had always been one of my best friends. Therefore, it was quite a shock to me to learn of his death. He was a tall, white-mustached man, straight as an arrow and with bronzed, clean-cut features. He had served for many years in India and had been present at the siege of Delhi and other important battles of the Great Mutiny.

The cause of death, as well as could be ascertained, was heart-failure. The colonel had been found dead in his chair about ten in the morning by a servant. Death had apparently taken place about midnight.

Naturally, knowing what a strong, healthy man the colonel had been, I was much surprised at the news. He was the last man whom I would have expected to die of heart-failure. However, at the time, I, as well as the doctors, suspected no other cause of death.

Of the Colonel's private affairs I had little knowledge. He was a rather reticent man, and seldom talked of himself. He had told me very little of his experiences in India, but from chance remarks of his, I gathered that they had been very interesting.

Among his possessions was a large uncut emerald, about the size of a small walnut.

[Untitled]

I then dismissed the matter from my mind, having several important cases on hand.

My subordinate, Lal Singh, a Sikh, reported the following morning.

"Sirdar," he said, "I have obeyed your orders. The turban was sold by one Ibrahim Marrash, a clothing dealer whose place of business is in the Chandui Chowk. He promptly identified it, and told me that it had been sold two weeks ago to one Indra Singh. Indra Singh is a wealthy and well-known Punjaubi, and is of high caste."

Indra Singh was a personal friend of mine, and therefore you may judge of my surprise upon hearing this. To verify it, I paid a visit in person to Ibrahim Marrash's shop, and received substantially the same story, with some added information, even to the price of the article.

"Indra Singh," said the dealer, "is an old customer of mine, and I have never sold him any but the best goods. Yes, I remember that turban well. I am confident that there is not another like it in Delhi. Sirdar, here are Russia-leather slippers such as a Maharajah might wear, and the price is just seven rupees!"

This affair was very perplexing. How came Indra Singh's turban into the merchant's house? I did not like to think that the Panjaubi was the thief. I knew him to be rich, and besides, he was honorable. High castes are not in the habit of appropriating other people's jewelry.

The Sapphire, in spite of the most stringent search, was not found, not did I come any nearer to discovering the identity of the thief. As to Indra Singh's part in this matter, I gradually became convinced that there had been some mistake in regard to the turban. And besides, the presence of his turban in Leja Puri's house by itself, was small proof of the Punjaubi's guilt.

Leja Puri, who appeared to set a great value on his sapphire, came often, and seemed much disheartened that no progress had been made. The jewel, he told me, had belonged to his father, and had had an eventful history. It had originally been the property of a high-caste Punjaubi family from whom it had been taken during the terrible days of the mutiny. This family, it appeared, had remained true to the English during those times, and in consequence their house, after the mutineers had taken possession of the city and murdered the English inhabitants, had been looted by a mob. The sapphire fell into the hands of a low-caste Mohammedan, and was purchased from this man for a small sum by Leja Puri's father. Leja Puri gave the name of the original owner as Phairon Singh. The mentioning of this name gave me the first clue to the sapphire's disappearance. Phairon Singh was Indra Singh's father. Investigation revealed that he had remained faithful during the mutiny, and that his house had been sacked by an angry mob. I also learned that such a sapphire had been possessed by him, and that it had disappeared at this time.

It did not take long to put these facts and the finding of Indra Singh's turban together. Taking all into consideration, I decided that Indra Singh was the thief.

First the sapphire had belonged to his father. Then by a low-caste it had come into Leja Puri's family. Lawfully, it was the Punjaubi's property, and Puri had no more right to it than the low-caste. I became convinced that Indra Singh, learning of this, and wishing for some reason to regain the sapphire, had entered Puri's house and stolen it. How he had come to lose his turban I could not surmise. There were very many other things that I did not understand in the case. However, everything pointed to Indra Singh as the thief.

Several days later I paid a visit to the Punjaubi, with the full determination of getting to the bottom of the case. Nothing could be proved by inaction. The only thing was to get the truth out of Indra himself. I was morally convinced of his guilt, but could not prove it unless I obtained his confession.

Indra Singh was a man perhaps thirty years of age. He was tall, even for a Punjaubi, and wore a heavy, black beard.

He greeted me cordially. I could detect nothing in his manner which might indicate apprehension. If he were indeed guilty, it was clear that he did not connect my visit with the sapphire, or else he was an adept at hiding his feelings.

I stated the object of my visit at once.

"Indra," I said, drawing forth the red turban, "does this belong to you?" He started at seeing the article, but beyond that betrayed no emotion. He hesitated a while before answering.

"Sirdar," he said at last, "It is mine." I proceeded to tell him where it had been found, and my suspicions in regard to himself.

"Yes," he confessed slowly. "I may not lie. It was I who stole the sapphire from Leja Puri." He stopped, drew a small metal case from his bosom, and opened it. Within lay a sapphire of perhaps six carats weight, and which I, who am no expert in such matters, saw plainly to be flawless.

"Six hundred years," he continued, "this stone remained in our family. It is of great value apart from its intrinsic worth—for a legend no one knows how old, deems that it will bring good luck to the possessor. Six hundred years—and then the mutiny, when India was drenched in blood, and a madness more terrible than midsummer heat lay upon all the land. The stone was stolen. Till the day of his death my father, Phairon Singh, sought to regain it but in vain. And after him, I, his son, took up the search, and carried it to the end which you have seen. It was no easy matter to trace the thief—why detail?—but success crowned my efforts, and I learned that the sapphire had been sold to Leja Puri's father, and that it was now in the former's possession.

"The only method of regaining it which suggested itself, was theft. There was much risk, but my courage, nerved by determination to regain the sapphire, was equal to the deed. I learned from Puri's servants where he kept his jewels, and selecting a dark night, entered his house. I found the room, broke open the case containing the sapphire and was about to leave when I heard footsteps in the next room.

"Fearing that I was detected, a panic seized me, and in my haste to escape, a loose fold of my turban became entangled and I left the turban behind. I afterwards regretted this greatly, fearing that it might furnish a clue and have always cursed myself for my carelessness. Doubtless the person whose footsteps I heard was totally unaware of my presence, and had no intentions toward me."

"Of course," said I, "as the jewel was stolen from your father, it is legally your property. The fact that the thief who sold it to Leja Puri's father does not entitle the latter to it. But there is another side of the case. You had no right to enter Leja Puri's house secretly, even for the purpose of regaining what was legally yours. Had you been caught in the act, there would have been little difficulty in convicting you for burglary.

"For over thirty years the sapphire was in the possession of the Puri family, having been purchased by Leja's father." I paused, and then went on.

"I have come here to urge you to return the sapphire. You will hand it over to me, I guarantee that the matter will be dropped. Leja will be only too happy to have it back, and will not make close inquiries as to the identity of the thief or the method of recovery."

I went on to inform him that if this demand was not complied with, it would be regretfully necessary to place him under arrest.

"I should be very sorry," I said, "for you have always been a good friend to me. But in the performing of duty, friendship is not to be considered, and my duty would be to arrest you for entering Leja Puri's residence for purposes of burglary."

Indra Singh thought the matter over, and recognized the justice of my remarks. I pointed out the situation to him in detail, and he finally, though reluctantly, assented, and gave me the sapphire. Fear of arrest perhaps had much to do with this but, from my knowledge of his character, I think that he really came around to my views.

Leja Puri received the sapphire. The tale which I told him of how I had discovered the thief, and of the jewel's recovery, I have always regarded as a masterpiece.

[Fragment of an essay]

". . . by lack of finish. A commonplace idea when well told is more acceptable than a brilliant thought poorly expressed.

Always go over your stories. Close and rigorous scrutiny will often reveal some flaw, and a flaw, no matter how small, spoils the story. Errors of grammar, spelling, and punctuation must be corrected, for, though the tale is good, an editor has no time to correct such mistakes. Thorough revision of structure, style, and punctuation will save you many postage stamps.

It is desirable that you should have some talent to begin with, but talent without perseverance is of little use. Success in literature, as in other things, is largely a matter of hard work.

Editor's Note: It is to be hoped that the rest of this exists somewhere. It would be quite something to know whether this was part of a general essay on "The Writer's Art," or part of a letter of advice to some fledgling author; it may also be general thoughts on the subject for his own reflection.

[Letter to Munsey's]

Frank A. Munsey Co.

Sirs:
Enclosed please find my manuscript entitled An Officer's Ghost Story,
which I am submitting to you. If not available at regular rates, please return.

C. Ashton Smith,
Auburn, Calif.
Box 5

Editor's Note: Regrettably the letter is undated. We do not know if it is a
copy of a note typed to accompany the manuscript, or the original returned
to him. The story survives (possibly only as a fragment) in the Clark
Ashton Smith Papers at the John Hay Library. Clark's poem "The Sierras"
appeared in *Munsey's* in September 1910 (his first published poem).

Lost Pages from The Black Diamonds

[This passage goes at the end of Chapter XVII (page 126). The manuscript consists of two 8- by 12.5-inch leaves closely written in pencil on both sides. The sheets are numbered on one side only, 167 and 169.]

"That is no mean comfort," said Mustapha. "The profit last year was only 11,000 pieces of gold, but trade was bad, the weather bad, and I had only eight ships. It was 9,000 pieces of gold the year before that, and I had only seven ships. The coming year I intend to buy five more ships and then I will have, at least, if trade is good, and the weather good, 30,000 pieces of gold. If things go on like this from year to year I will soon be one of the richest merchants in Bagdad."

"You are a fortunate man, Mustapha."

"Perhaps you think so, but at the present time I shall bother myself little about fortunes. My mind is too full of plans for revenge to have much time to give to thoughts of gain."

"Well, I am not as rich as you, Mustapha, but my trade increases more and more every year, though I have only four ships. I possess 20,000 pieces of gold at the present date and I hope to have 5,000 more next year. Besides my ships and stores, I am the master of a tailoring establishment, that is, a number of tailors working for me, and in my pay, and from that I make 500 pieces of gold a year. I supply them with the cloth, they make the clothes and sell them, I receive the profit, and pay them out of it."

"Well, you are quite prosperous. I can remember a time when my father was no richer than you. But trade gets better every year and the merchants of Bagdad get richer year by year. The whole country is more prosperous too, and I intend to start a caravan or two, to trade with the Arabians and Persians. Heretofore I have done all my trading with the distant lands of China and other countries in that part of the world, but next year I shall follow the example of most of the merchants of this great city and trade more at home. The risk is not so great, and neither is the time and expense, and I have heard that the profit is just as good as that earned by trading by the sea. I shall also trade with Arabia and Persia by ship which is much quicker than caravan-trading, and I would advise you to do the same. You will make nearly as much out of it as I."

"I have long intended to do it, Mustapha, but I could not quite make up my mind to such a course. I shall do so next year, though, and as soon as I can spare the money. I owe several debts and they will not leave me more than half my fortune when I have squared them. The rest of the money will be for provisioning my ships and paying the officers and sailors, and when I am all thru, I fear I shall have only a few thousand."

"Why don't you borrow? I will lend you ten thousand just for friendship's sake and give you ten years to pay it back in, with no interest."

"What a friend you are, Mustapha. It is just what I shall do if you will lend me the money. When can you do so?"

"Any time you want it. To-morrow afternoon will be a good time. I shall be at my home then. Can you be there at two o'clock?"

"Certainly, I shall be there right on the minute."

"Then it is agreed. Hand me parchment and ink and I will give you a written agreement."

The parchment and other necessary things were brought, and Mustapha seated himself and wrote the following:

"I, Mustapha Dagh, do hereby lend to my friend, Balbec Khan, the sum of 10,000 pieces of gold. This amount is to be paid back within ten years, and there is to be no interest upon the same.

"Signed,

"Mustapha Dagh"

Then Balbec wrote below in his own handwriting:

"I, Balbec Khan, do hereby agree to Mustapha Dagh's agreement above. I promise to pay back the ten thousand pieces of gold within the agreed the ten years.

"Signed,

"Balbec Khan."

"Put this away and see that nothing happens to it," said Mustapha when the document was finished. "When you have paid back the money you will write below what is already written: 'I, Balbec Khan have paid back the ten-thousand pieces of gold lent to me by Mustapha Dagh, within the given time.' Then you can destroy the record if you wish."

"Well, it is time to go to bed," said Balbec. He then deposited the document in a safe place and led his guest to the room where he was to sleep for the night.

It was long after midnight when Mustapha fell asleep and he did not awaken till seven of the following morning. He arose and dressed and went downstairs to the dining-room where he found Balbec awaiting him before sitting down to breakfast. Balbec was a bachelor and led a somewhat lonely life, eating breakfast alone, except when he had company or some of his friends stopped in.

"Well, you are not an early riser," said Balbec, impatiently. "I always make a point of rising at six, no matter what time I go to bed the night before."

"I always sleep till I awake," was Mustapha's quiet answer. "I do not see how you can awake at six in the morning if you go to bed at 2 o'clock of the previous night, unless you have somebody to wake you up."

"That explains it, my dear Mustapha. It is nothing but habit that make me awake at six."

"I have never formed such a habit, so you see I awake at the time I have had enough sleep. I let nature take care of my sleeping and waking, not my habits."

"Of course, everybody doesn't have the same methods. It would be madness to expect such a state of affairs. Every door has two sides, as anyone knows, and a square box has four. If one has two sides, and the other four sides they can't turn it around without making the door as thick as it is wide, and taking the box to pieces and making a door out of it. You can't wash off a leopard's spots, no matter what you use, nor can you make silk out of wool or cotton."

"Quite an admirable argument, my dear Balbec. You have defeated yourself by your own reasoning. Some swords have two edges, you know, and each edge is equally sharp."

"Come now, no more of this fine talk. Our breakfast is growing cold."

With that they seated themselves at the table and ate a hearty breakfast. When the meal was finished, Balbec said, "I have the disguise ready for you and if you will come with me you may put it on now and see if the fit is good."

He led the way to another room where a wig, false whiskers, and a suit of clothes resembling those worn by the middle class of Arabians lay on a chair. The wig was coal-black in color, and the hair was long and rough. So were the whiskers. The clothing consisted of a white turban, a long Arabian cloak, sandals, and the other articles of desert clothing.

When Mustapha had dressed himself in these articles, wearing his real clothes beneath, except his shoes, as he had to put on the sandals in their place, and his red turban, which he exchanged for the white one, Balbec told him that he would have to paint his face a darker hue. This was done with a kind of pigment, and the same was applied to his hands and feet.

Balbec then gave him a long staff like those carried by the Arabians and an Arabian sword which was little different from the Turkish scimitar.

"Now you are all right," said Balbec, surveying Mustapha's make-up with the eye of an artist. "I give myself credit for what I have done. The rest you'll have to manage for yourself. I shall not try to give you any more advice. You yourself know just how to act in what you are to do today."

"Yes, you have done well, and I shall not forget it. Send a messenger to my home to tell them that I have returned. Do not forget that you must be there this afternoon. Good-bye."

"Good-bye, and good luck go with you, Mustapha," said Balbec, as Mustapha walked out of the room and into the street. The merchant stood in his doorway watching his young friend, till he was out of sight, and then turned and went in, closing the door behind him.

This picnic photo and the color shot (rear cover—Clark's favorite of himself) I took at Pacifc Grove. The age ten photo of Clark (rear cover) is the property of Gene Scott and is a school photo from the little one-room that Clark attended, Long Valley School.

This shot by the shed was taken during Clark's last visit to the cabin before the fire, and was taken by Carol, when she could get him to stand still long enough. Clark was making fire-breaks.

Clark Ashton Smith: A Memoir

W. C. Farmer

Traveling home from Mrs. Griffith's first grade class at Auburn's Union Elementary was always an adventure. First there was the steep descent into the "Cooper Amphitheater" (I wonder who remembers that it had a name?) Oak wooded hills, with dried leaves so thick you could slide on them going down, made the ascent doubly difficult. The strange bridge and stage that seemed never used, you had to cross at the bottom (were there Trolls by this bridge?). On the brightest afternoon this deep gulch was gloomy; and then, like reaching the peak of the Matterhorn, there it was— High Street, just below the olive grove by the remote castle, Placer High School. From there on it was downhill until the steps in the WPA wall up to the old house where my four-striper Dad, Mom, and I rented a little apartment toward the back. The sidewalk was paved all the way but for about 100 yards beside a densely overgrown acre that the big third and fourth graders bravely entered but was the "forbidden forest" to me. Once, as I stepped onto the rocky, unpaved sidewalk, a sense of foreboding over-took me. There seemed to be a "presence." Had there been hackles at the back of my neck, the sensation there suggested they would have been up. Did I dare look back? No, best not to. Walking a bit faster, the foreboding became fear, and halfway along, by the darkest part of the wood, I looked over my shoulder; and there, striding toward me at a great rate, was a tall, gaunt figure like I had never seen. The boots arrested my attention: logger boots tightly laced to the knee, with great soles and heels moving to a rhythm that in 1943 seemed like the "goose step" in the newsreels; khaki pants and shirt, black belt, coat like burnt umber, threatening moustache, piercing eyes, and above all a black beret; arms clutching a large sack (what—or who—was in it?). Fear turned to terror, and I ran as fast as my five year old feet could take me. Yet, to no avail—he gained, and gained, only walking though I ran! As suddenly as I had seen him, he had over-taken me—then passed—and took my fear with him. I stopped and watched in amazement as he rose out of the swale, crested High Street, and turned left out of sight with a speed I had never witnessed. And so I met, for the first time, the poet Clark Ashton Smith.

Over the next few years, I saw this apparition occasionally and most often emerging up the steep incline from "Old Town" on his way out Fol-som Road (strange to reflect, I never saw him going down). On these occa-sions he always carried a brown paper sack (pre-plastic days) with the neck of a bottle sticking invariably out the top. As our eyes would meet, he seemed to have a wry smile attempting to emerge, but getting no further than a crinkling of wrinkles on the right side of his mouth and a little lift and twitch of the moustache—he *knew!*

In 1946, the War was over, and my Dad was now stationed at the Presidio in San Francisco, but rather than leave the lovely mountain village, we bought a little house (second on the left) in a little development that extended High Street a slight jog to the left of where it had formerly ended and directly below Ethel Heiple's house. Where High Street intersected the road from Old Town, a new noisy Nazarene church was built on the strength of revivals that kept the neighbourhood awake late for weeks on end. Eventually they calmed down and became almost as respectable as we Methodists who inhabited the oldest church in town. Ethel had been a member there forever, and her youth group had done what amounted to the only theatrical productions there were in town in her day—other than the burlesque and traveling shows which came by the old Opera House, now a three-lane bowling alley. Lola Montez and John Philip Sousa had performed there. How I wished I had seen them! The old place still had its box seats and velvet drapes when I would go with my Dad for bowling tournaments. I had started violin at age five, and soon learned that the "Orcs" in the 7th and 8th grades took a jaundiced view indeed of such sissy stuff. Nevertheless I persisted, and gloried in being the top student, though the prettiest girl in class (whose Dad taught school!) often beat me out by a little. Eventually, I graduated from the 8th grade myself (having avoided the transformation into Orc) at a ceremony held in that amphitheater. That may have been the last such event ever held there. Our speaker was an officer in the Salvation Army—"O quae mutatio rerum."

As I had become good friends with Ethel Heiple (she taught me to play canasta during that "craze") and had begun voice lessons with the great oratorio artist, Frank Pursell, some folk began to suggest greater things for me than spending my life idling about. I had read steadily for years, and in early 1953 in my sophomore year, my World Lit teacher, Mr. Chaney, suggested I drop out of high school and enter a program for gifted kids at the University of Chicago. That idea lasted two seconds at home, but the world of really fine writing had opened for me in freshman and sophomore English. Where I had read voluminously, I began to read voraciously—add an excellent Latin teacher into the mix, and I had begun to have reason to regard myself as rather bright. In discussing some of the things I had read with Ethel, she asked if I knew Clark Ashton Smith, and lent me a couple of his books. I soon discovered that she knew him well (she always called him Clark, never "Ashton" or "Clark Ashton"). Ethel was in the magazine business in her retirement—really kind of took over

Clark's mother's business after her passing. Clark had often stopped by over the years, it seems ostensibly to visit, but more often to do a little repair or yard work for Ethel unasked.

I acquired my driving permit in 1953 and, in a 1938 Model A Ford with V8 wheels and a sheet metal top (Dad got tired of having to tar the top every year), with Ethel as navigator, we headed out to the ridge to visit Clark—my first formal introduction. Ethel lost the road, but we got to where we could see the tree, the rock, and the cabin; so, thanks to that old car's first gear (easily equivalent to a compound low on a jeep), I swerved out across the open field, avoiding large rocks, gunned up the hill and came to a halt as Clark emerged from the cabin, no doubt wondering at this noise that had invaded his solitude.

My first visit with him is vague, but I remember liking him very much—possibly because he was so gracious and courtly with Ethel. She had told me many tales of Clark, including his having educated himself by reading everything in the Carnegie Library, and how he sold stories but lived an extremely penurious existence chopping wood, picking fruit, and so on. I was able to tell him how much I enjoyed the stories I had read, especially "Xeethra" and "Genius Loci," but that the poems I had found strangely moving and beautiful. We became fast friends.

Over the years I was in high school, I had several opportunities to visit Clark and Carol (he had just married), though that was limited to their infrequent visits to the Auburn property from Pacific Grove to check up on the place, make fire breaks, etc.

Once I began attending Sierra College (then next to the high school), I was able to get together more often. What times we had! "A loaf of bread, A jug of wine . . ."—vintage Loomis Burgundy, sixty-nine cents a gallon. Frequently we visited Marilyn Novak's amazing old place in Newcastle. She had had an antique/resale shop in Old Town Auburn and was a longtime friend and a sharp, witty, well-read conversationalist. This might be a good place to talk a little of the artistic ferment that somehow swirled around a little place like Auburn in the 1930s and '40s. An old "Happy Hour" acquaintance of Clark's was "the Count," Emilion Aloysius Walther Hebenstreit, who was in fact an Austrian Count who had fled Europe in World War I days with his wife, Inez Marie Koster, a well-known operatic soprano, and opened three mine tunnels in his 40-acre property several miles beyond Clark's, not far from Rattlesnake Bar and the areas where Clark gathered the material for his carvings. When I knew Emilion, he had three little chalets built in a hidden gully below the mines, and water from the 800-foot tunnel filled tanks that provided the houses with water. He was, in every sense of the word, the quintessence of European royalty: tall, immaculate, great shock of white hair, cigarette holder, leather elbow shooting jacket, and a debonair connoisseur and bon vivant, elegant—and a great, good friend. From Emilion, Clark had adopted the use of the cigarette holder using Dunhill filters; but not just any old holder: the Count used an elegant holder with an ejector! Clark's first cigarette holder was a gift from Emilion. Emilion had shown him the filter after three cigarettes, and Clark needed no more convincing to decide not to put that slimy junk in his lungs.

Clark and Carol and I visited the Count twice during the years I knew him. On those occasions, Emilion and Clark would remember Inez and her vocalizing about the place. I had already studied voice for some years and was singing operatic music, and would be invited to entertain with some well-known piece. Emilion always urged Clark to take up his pen again, was always courtly with Carol, and freely flowed the May Wine (Havemeyer's in stone crocks—wonderful!). Back at the cabin, we might have an evening of poetry reading. I had gained a little reputation back East as an actor and interpreter, and Clark enjoyed particularly Dylan Thomas' "Lament" (brandy and ripe in my bright base prime . . . no spring-tailed tom in the red hot town with every simmering woman his mouse! Etc.), and he gloried in the splendour of G. M. Hopkins skill in works like "The Windhover." We debated for some hours one evening what to call lines in Hopkins that sound like what something looks like (as a skate's heel sweeps smooth on a bow-bend, etc.)—obviously could not be onomatopoeia, and no appropriate term using Greek roots came to mind, so we decided that, since Hopkins was about the only poet who could pull it off, it would be best not to try to categorize the technique, but just enjoy it.

During the Depression, another person who made it to Auburn and crossed paths with Clark Ashton was Pulitzer-Prize winning composer, Ernst Bacon. Ernst had become a close friend of mine, and a hiking buddy while I was an undergraduate at Syracuse University in upstate New York. Lo and behold! Ernst had, under the auspices of the WPA during the Depression, been given the job of creating an orchestra in San Francisco in order to keep some kind of artistic presence alive. Marion Sully, daughter of Genevieve, was (as Ernst described her) a "damn good fiddle player." Ernst was known for having an eye for beautiful and talented women, and Genevieve Sully and her circle of friends entertained Ernst on many occasions. Clark would often be at the Sully place cutting wood, or whatever could be found for him to do that would help him out, so naturally, he and Ernst met. Auburn at that time had a small orchestra, chamber groups, and a long-standing theatrical tradition. While Clark to my knowledge probably never heard a symphony or opera in a great hall in a great city, he deeply appreciated the profound capacity which fine music has to move the spirit, having heard the local people, many of whom were distinguished talents, perform. Ernst Bacon was a devoted outdoorsman and loved the High Sierras. His circle in the 1930s included Ansel Adams (a best friend) and Peter Hurd, both of whom made it up to Auburn, naturally visiting the canyons, rivers, and local watering holes. Once Ernst took his good friend Carl Sandburg to Yosemite. Their itinerary included visiting Auburn and its literary lights, but, alas, events intervened and prevented that visit. Clark and Carl! Wouldn't that have been a time to be a fly on the wall!

Helen Holdredge, author of the then infamous book, *Mammy Pleasant,* owned a summer "cabin" (the place was huge but rustic looking) out toward Folsom, and, not knowing her unlisted number, Clark, Carol, and I drove out to see her once; regrettably she was not home. I never inquired with him how he had come to know her, and I have since wished I had followed up and tried to meet this very interesting lady. It is possible that Clark had known her as part of the Carmel–San Francisco literati of his youth. Those who like to track down interesting information might enjoy following this lead.

In the fall of the year Clark died, I was seeking a place to live while attending graduate school in Berkeley, and through personal contacts met Bertha Damon, author of *Grandma Called It Carnal* and *A Sense of Humus.* Bertha was then about twenty years older than Clark and remembered him well from the time he first burst upon the literary scene. She had read and loved his poetry, but the fantastic tales were not to her taste. Her first contact with him was in the general literary milieu of the Carmel–San Francisco connection. I don't know if Clark read her books, but it is likely, since he made a point of reading California authors. Bertha's first book came out in 1938, and I'm sure Clark would have remembered her from earlier days.

I mention these rather famous folk by way of indicating that, though isolated in the foothills, and no longer among the lively literary community of the time (and indeed it had much altered from the elevated Victorian-era writing that had nurtured Clark's early efforts), yet he was remembered, known, and sometimes sought out by those who appreciated him.

In the fall of my senior year at Syracuse University, Clark's correspondence with George Sterling was purchased by the New York Public Library for a pittance (the figure I remember was $800.00, though that may not be correct). I was asked to deliver the documents, which I faithfully did. I was much put off by the haughty demeanor of the curator who took them and placed them in a box under a pedestal lectern. I was, of course, a kid of twenty and full of enthusiasm for Clark Ashton Smith, and was politely informed that their interest was in Sterling, but that it was nice to have both sides of a correspondence, thank you very much, and now run along, little boy. I stewed about that for some time, because to me, Ashton was ten times the poet Sterling had been. It would seem that things have come full circle, and wherever he may be, Clark has to be getting a quiet chuckle seeing his works at last appreciated and valued.

A real tragedy happened in Auburn after the sale of the Smith land at Sky Ridge to developer Greeley Herrington. He had paid $800 for the 40 acres. I was driving Clark and Carol about in my Model A Ford, Clark, as always, in the back seat rigid with a scarce suppressed terror. We shopped at a couple of places, then parked up the hill from the Auburn Post Office across from the Auburn Hotel. As we were getting out, Clark missed a weight in his coat. His change purse was gone. Carol always called it his "pokey purse" because it so reluctantly opened. Yet it was indeed gone, and the money from the sale of the property with it. We searched around the car, retraced our steps to all the places we had been, for I knew that for Clark and Carol such an amount was rarely seen and the loss truly tragic. Yet Clark, though clearly stricken, said that his little fortune must now be in the hands of a latter day Aladdin on the other side of the world.

Most of our adventures in the car turned out far better. Once shopping at a J. C. Penney store after what was already a harrowing trip for Clark (I can't imagine him in this gadgetized era we live in), he was faced with having to go down an escalator. Carol went first, and I brought up the rear. As we approached the dismount step Clark took a leap worthy of the Olympics, and his long legs took him a good twelve feet safely away from this malevolent device that seemed to be eating the steps. We found another way back to the car.

That same afternoon was greatly improved by a black bread, cheese, and burgundy picnic on the beach down the hill from the Pacific Grove house, where Clark achieved that slight glow that went with good fellowship, good wine, good food, and great conversation. Back in the house in the evening we played a game we often enjoyed (though my skills are now atrophied from disuse) wherein one person would give a line or two from any poem, and the person next must remember the next line, and so around until we had finished. Clark was the only one who never slipped. My most vivid memory of this game came one evening when we got into a well-known poem, and Clark filled the missing lines, and I blanked out on the author's name. Clark quietly muttered, "Charles Lamb." I have never known so prodigious a memory, for I knew that Clark had not read Charles Lamb since he had gotten to the "L" section of the Carnegie Library as a boy, more than fifty years before. The next evening, following a day of rest, we read through Clark's play, *The Dead Will Cuckold You.* I had earlier typed (an archaic practice using a strange machine known to be an ancestor of this thing in front of me) the play, making two carbon copies (what on earth are those?). Each of us took appropriate parts and had a rousing good time, managing to empty the remainder of the Burgundy.

It was during my last visit to Pacific Grove, in July of 1961, that Clark at one point emerged from the dug-out basement with a stack of musty manuscripts which he placed in my hands as I stood at the door. He held them by both sides and, in a kind of ceremony, passed them on to me. In the past, Clark had given me several copies of unpublished poems and had signed them for me; my copy of *The Star-Treader,* signed in his youthful script in 1912, and signed again "For Bill Farmer, this pale-bound volume of yesteryear, From Clark Ashton Smith—Sept. 14th, 1958" with its original dust jacket, remains one of my most prized possessions, given just before I departed for New York for my first year at Syracuse. Yet the stack of holographs came in a different way—perhaps Clark sensed that his time was short.

The burning of the cabin has been written of elsewhere, and I heard Carol speak of moving to Peru. Clark, in retrospect, had been struck a death blow, I think. His grief, so evident in his eyes, was never allowed to compromise his courtesy. We spent the day, just wondering why? Marilyn Novak (she had lost her Nikki) had dinner for us all and we sat outside with wine-coolers and just talked and talked until dark. Carol and Ashton stayed at Marilyn's that night.

In July of 1961, Clark made his last trip up to Auburn. We spent some time together, though Clark would not go back to the property as an unbearable thing to contemplate. His whole life, as it were, had been bulldozed level. To return to the canyon-side where in his youth no lights from town depleted the deep heavens in which his young mind swam freely, and see it platted and subdivided was too much to ask. Carol thought he would want to go and didn't quite understand, and that, in itself, is a measure of how genuinely distraught they still were about the vandalism.

I have often been asked recently, "What kind of man was Clark Ashton Smith?"—was he a "regular guy"; did he dabble in the occult, or become a Buddhist, or was he a nihilist? No one can really get inside another man's head that far, but I can share the man I knew: If by "regular guy" is meant a sports-addicted, beer-drinking, gas-passing dirty joke teller—no. Yet he had a wry sense of humor, as can be readily found in his writings, and he loved a naughty but witty tale. He despised sarcasm and mockery as a source of "humor," but reveled in satire and irony. As to involvement with the occult, he knew the jargon and read the books—but when asked what he thought of Anton La Vey, his answer, as usual, was brief: "Phoney!" Clark was not an occultist but had a very considerable respect for real evil; he acknowledged its existence as a palpable reality, and not just as a value judgment upon random events. He had read the writings of the Buddha, respected them as any contemplative mind would, yet agreed that the Western notion of vicarious sacrifice was more humane when practiced than simply feeling deep sympathy for life's pathetic victims. It is reasonably clear in his earliest writings, of which this book is an example, that he had early on absorbed the Victorian era's understanding of Christian morality, decency, and sanctity of one's person. Yet the failure of most "Christians" to even begin to approach the standard they espoused turned him away from the dominant Protestantism of his environment. Once he remarked that Ethel Heiple most nearly fit his idea of how a Christian should appear to the world. She did not "sound a trumpet" before her as she did her alms, she just did them—caring for his mother, slipping him a little food to take home, or medicine.

All persons of high intelligence go through periods in their youth where their enthusiasms take them into strange and exotic realms of thought. However, since I am often asked, I shall take just a moment to reflect on where Clark may have been in his personal philosophy when I knew him just past age sixty. I made the observation one evening that some of his "malevolent" forces appeared to be simply "being themselves" and were not good things that had become corrupted. A dangerous plant or creature ("The Weaver in the Vault") can hardly be blamed for being itself. Yet Clark's evil existences seemed to have, even so, a deliberate antipathy to man. This led us to a discussion of "dualism." I had only the previous year done some extensive study of Zoroastrianism at the University, and mentioned it as an example of a thoroughgoing dualistic system: Ahura Mazda, god of light (his first "emanation" is Mithra—born on December 25th), and Ahriman, god of darkness and directly opposite. In other words, in this philosophy, evil exists as a thing unto itself and is not defined in terms of corrupt goodness. By contrast, for example, in Christianity the evil entity, Satan, is the opposite not of God, but of Gabriel, a being essentially like himself within the mythic archetype. Clark was deeply familiar with this middle-eastern "religion" which predated Christianity and Islam by many hundreds of years. His point was that his experience led him to conclude that no matter how insensate something that is dangerous or inimical to man (a shark for instance) may appear, there is a deeper impulse moving this entity in such a fashion as to maximize its opportunities for exercising a profound enmity toward humanity.

Clark was also strongly attracted to the concept of the transmigration of souls and reincarnation, though I think he never quite felt comfortable landing absolutely in that spiritual quagmire. In thinking back over these many years about the older genius I knew as a young and artistically inclined youth, now seasoned by years of study and bearing the scars of experience—like Zorba, all in the front—I think I can safely say that Clark just *was*. A true original, not *sui generis,* but consuming the spirit of things around him, assimilating them, making them one with himself; sifting out what suited him best and discarding the dross, yet bearing always the memory of wounds of soundless depth, and loves that rode comets around the sun to remotest space.

To tell you what informed the man and his work is perhaps too much to ask and beyond real knowing; I do know that Poe excited his imagination in the direction it would retain, MacDonald showed him how to create fantasy, and Robert Graves revealed to him, as he said, that his whole life had been in service to the "White Goddess," without knowing her name. Beyond that I can tell you of the last time I saw Clark alive. In that hulking Packard, Carol at the wheel, Clark prepared as best he could for the terror of the trip from Auburn to Pacific Grove (and with Carol driving, anyone should fear), the engine idling as Carol rattled on about someone they knew who was sitting on the promontory in Monterey counting spirits and being concerned with a recent increase in numbers flying by, the skies being so thick with them that he couldn't keep up. To which I responded in my arrogance that I thought such stuff was hogwash. And Clark, from the back of the car looking straight ahead, said, "He is very brave." And Carol, not getting it, smilingly said, "Yes, he is very brave," and off they roared. In the fall, just before beginning a term in graduate school at UC Berkeley, that car screeched to a halt in front of my house, and a disheveled and distraught Carol fell into my arms saying, "Ashton is gone!" Yet, dear reader, having reached this point in my memoir of Clark Ashton Smith, perhaps you will find, as I have, that he is not gone at all, but present in these pages as a boy author seeking a voice that is forever reserved for those especially gifted to hear his music. I hope you make friends with him; I liked him a lot—I still do.

13 November 2002
Corpus Christi, Texas